100 Reasons to Celebrate

We invite you to join us in celebrating
Mills & Boon's centenary. Gerald Mills and
Charles Boon founded Mills & Boon Limited
in 1908 and opened offices in London's Covent
Garden. Since then, Mills & Boon has become
a hallmark for romantic fiction, recognised
around the world.

We're proud of our 100 years of publishing
excellence, which wouldn't have been achieved
without the loyalty and enthusiasm of our
authors and readers.

Thank you!

Each month throughout the year there will
be something new and exciting to mark the
centenary, so watch for your favourite authors,
captivating new stories, special limited
edition collections…and more!

Fortune's Vengeful Groom
by Charlene Sands

SECRET MARRIAGE EXPOSED!

Although the almighty Fortune clan will probably blow a gasket about us splashing more headlines about them, this was just too delicious to pass up. Looks like another skeleton has emerged from Eliza Fortune's gold-plated cupboard. And, according to our top-secret source, this sainted Fortune socialite has fallen off her pedestal for good this time.

Her family is still trying to live down her *last* romantic debacle – remember how the Sioux Falls airwaves were burning when Eliza caught her mayor-wannabe fiancé in bed with his campaign manager right before their wedding? Well, now it looks like history has repeated itself...

Turns out Eliza had a quickie marriage with ex-wildcatter Reese Parker six years ago that bit the dust when she supposedly caught her brand-new hubby cheating on her! This suave, self-made millionaire is a far cry from the rugged rodeo rider she once knew, but apparently he's still her dirty little secret. Though why someone would want to hide this strapping oilman is beyond *moi*.

Perhaps a spark of attraction still flickers between this feuding duo?

Mistress of Fortune
by Kathie DeNosky

SASSY SOCIAL CLIMBER TO WED BLACK SHEEP FORTUNE HEIR...?

You heard it from us first... Casino magnate Blake Fortune has bedded PR assistant Sasha Kilgore and just might be planning to pop the question! But don't break out the bubbly quite yet – a sordid sibling love triangle could be looming.

Not long after Sasha and her handsome boss, Creed Fortune, were spotted dancing cheek to cheek at his brother Case's wedding reception, she was caught getting hot and heavy with Blake Fortune during the grand opening of his newest casino.

Sounds like Blake's stolen Sasha Kilgore right out from under his brother Creed's nose.

(Not that she's complaining, because rumour has it that she's been lusting after Blake since adolescence!) It's a well-known fact that Case and Creed Fortune have been at odds with their wayward half brother, Blake, for years. But who knew that brotherly rivalry would reach such epic proportions? Hmm...I wonder if poor Sasha is privy to the fact that she's being used as a pawn in this shameless show of macho one-upmanship.

Until next time!

Fortune's Vengeful Groom
CHARLENE SANDS

Mistress of Fortune
KATHIE DeNOSKY

™ MILLS & BOON®
Pure reading pleasure

First published in Great Britain 2008
by Harlequin Mills & Boon Limited,
Eton House, 18-24 Paradise Road, Richmond, Surrey TW9 1SR

The publisher acknowledges the copyright holders of the individual works as follows:

Fortune's Vengeful Groom © Harlequin Books S.A. 2007
Mistress of Fortune © Harlequin Books S.A. 2007

Special thanks and acknowledgement are given to
Charlene Sands and Kathie DeNosky for their contribution to
FORTUNES mini-series.

ISBN: 978 0 263 85892 1

51-0208

Printed and bound in Spain
by Litografia Rosés S.A., Barcelona

FORTUNE'S VENGEFUL GROOM

by
Charlene Sands

THE DAKOTA FORTUNES

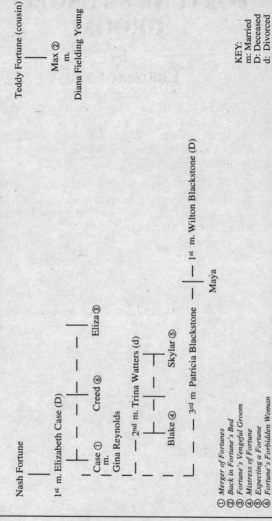

Nash Fortune

1st m. Elizabeth Case (D)

Case ① m. Gina Reynolds

Creed ⑥

Eliza ③

2nd m. Trina Watters (d)

Blake ④

Skylar ⑤

3rd m Patricia Blackstone — 1st m. Wilton Blackstone (D)

Maya

Teddy Fortune (cousin)

Max ② m. Diana Fielding Young

① Merger of Fortunes
② Back in Fortune's Bed
③ Fortune's Vengeful Groom
④ Mistress of Fortune
⑤ Expecting a Fortune
⑥ Fortune's Forbidden Woman

KEY:
m: Married
D: Deceased
d: Divorced

CHARLENE SANDS

resides in Southern California with her husband, school sweetheart and best friend, Don. Proudly, they boast that their children, Jason and Nikki, have earned their college degrees. The "empty nesters" now have two cats that have taken over the house. Charlene loves writing both fun Historical romances with lively characters that warm your heart and sizzling Desire books with alpha heroes and feisty heroines. When not writing, she enjoys sunny California days, Pacific beaches and sitting down with a good book.

Charlene invites you to visit her website at www. charlenesands.com to enter her contests, stop by for a chat, read her blog and see what's new! E-mail her at charlenesands@hotmail.com.

To the V-alley Girls, Carol Pettis, Ellen Lacey and Charleene Feldman, dear friends and striking women who roll with the punches making my Tuesday mornings a real blast. Your love, friendship and open-hearted support bowl me over!

One

"It's a stroke of brilliance, Eliza. The place looks great. Nobody does a fund-raiser like you," Nicole Appleton whispered into Eliza's ear.

From up on stage, Eliza Fortune smiled with satisfaction as her gaze traveled around the large ballroom filled with invited guests, the men dressed in authentic three-piece suits and the women in elegant gowns of the Old West. She'd designed and decorated the ballroom for the event. "Thanks, Nic. It was a labor of love."

"Well, you've outdone yourself this time. Everyone is having a wonderful time and your Basket Dinner Auction idea is going over well. You're raising thousands of dollars for the reparations to the Old West Museum."

The auctioneer announced another dinner basket to be auctioned off. Chloe McMurphy stepped up to the podium and lifted the flap on her basket, retrieving a pledge card to give to the auctioneer. "This lovely young lady will provide dinner for two, three or four. Her specialty is fried chicken and the best dumplings in Minnehaha County. And an added bonus of home-baked apple pie. Now that's what I call a real fine South Dakota meal."

Eliza tensed suddenly and glanced at her friend with apprehension. Only she and Nicole remained up on stage. All the other dinners had been auctioned off. "I hope someone bids on my basket."

"You've got to be kidding. Who wouldn't want to have a dinner cooked expressly by Eliza Fortune? At the Fortune estate, no less. I bet your dinner pledge goes for the highest bid of all."

Eliza scoffed. "Only if my father or brother decide to take pity on me. My family's out there somewhere and they know I'm not the best cook."

"Won't matter," Nicole said adamantly. "You're gonna raise a lot of money tonight—and *not* from Nash or Creed Fortune. Everyone knows how dedicated you are. They saved the best for last. And that's you."

She mouthed a silent thank-you to her friend, then took note of Mr. Phillips at the podium crooking his finger at Nicole. "Oh, look. It's your turn to go up to the podium, Nic. Good luck."

And as her friend approached the auctioneer carrying a white wicker basket adorned with a large red taffeta bow, Eliza settled back on the wooden bench seat to wait her turn.

Being a benefactor, as well as Sioux Falls Historical

Society chairwoman, she'd had no trouble convincing Siouxland's Old West Museum's president to donate some of their Western gear to help her transform a chandelier-ensconced ballroom into a springtime scene straight out of the Old West. Lariats, silver saddles and wagon wheels filled the perimeter, while bound sheaves of grain and husks of corn draped the walls. The dinner tables, though set with elegant china, rested on blue gingham tablecloths with tall, lumbering sunflowers as vibrant centerpieces. A sunrise backdrop and a large buckboard wagon filled with straw sat upon the stage just behind Eliza.

When all was said and done, Nicole's bid ranked up there with the highest so far. Her dinner pledge of roast lamb and potatoes with carrot soufflé and crème brûlée for dessert garnered over three thousand dollars. Eliza joined the group in applauding the generous bidder.

"And now, ladies and gentlemen, you have the distinct honor of bidding on Miss Eliza Fortune's dinner basket. As you all know, Miss Fortune has worked tirelessly to put on this fund-raiser and it looks like she's made it a tremendous success." Mr. Phillips reached for Eliza's hand and guided her to the podium. Eliza handed him her pledge card from her gold-trimmed basket and stood as he read her offering. "Ah, I see the winner will have a great treat in store for them. Eliza has pledged to cook any meal of your choosing, beginning with hors d'oeuvres and ending with a decadent dessert with as many courses as you desire. So let's begin the bidding at five hundred dollars."

Eliza stood smiling at her guests, while inside a tremor of apprehension coursed through her body. And only once the first bid was announced for five hundred dollars—*not* by her father or brother—did she finally relax. As the bidding continued, she grew more and more confident.

"We have a bid for thirty-five hundred dollars. Do I hear four thousand? Anyone for four thousand dollars?"

Pleased that she'd garnered a respectable sum of money, Eliza was ready to walk away from the podium. She needed to coordinate the country band's performance on stage so the dancing could begin.

"Going once, going twice for thirty-five hundred dollars and…"

"Thirty-five thousand dollars."

"I'm sorry, sir," the auctioneer said, "we already have a bid for thirty-five hundred dollars."

"I said thirty-five *thousand* dollars," a commanding voice echoed from the back of the room.

All conversation stopped in the grand ballroom, as heads turned in the direction of the voice.

Eliza stood perfectly still. Her smile faded, while her heart pounded up in her ears. She knew that voice. She would never forget the low, raspy timbre that would send her nerves spiraling out of control. She shut her eyes briefly, willing her body to calm.

It couldn't be, she told herself.

But she knew better.

She had always known that this day would eventually come.

Mr. Phillips glanced at Eliza with a baffled expression, but when she offered no help, he turned back to his task. "Uh, sorry, sorry, indeed. The bid stands at thirty-five *thousand* dollars," he emphasized. "Going once, going twice, sold to the gentleman in the back of the room!"

Just like that, Reese Parker stepped into her line of vision.

And back into her life.

After six years.

Their gazes locked from across the room. For a long moment they just stared at one another. His eyes held no warmth, his face no joy. He hardly looked like the gentle jeans-clad rodeo rider she'd met one summer in Montana.

Oh, he was as handsome as she remembered. Maybe more so now, with a chiseled jawline and dark, piercing eyes. But this man looked as though he belonged here amid South Dakota's wealthiest patrons, dressed in a dashing ink-black Western tuxedo with lines cut to perfection. A golden nugget clasped the bola tie that lassoed his neck and settled into a single-breasted brocade vest. A black felt Stetson covered shocks of short-cropped sandy hair and, as if he needed it, snakeskin boots added flair to the whole look.

Heavens, he could have stepped off the pages of *GQ*.

Eliza was aware of the hush that settled onto the crowded room. But she couldn't tear her gaze away. She simply looked at the man she had once loved.

Goose bumps erupted on her flesh.

Memories poured in, and her breath caught as myriad emotions ran havoc through her system, but the one that remained, the one she couldn't banish, washed over her like a deluge of rain.

Anger.

Mr. Phillips took his cue then and concluded the auction, asking that the bidders make good on their bids at the reception table, while the HoneyBees made their way on stage.

Eliza was grateful for the reprieve. She broke eye contact with Reese and scurried off backstage. A gentle hand grabbed her from behind, startling her.

"Eliza, where are you running off to?"

Eliza turned around, relieved to see that it was Nicole. She blinked and couldn't formulate an answer. The last few minutes had seemed like a dream. No, she corrected, a nightmare.

"That gorgeous guy bid a ton of money on you, Eliza."

Eliza couldn't fake a smile. "I know."

"And you two couldn't take your eyes off each other."

"I know that, too."

"So? Are you going to tell me who he is? You must know him. Either that or he's flirting big-time."

"No, trust me, he wasn't flirting." The very thought was absurd. She didn't know exactly why Reese had come to Sioux Falls, but she couldn't entertain any warm thoughts about him. He had nearly destroyed her with his betrayal. No one knew the whole truth, and she'd hoped to keep it that way for as long as possible.

"Who is he, Eliza?" Nicole pressed. "Please tell me."

Eliza had kept her secret for six years. Her own humiliation aside, she hated to think of the damage her revelation might do to the Fortune good name.

Good Lord, but she'd been a fool in the past. If the truth got out, Eliza would lose all credibility with her numerous charitable organizations, not to mention the headlines it would cause. One scandalized romance was enough in a girl's life. She'd managed to survive it, but this one she doubted she would ever live down.

She heaved a sigh. Keeping this from her best friend had been hardest of all. She stared into Nicole's earnest amber eyes.

"Something's going on, Lizzie," Nicole whispered, using her childhood name, reminding Eliza that she and Nicole had a long history of devoted friendship. They'd been close for more than half of Eliza's thirty-one years. Eliza had wanted to tell her countless times. She decided she'd kept her emotions bottled up long enough. Besides, if the manure were destined to hit the fan, at least she'd have an ally in Nicole.

She spoke the words she'd never said aloud to anyone in Sioux Falls, especially her family. "His name is Reese Parker and…he's my husband."

The South Dakota air made Eliza shiver, but she put up with the nighttime chill in order to catch her breath. She'd hurried out of the grand ballroom after speaking briefly with Nicole, finding this little hideaway terrace high atop the Fortune Seven Hotel to collect her thoughts. The magnificent view of the landscape had always helped put her at ease. But tonight it wasn't working.

Oh, God. Oh, God. Oh, God.

Reese was in Sioux Falls.

She doubted it was a coincidence that he'd shown up in her hometown.

I was passing through town so I thought I'd look up my...wife.

She shivered again.

And felt a wealth of warmth swarm her body as a man's jacket enveloped her shoulders. She turned quickly and came face-to-face with her husband. "Reese."

"Eliza." He stepped away from her as if he couldn't stand to be near her, yet he'd just seen to her comfort. The tuxedo jacket smelled of him, an erotic mix of musk and pine.

"You...look different," she said, fumbling for words.

"I am different," he said curtly as he removed his Stetson.

His hair was just as she remembered—thick, short and neatly groomed. How often she'd run her fingers through those locks just to muss up those perfect strands.

Eliza's heart hammered again. Even with this awkwardness, Reese held true to his manners. But he didn't look like a rugged rodeo rider right now, the man whose dimpled smile could send her body humming. There was nothing soft or gentle in the way he looked at her.

But he did look his fill, his gaze traveling over her body with a laziness that could be mistaken for arrogance. Suddenly Eliza was aware of the revealing gown she'd had designed especially for tonight. In keeping with the Western theme, the creamy satin gown dipped low in the front, the bodice forming her figure and cinching in at her thin waist. Shiny golden threads created an intricate pattern throughout and gilded wide lace teased her bosom and wrists. *To match the golden highlights in your blond hair, Eliza,* the dress designer had said.

Now, with his eyes upon her, Eliza felt exposed and vulnerable to his scrutiny. His gaze lingered on her chest, making her think back to a time when more than his eyes had devoured her.

She trembled again, and this time the night air wasn't the cause.

"It's not that cold, Eliza. Ice must be running through your veins."

Eliza had almost forgotten herself. She wouldn't let Reese get the better of her. She'd walked out on him once and she'd do it again. "What are you doing here?"

He smiled then, but not the gentle smile that softened his eyes. No, this smile was thin-lipped and hard. "We have to talk."

Eliza began shaking her head. "No. We can't. I have to get back inside."

"Tomorrow, then. During the dinner you're going to cook me."

Eliza removed his jacket and tossed it to him. "You're joking."

He caught the jacket with a nonchalance that angered her. Reese had always been fast with his hands. "I seldom joke."

But he had, years ago. They'd spent one glorious summer laughing and joking and making love. It was his quick wit and ease of manner that had attracted her to him initially. That and his hard, lean, gorgeous body.

"I can't possibly cook you dinner, Reese. I'll have someone else…"

"No. It's you or nobody." His dark eyes held hers firm.

Eliza thrust her chin up. If he wanted a battle of wills, then she'd oblige. "Then I'm afraid it'll be nobody. I have to get back inside." She turned to leave, but his hand snaked out to catch her wrist. He spun her around, and she faced narrowed eyes and a set jaw.

"You're bought and paid for, darlin'. To the tune of thirty-five thousand dollars."

Eliza's eyes widened with surprise. She'd been so distraught at seeing Reese again she'd forgotten all about the enormous donation he'd made. "You don't have that much—"

His brows shot up. "I do."

He caught her staring at the fine cut of his tuxedo, his tie clasp made of solid gold and his handcrafted snakeskin boots. She wiped the curiosity off her face, wishing he would leave. She didn't care how much money he had now. Seeing him hurt too much. She'd managed to tuck away reminders of his betrayal, but now that he was so near, all of it came rushing back with frightening force.

"Let go of me," she said breathlessly.

He released her immediately.

"I'll be over tomorrow night at eight."

She shook her head again. "It's not a good idea, Reese."

"They don't know, do they?"

He was smug enough not to have to explain. Eliza knew that he spoke of her family and the secret marriage she'd kept from them. She shook her head slowly.

"Six years, and you still haven't owned up to the truth. You must have really been…hell, never mind."

"Reese, you can't come over tomorrow night."

He scowled. "Would you rather I went to the press? News of the Fortunes was splashed all over the *Tribune* this morning. You'd think this damn charity event was the second coming or something. Wouldn't they just love to hear about the sainted Eliza Fortune's *misfortune* one summer in Montana? How she got down and dirty with a local cowboy?"

It hadn't been like that. That summer had been magical until… She drew oxygen into her lungs. "Is that a threat?"

He jammed his Stetson back on his head. "Damn straight, darlin'. I don't make them lightly."

Eliza pursed her lips to keep from lashing out. She'd lost this round with Reese. She couldn't afford for him to make good on his threat. It had taken several years to live down her last romantic debacle with a man who had aspirations of becoming Sioux Falls' youngest mayor. She'd been engaged to Warren Keyes for six months and broke off the engagement two weeks before the wedding.

Local news stations and leading headlines in the *Tribune* had kept a running tally on their breakup for weeks, and Eliza had come out the loser. Her head throbbed as she recalled the pain she'd endured finding her fiancé in bed with his campaign manager. No one knew the entire truth except her family. She'd kept quiet about his infidelity, not out of any concern for him or his campaign but because she hadn't wanted the public humiliation. Pity was the last thing she'd needed. It was bad enough that she'd suffered public scrutiny, being described as "flighty," "fickle" and "confused" when she'd walked out on him.

But what she'd really been was hurt, the injury to a young girl's heart almost too painful to bear. Warren had used her and her family's name to attain status in the community for political gain.

She'd run away then to Montana and had met Reese Parker. The ruggedly handsome cowboy had swept her off her feet. She'd fallen hard for him, and they'd had a summer affair that led to a quick wedding. Now, if the truth got out about her marriage, the term *rebound* would take on a whole new meaning.

"Dinner at eight," he said without compunction. "I doubt you remember my favorite meal, but this really isn't about food, is it?"

With that, he strode purposefully off the terrace. Eliza watched the glass door slam shut in his wake.

"Pot roast and potatoes with creamed spinach," she muttered softly.

Then trembled again.

Reese paced his penthouse suite, striding back and forth with suppressed rage. Eliza Fortune Parker, his wife, had tried to cast him off once again tonight. This time he wasn't having any of it. She'd see him on his terms, whether she liked it or not. And she hadn't liked it.

No, his appearance at her fund-raiser tonight had put a wrench in her nicely tuned life. Reese could take some satisfaction in that. He'd seen fear in her eyes, and that suited him just fine. Let her fear him and what havoc he could cause her.

She'd caused him enough grief to last a lifetime. Reese shoved his hand into his pocket, coming up with the note she'd written him six years ago, the crinkled, worn parchment he'd been given by a hotel desk clerk a constant reminder to him to succeed in life. Hell, he'd practically used the note as his bible, his guide to never give up. To never let anyone best him again.

He glanced down at the delicate writing, smudged now and bleeding blue ink.

The marriage was a mistake. I'm going home. I don't want to see you again. Ever.

Ever.

Damn her. He'd stayed away long enough.

He knew every cold, harsh word of that note by heart. It was time to end it all, and too bad if it didn't fit into Eliza's plans.

Before his father died last month, he'd made Reese promise that he'd get his affairs in order. With unspoken words, he'd immediately known what his father had meant. Normally, Cole Parker didn't pull punches. He'd been one up-front tell-it-like-it-is kind of man. But his father had known that Eliza Fortune Parker had been Reese's one weak spot so he'd trod carefully.

It's time, Reese, he'd said, almost on his last breath. *Take hold of your life, son.*

His father had been right. It was time.

But Reese would take his time, making Eliza squirm, upending her perfect little world, showing her that he wasn't the sweet-natured, bronc-busting cowboy she could tie up in knots, anymore.

God, he'd been a fool thinking that the rich, pretty socialite would be happy with a down-on-his-luck cowboy.

Reese winced and crumpled the note, shoving it back into his pocket.

Man, but he'd loved her. She'd come to Montana and he'd seen something unique in her, something beautiful in her heart. She'd turned him on with that body of hers, wearing clothes that hid her perfection. His imagination had taken wild rides, until he'd known he had to have her. And once they'd made love, it had been better than good. So damn much better than anything he'd ever experienced.

When Reese's cell phone rang, he checked the number, then smiled. "Hey, Garrett."

"Where are you, bro?"

"In the Providence Hotel."

"Top floor?"

"Penthouse." Reese could picture his brother's grin. They'd often joked that once they struck it rich, they'd never stay in anything but the best—a result of too many sleazy motels with torn sheets and rodents as bed partners.

"I take it that's not a Fortune acquisition?"

"Hell, I had to drive across town to find a decent hotel they didn't own."

"You're home early. I take it the night didn't go well?"

"On the contrary. I accomplished my goal."

"Which was?"

"You wouldn't approve, Sir Galahad."

His brother sighed. "So, how is Eliza?"

Beautiful, sexy, cold as ice. "She hasn't grown fangs or anything."

"Ah, still a knockout."

Reese didn't answer.

"Hey, I'm on your side, Reese. We're family. But I liked Eliza from the moment I met her."

"You only met her one time."

"True, but I could tell she was crazy about you. I thought you were a lucky man. And Pops, well, he wanted you to sort out your life, Reese."

"That's what I'm doing. I plan on getting her out of my life."

There was a long pause. "Are you sure that's what you want?"

Reese let out a bitter laugh. He knew his brother only meant well, but what option did a man have when his wife walked out on him without any explanation. She'd kept their marriage a secret because she'd been ashamed of him and his status in life and feared her family wouldn't approve. She didn't care enough about him to fight for what they had. He'd been broke, making his way through the rodeo circuit and pouring all of his money into his venture. But Eliza hadn't stuck around long enough to see his dream come true. When she'd had enough, she'd simply walked out. Without taking a backward glance. Well, he's making her take a good long look now. "I'm sure."

"Okay," Garrett said quietly, and Reese knew his brother only had his welfare at heart. "Hey, want some good news?"

"Shoot."

"We had a blowout in Cinder Basin. A real gusher.

Your instincts were right on. That makes seven straight oil strikes, Reese."

Reese's mood lifted. "Pops would've liked to hear the news."

"He knows, Reese. He's overseeing our operation from up above."

"Yeah."

Reese had ridden the rodeo circuit to sustain his dream, using his winnings to help finance his venture as a wildcatter. He'd worked long and hard coming up with nothing but dry holes his first three years. The standing joke was that he couldn't find oil in a gas station. But then his luck changed and his rigs started paying off. He became a respected oilman, hitting five straight blowouts that year, and his success continued to mount every year, his ratio of blowouts to dry holes ten to one. It hadn't taken him long to form his own company—Parker Explorations being one of the most prosperous oil companies in Montana.

"Thanks for the call, Garrett. I'll be dreaming of black gold."

"You're going to need it with that house you're building."

Reese agreed. "Yeah, it's a money pit, but it'll be perfect when I'm through."

"Perfection has its drawbacks at times."

How well he knew that. At one time he'd thought he'd found the perfect woman, the perfect wife. They were to have the perfect life. Eliza had crushed that idea and left him a broken man. It had taken him a long time to dig himself out of that hole. But now he was back on top and nothing was going to stop him. He had the *perfect* plan for getting back at his wife.

"Yeah, but when you get it right, there's nothing that compares to it."

Two

"Here are the books you requested, ma'am." Ivy Woodhouse, the Fortunes' chef, handed Eliza three cookbooks as she sat in the great room just off the kitchen. "Are you sure you don't need my help for that special meal you're cooking tonight?"

Eliza glanced up at Ivy. "No, but thank you for the offer. I plan on doing this myself," she said.

Even if it kills me, she thought. She couldn't risk having the cook or anyone else around when Reese came over tonight. "In fact, since my father and Patricia won't be home this evening, why don't you take the night off."

Ivy's brows rose in surprise and she paused briefly before answering. "Thank you. Shall I set the table for you, miss?"

"I'll take care of it. Enjoy the night off, Ivy," she said as the cook thanked her again and left the room.

Eliza leaned back against the sofa, planning her dinner outside on the veranda, where no one would bother them. She remembered the chills she'd experienced last night when Reese had joined her on the hotel terrace. Most of what she'd felt had little to do with the weather. She'd been shocked and then angered by his appearance, which she believed was the exact reaction he'd wanted from her. He'd made her darn uncomfortable last night.

Now she had the chance to return the favor. If she could make Reese uncomfortable enough, maybe the evening would end quickly. She'd be willing to endure a slight frost to get rid of Reese. His presence here in Sioux Falls made her jumpy, but having him show up at her home tonight could surely do her in.

As luck would have it, her father and stepmother had dinner plans this evening. As for the rest of the family...hopefully they wouldn't make an appearance, either.

Eliza opened a cookbook and began flipping pages.

Her father took a seat in his wide velvet-tufted wing chair, facing her. "Good morning, honey."

Eliza lifted her face and smiled. "Hi, Dad."

Nash Fortune, never one to miss a sign, sent a worried look her way. "Tired today?"

"Not really," she said, telling a little fib. She'd spent a restless night worrying about what Reese's appearance in Sioux Falls might mean, and she feared the lying would only continue.

"You worked very hard last night, Eliza. The fund-raiser was a huge success. And, as a father, I couldn't be more proud of what you managed to accomplish."

"Thanks, Dad, but it wasn't all me. I had a great deal of help and—"

"And you're the one with the ideas, the guts to pull it together, to make it all work, right down to the final dotting of the *i*'s and crossing of the *t*'s. I understand you've outdone yourself this year, bringing in more money than the museum had ever hoped."

"Yes, I'm happy we raised the funds they needed for the repairs."

"The gentleman who bid on your dinner put you over the top."

Eliza slammed the cookbook closed, took a deep breath, then nodded.

"Do you know who he is? Where he's from?"

Eliza's heart raced with dread and she cursed Reese for putting her in this position. Her mind fumbled around for just the right words. "Montana, I believe. He's passing through Sioux Falls."

"Just passing through?" Her father scratched his head, then furrowed his brows in a gesture Eliza knew so well. When Nash Fortune wasn't buying something, he couldn't hide the expression on his face. His instincts were usually right on, but the man didn't have a poker face. "Why would he donate so much money if he had no stock in Sioux Falls? No one I questioned seemed to know."

Eliza clenched her teeth. Her father had asked people about Reese Parker? "It's a good tax deduction," she said, keeping her comments noncommittal, "and a wonderful cause, Dad. Maybe he's generous by nature."

He didn't seem convinced. "I suppose. Too bad I won't be meeting him tonight. Patricia's been a little down lately, so I thought a romantic dinner for two at her favorite restaurant would help lift her spirits."

"Patricia mentioned that you wouldn't be home tonight for dinner. I think she's excited about some alone time with you."

Eliza envied the love her father and Patricia shared. He was devoted to her. And after losing Elizabeth— Eliza's mother—early in life, he'd rebounded with a disastrous marriage to Trina Watters before finding true love again with Patricia. Eliza had once thought she'd found that same kind of love, but nothing with Reese had worked out as she'd hoped.

Her father glanced down at the cookbook still in her lap. "So what kind of fabulous meal are you planning for tonight?"

"Don't say *fabulous* and *meal* in the same sentence when you're talking about me. I'll be lucky if I don't poison the man."

Now, there's a thought.

Her father's lips twitched, but he didn't comment any further. Nash Fortune was a wonderful husband to his wife and a caring father to Eliza, but he never showed her much outward affection. She knew her father loved her, but he'd also held high expectations for all his children. Case, Creed and Eliza all did their best never to disappoint him. They'd wanted his approval as much as his love. But Blake and Skylar, her half brother and half sister, were a different matter.

And now, with Reese Parker on the scene, the truth of her six-year secret marriage might hurt her family, disappoint her father and splash unfavorable headlines in the newspapers about the Fortune name.

Eliza shoved that thought aside and instead focused on something else. "Was my mother a good cook?"

Her father stared off for a moment as if reliving another time in his life. When he spoke, his voice broke with a certain reverence mingled with pain. "Your mother was good at everything she did...."

Eliza listened carefully, noting the momentary winsome look on her father's face. It was an expression she'd seldom witnessed.

"Except cooking," he finished.

She released an amused sigh. "Oh, Dad, really? I take after her?"

He looked into her eyes. "She was smart and dedicated to what she believed in, pretty as a picture—and couldn't cook worth a darn. Yes, you take after her."

Eliza had heard some of these things before, but she never minded hearing them again. It made her feel closer to a mother she'd never known. She'd wanted so much to know the kind of unconditional love that she'd seen among her girlfriends with their mothers.

"I loved her dearly, Eliza. You know that."

She nodded. "I do know that."

Her father stood, then and placed a rare but much-needed kiss to her forehead. "Good. And, honey, no matter what you cook tonight, if the man is a real gentleman, he'll eat it without complaint."

* * *

"Except the man isn't a gentleman," Eliza said to Nicole over the phone hours later. "And the weather gods aren't cooperating, either. A light mist is falling. We can't eat out on the veranda as I'd hoped."

"So why not use the dining room?"

"No, I can't do that. *Family.* Patricia and my dad will be gone, but I can't chance anyone else popping into the house and overhearing our conversation. I've set everything up in my design studio. If the rain stops, then we can go out onto the veranda."

Her gaze traveled around her beloved room, where she'd spend hours dreaming up designs and wishing that one day she could open her own studio. She realized suddenly—and perhaps too late—how the room appeared. In an effort to conceal the mess, she'd arranged beautiful lengths of silk and satin cloths, draping them over bolts of fabric, design charts, spools of thread and ribbon. With soft lighting, her work area hidden and colorful material flowing in an array of delicacy, she'd unintentionally created a dining area that one might conceive as seductive.

"I think this might be a mistake, Nic," she said slowly, trying to calm her impending panic.

"You'll do fine, Lizzie. You always do. Just keep your head up, your mind on something else and you'll get through this evening."

That had always been her problem with Reese. Whenever he was in the room, she couldn't focus on anything *but* him. She'd met him right after watching the rodeo and walked up to him in a meet-'n'-greet line to shake his hand. He'd held on to her hand a little longer than the other cowboys had and looked deeply into her eyes with a certain sweet promise, then released her to shake the next person's hand. She'd been fascinated, transfixed in the moment—and disappointed when she'd left the rodeo without seeing him again.

So when he slid in the seat right next to her that night at her hotel bar, she'd been captivated by his slow and easy manner, quick wit and undeniable sex appeal. She'd fallen hard for Reese Parker, and she'd realized right then, that what she'd felt for Warren Keyes wasn't love at all. She'd dismissed her feelings for him quite easily after meeting Reese.

She'd had the real thing with Reese—or so she believed. And when he'd betrayed her, her world had crumbled apart.

"Thanks, Nic. I don't know what I'd do without you." She'd never regret telling her dear friend the truth. She'd been a godsend today, coaching her through the cooking and giving her moral support.

"So, are you wearing a knockout dress?" Nic asked.

"No, just a plain black cocktail dress with simple lines. I don't really care how I look to Reese."

Nic sighed. "Eliza," she said, taking a serious tone, "you were married to him. I mean, you're *still* married to him. A woman who's been placed in your situation would surely want the man to eat crow…at least for a little while."

"It's not crow, Nic. It's pot roast. You helped me with the recipe, remember?"

"Is that a joke coming from my worried friend? Maybe there's hope for you after all. Besides, I *know* that black dress you're talking about. And it's killer on you. You could make a burlap sack look great with your figure."

Eliza closed her eyes briefly, wondering if Nicole had a point. After all, why had she chosen Reese's favorite meal to serve unless a small part of her wanted him to see what he'd missed out on these past years. A small part of her wanted him to recognize that he'd thrown away an abiding love. Maybe she had chosen a dress, though conservative in design with a high neckline and a decent hemline, that seemed to set off her curves. With Eliza's body, unless she truly did choose a sack to wear, she could hardly conceal her womanly form.

When the doorbell rang, she froze. I need more time, she thought. I'm not ready for this. "He's here," she breathed into the phone.

"Eliza, keep your cool. Be honest with him. And whatever you do, don't…"

"What, Nic? Don't what?"

"Don't fall for the guy again."

"Not a chance. I'm immune to his charm now. I've learned my lesson with Reese Parker."

She clung dearly to those thoughts as she descended the stairs and greeted her estranged husband.

Reese Parker stood outside the Fortune estate, barely containing his temper. The last time he'd been here, he'd been effectively tossed off the property. Now he was an invited guest. Hell, not exactly. It had cost him to get this invitation, but it would be well worth the money paid to see Eliza's reaction when she learned the truth about him. She'd toyed with his affections in the past, then cast him aside. Reese would only give her a dose of her own medicine.

He rang the doorbell, and when the door opened, he was surprised to find a nervous Eliza standing there instead of one of the staff. "Still keeping secrets, darlin'?"

Her chin jutted up, angling her nose in the air, but she couldn't conceal the rosy color flaming her cheeks. "I thought we could be civil to one another tonight."

Think again, he wanted to say, but she did have a point. Nothing would get settled if they couldn't stand to look at each other all evening.

Although looking at Eliza had never been his problem. She'd captured his attention from the moment they'd met. Tonight, she dressed in a classy black dress that attempted to hide a body he'd tried damn hard to forget. With blond hair caressing her shoulders and those soft blue eyes—glaring at him right now—Reese remembered her all too well, *in* and *out* of her clothes.

He stepped inside and handed her a bottle of Dom Pérignon.

A faint smile crossed her lips when she glanced at the bottle he'd given her.

When I make my first million, we'll celebrate with Dom Pérignon.

Reese had always wanted the best for her, no matter the cost, and now that he could afford it, he knew the champagne would taste bitter to them both.

"I keep my promises," he said quietly.

Eliza nearly dropped the bottle she held. "Except the most important promise of all," she said, handing him back the champagne. "Dinner is waiting."

Reese set the bottle down on an entry table and arched his brows. He hadn't really wanted to drink champagne with her. No, his intention was to make a point, and he wasn't entirely sure he'd succeeded.

Eliza led him up a wide winding staircase to the second floor. It irritated him to no end the pains she took in order to keep their marriage a secret. She'd probably arranged for the entire family, as well as the staff, to be gone this evening. Fine by him. He wasn't overly fond of the Fortunes anyway, from the little Eliza had shared with him about her family. And now she was tucking them both away somewhere on the second floor.

"You have a dining room up here?"

Eliza rolled her eyes. "We need privacy. We'll dine in my studio."

"Ah, worried that your father or brother might stumble upon the domestic scene? Wonder what they'd say to see you actually dining with your husband?"

"Shhh. Please, Reese. Keep your voice down."

Reese clammed up, but not to ease her distress. His plan of action called for charm and wit, not anger. He'd had six years to stew and now he'd have to control his boiling point.

He followed her into a large room that appeared welcoming and warm, a room that clearly wasn't ordinarily used for dining. Yet she had a table set beautifully with all the finery he'd have expected from a Fortune and she'd obviously gone to some trouble to conceal a work area using drapes of material. Reese felt himself relaxing some. "This is nice."

Eliza shut the door behind them, then let out a deep sigh of relief. "We can talk in here without…"

Reese raised his brows. "Without?"

"Interruption. Would you like to have a seat?"

So formal, he thought. Had she forgotten how it'd been with them? The laughter, the sweet promises, making love anywhere and everywhere, including the backseat of his truck. Reese shoved aside an image of Eliza straddling him on a chair not too unlike the one she so properly offered him just now. She'd been beautifully naked, gripping him tight and rocking that chair for all it was worth.

He removed his jacket and loosened his tie.

Eliza approached, coming up close enough for him to catch a whiff of her scent. The familiar exotic perfume teased his nostrils, bringing back even more memories. She still wore the same fragrance that had lingered on his clothes for weeks after she'd gone.

"I'll take that," she said, reaching for his suit coat.

He handed her the jacket and sat down. Within a few moments, she joined him at the small round table. When she uncovered the dishes, he glanced down at the meal, then lifted his gaze back up to her. "Pot roast and all the fixings."

"Yes," she said, meeting his eyes as though meeting some sort of challenge, as well.

Reese studied her for a second, while something fierce slammed into his gut. She remembered. Damn her. They'd had a good thing, and she'd destroyed it—and him, nearly—when she'd walked out of their marriage. Well, he was here to set things straight. He tempered his anger with the knowledge that he would do just that. Then he'd be gone.

Reese took a bite of the roast and nodded. "This is very good."

Eliza's lips trembled into a little smile. "Thank you. I, uh…my cooking ability hasn't improved much, but I'm happy with the results."

Reese swallowed and leaned back in his seat. "Are you saying you cooked this meal?"

She nodded. "It was a huge donation, Reese."

"So you figured you owed me? You figured—"

"I'd do the same for anyone who made a bid," she said in a rushed breath. "It's only right."

Too bad his wife had a slanted view of what was right or not. She'd honored her pledge to cook a meal for a hefty donation, but she hadn't the decency to tell him to his face that she'd missed the good life and was leaving him high and dry six years ago. Reese let her comment drop for the time being.

He scanned the room again, this time with discerning eyes, noting the objects partially hidden behind draped fabrics. "So what is this place?"

Eliza's eyes brightened for the first time tonight. "It's my studio. I do interior design. It's something I've always enjoyed."

"Are you in business?"

She shook her head. "No. Maybe someday," she said on a wistful note. "I've decorated the third floor of the estate. And I use my talent for charitable events at times."

Reese forked another mouthful and chewed thoughtfully, wondering about Eliza's life. Didn't sound as though she lived on the edge anymore. The Eliza he'd known had been part risk taker, part sexy bed partner. She'd been carefree and happy—or so he had thought until he'd realized that he had been her entertainment that one summer.

Now she spent her time raising money for good causes, but it seemed, from the light that sparked in her eyes just then, that she wasn't pursuing her true passion. He'd noted the longing on her face when she'd let down her guard.

He glanced at her full plate. "Not hungry?"

She lifted a quick smile to him and picked up her fork, ready to stab the meat. Then she lowered the fork down none too gently. "Reese, why'd you make such a large donation last night?"

He smiled. "Because I can."

Eliza's blue gaze met his. He'd always thought she had the prettiest eyes. That hadn't changed, only now he knew what kind of deceit those eyes could conceal.

"How can you? What's changed in your life?"

"I told you one day I'd strike oil, darlin'."

She slumped back in her seat, stunned. "You mean… you did it? You actually… I never thought…"

"That was the problem, wasn't it? You never believed in me. You never thought I'd fulfill my dream. All you saw was a silver-buckled rodeo cowboy without a dime in his pocket." His tone turned gruff. "But after you left, I made it my mission in life. I partnered up with my brother Garrett. We pooled our resources. With his business sense and my gut instincts we struck oil after two years. Now Parker Explorations is a successful wildcatting company in Montana."

"You own your own company?"

Judging by the look of awe on her face, she appeared truly surprised. Reese had wanted that reaction from her, but now it seemed that her lack of faith in him achieving his goals just irritated him even more. He'd wanted to shock her and rub his success in her face to gain well-deserved satisfaction. He'd done all that, but it wasn't enough, damn it. "Let me get this straight. You married a rodeo cowboy from Montana and never in your wildest dreams did you think I'd amount to anything. I had no money, and that just wasn't good enough for you. After our little summer fling, you got tired of playing the penniless wife and headed for home. I get that now. But you should have stuck around. My company is one of the fastest growing in Montana, and now I'm finally setting down roots. I'm staying in one place for a change and building my own estate just outside of Bozeman. So let's just call our marriage what it really was—a foolish notion. Or how did you say it in your note? *A mistake.*"

Eliza blinked, then stared at him as if he'd gone raving mad. "Reese! What are you talking about? I didn't run out on you because of *money*. And I certainly wouldn't have married you if I hadn't lo—"

"Hadn't what, Eliza?" he probed, shoving his plate away and leaning in with elbows braced on the table.

She hesitated for a moment and then on a long-winded sigh finished, "Hadn't thought it would last forever. I'd planned on staying married, but you…you were the one who made that impossible. How could you think I'd stay in a marriage to a man who'd been unfaithful? After less than three months together, Reese! I'd trusted you. And you, you…"

Reese tossed his napkin onto the table and bolted out of his seat. "What?"

"Don't pretend you don't know what I'm talking about."

"I *don't* know what you're talking about! I was never unfaithful."

Eliza sat perfectly still in her seat and spoke slowly. "I'm not a fool, Reese. But apparently you thought I was. That last night, when I left you to go home for my father's surprise birthday party, I came back to our hotel room unexpectedly and saw her."

Completely baffled, he asked, "Saw…*who?*"

"The rodeo queen. Suzette, SueBelle, Sue…something. She was in our bed. *Our bed!*"

Reese slumped back into his chair as faded memories came back and he recalled that night. He'd kissed Eliza goodbye in front of the hotel, hoping she'd go home and finally have the courage to tell her family about him and their marriage. He'd met up with a friend from the rodeo named Cody Pierce and together they'd gone to the bar for a drink. Aside from missing his wife already, he'd had an event that next day so he'd decided one drink would have to be it. "Her name was Susanna."

Eliza nodded scornfully. "So you don't deny it?"

"Damn straight, I deny it. I never touched that woman. No, that's not true. I did touch her…."

Eliza's expression blackened.

He was so damn angry with her right now that he didn't give a damn what she thought, but he hated being accused of something falsely. "I was at the bar with Cody that night. You remember him. He's the big, good-looking bull rider who always managed to flirt with you."

Eliza opened her mouth to respond but clamped her lips together, apparently deciding against it.

"We spotted Susanna in the corner, drinking herself into oblivion. She was really wasted. It seemed her younger brother had gotten in a bad car wreck and she couldn't catch a flight out of town until the morning. She was pretty upset and then announced that she'd drive herself all the way to Texas if she had to. When she stood up to leave, she would have collapsed if Cody hadn't caught her. We both knew if we left her, she'd do something stupid. Since you were gone anyway, we put her in my bed, talked to her awhile and waited until she fell asleep. I bunked with Cody that night."

"Sounds like a good story," Eliza said bitterly, "except when I entered the room, she called out your name."

"And did I go to her? Did you see me? Hell, no. Because I wasn't there. It was after midnight when we finally got her to sleep. And when I went to check on her just after dawn the next day, she was already gone. She couldn't have spent more than a few hours in our room. I was never alone with her."

"But…but I thought… I came back so unexpectedly, and when I saw her…I assumed—"

"I know what you assumed," Reese said, barely managing to contain his hurt and anger. He'd given Eliza everything he had to give, but still she hadn't trusted in him. She'd instantly thought the worst, without even bothering to stay and confront him to get to the truth. "Did you really think I'd be unfaithful to you? Where were you for those three months we had together? Didn't you know how I felt about you?"

Eliza closed her eyes slowly, her face void of expression.

"What brought you back that night, anyway?"

She opened her eyes, the pretty blue tarnished with regret. "My…my father took ill. It was nothing serious, but Patricia decided to postpone the party. And I was so happy to come home to you that night that I rushed inside that room and then…saw her there."

"So you wrote me a note."

She stiffened and then sank her hand into her hair. "Yes. But first I ran. I couldn't help it. I had to get away. I came back just before dawn after crying my eyes out in my car. I decided to leave the note with the front desk clerk."

"Why? Why not blast me right then and there if you thought I'd been unfaithful? At least the truth would have come out. And we wouldn't have wasted six years of our lives."

"I couldn't," she said, the regret in her eyes turning to pain. "I couldn't because… You know that I had a broken engagement right before I met you."

"Yeah, that's about all I know. You never gave me details."

"You didn't seem to want any."

"What for? I only knew that I wanted you. I didn't care that some loser let you go."

"But you see, it's so much more than that. He hurt me in ways that I can't describe. And then when I thought you had betrayed me, too…I couldn't face it. Or you. And I couldn't face another disastrous scandal. I'd put my family through enough that year, breaking off that engagement. The headlines were cruel and probing…and I just couldn't put my family through that again."

"So you walked?"

She nodded.

"And it never occurred to you that I might have been innocent?"

Eliza lifted her eyes to meet his squarely. She breathed out, "Not once."

"Not once," he repeated. He tamped down rising rage. *Not once* had she even thought it possible that what she'd seen had been something harmless, something that could have been easily explained if she'd only sought the answers.

She continued in a quiet tone, "It was like I was re-living a scene from my past. First Warren's betrayal, then yours. We'd been engaged for months, and two weeks before our wedding date I found him in bed with his campaign manager. He hadn't expected me to show up when I did, either. But when I caught him, I realized that he'd used me and the powerful Fortune name for his campaign. He wanted to be Sioux Falls' youngest mayor. I guess I never really got over that betrayal."

"So you thought I was just like him?"

"No…yes. I don't know," she said, tears misting in her eyes.

"I never asked you for anything. In fact, I refused your money time and again. That's not what I wanted from you. I only asked that you love me. But you didn't. Maybe you weren't ready to get married, Eliza. Maybe you still loved this guy and only used me to get over him."

"No! That's not true." She rose from her seat and implored him with fire in her eyes. "I didn't love Warren. Not the way I loved you. He got what was coming to him when he lost the election, and I knew a moment of satisfaction in that. But it all seemed so trivial to me because when I met you, I fell in love and didn't care a thing about Warren anymore. I never thought of him that way again."

"Except the moment there was a hint of doubt about me, you cast that so-called love aside. No, Eliza. I'm not buying it. That's not what love is about."

Eliza's indignant expression faltered.

Reese hadn't expected this. No, he'd always thought she'd walked out on him because he couldn't provide the money and lifestyle she'd been accustomed to. They'd spend their days traveling the rodeo circuit, spending their nights often in a different motel room, in a different city. He'd been so sure that she'd gotten tired of the instability and the lack of luxury.

Now he was blown away by her allegation. She'd really believed that he'd deceived her and he'd had an affair the minute her back had been turned. This truth was a fresh injury to an old wound, one he'd nursed through the years until he'd thought it healed. Now she'd opened that old scar up and plunged it deep with a new sharp and gutting accusation.

Even now, as he gazed into her solemn eyes, he read doubt and mistrust there. What did it matter that she didn't believe him? After all, he hadn't come here expecting a happy reunion.

"What now?" she asked, and he noted worry on her sullen face. She didn't want their marriage exposed; that much was evident.

He approached her, his gaze holding hers. Eliza backed away from him and he smiled. And the more she backed away, the closer he came, until she bumped into a worktable draped with white satin. He grabbed her hand and drew her near, while the other hand reached up to caress her face. She stared at him. He skimmed a finger down her cheek, tracing the delicate lines. Her skin felt smooth and utterly soft, just as he remembered. He skimmed his hand farther down, grazing her throat and then stroked lower to flatten onto her collarbone.

She drew in a quick breath, the gasp reminiscent of the passion they once shared. Heat was still there between them, simmering from their bodies. And want was still there, too. Her pulse pounded under his palm.

He slid his hand to her breast, spreading out to cup her fully. Even through his anger and hurt, the remembered feel of her created havoc below his waist.

He flicked his thumb over her pebbled nipple.

She made a sound in her throat, a little cry that drew him to full erection.

He leaned in, pressing her body to his, his mouth angling toward hers. "Now, darlin', I give you something to worry about."

Three

If she pushed at him, she knew he'd release her and back away. But Reese's heat surrounded her. His eyes held her captive. And those lips, hovering so near, tempted her beyond reason. Eliza's body responded to his.

It always had.

So when he freed her breast and splayed both hands around her waist, tugging her closer, she allowed it. And sighed when his erection rubbed into her belly.

Her mind flashed images of making love with Reese in all ways and all positions imaginable. They'd been hot for each other. They'd never let up.

They'd been madly in love.

"Kiss me, Eliza."

And there it was—the low timbre of Reese's command. He'd always brought her pleasure. He'd been an incredible lover, a man who spoke to her in bed, telling her what he wanted and what he would do to her.

He'd been sinfully erotic, sexier than a man had a right to be. He'd brought her fulfillment each and every time.

Yes, yes. She wanted to kiss him and bring back all those heated, glorious memories. Just this once, she told herself because she knew she and Reese had no future together. They'd hurt each other far too much to ever hope to heal past mistakes. And she'd never reveal him as her husband.

Never.

She lifted her mouth to his. The moment their lips touched, Reese took over, and she flowed farther into his arms, remembering how he'd always taken care with her.

He held her close and gently, but his kiss was harsh, pressing her lips roughly, and the mix of his musky scent and demanding body was the sweetest torture she'd ever known. He took from her and took some more, his lips crushing hers without tenderness or regard.

And just when she meant to push him away, realizing the punishing terms of his kiss, he softened his assault and the blending of their mouths turned into something she'd never expected to feel for Reese again—desire.

It burned through her.

She stood in his arms, stunned by her reaction.

She'd spent the last six years hating him for his betrayal, and in less than six minutes he'd made her want him again.

"Open for me, baby," he rasped out.

"Reese, this isn't—"

He mated their tongues, and her protest died quickly as old rhythms came back. The taste of him and the heady way he moved his mouth on hers sent shocking tingles down to her feet. She fell deeply into the kiss, unmindful of reason, throwing caution to the wind.

Don't fall for the guy again.

No, no. She wouldn't. She'd promised Nicole and herself. But she couldn't deny how alive he made her feel. More alive than she'd felt these past six years.

Reese broke off the kiss after long moments. "Still so pretty," he said, his breath caressing her lips. "Still taste so damn good."

Eliza's heart raced. A shocking thrill coursed down her body, making her tremble with need. His seductive tone had always promised a wild night tangling in the sheets.

"Touch me," he said quietly.

She lifted her hand to his face, her fingers outlining the strength of his jaw. She felt the contours, the slight stubble that shadowed his features, and remembered how that stubble would brush her thighs, creating rough friction against her legs right before he'd...

He bent his head and took her mouth again in another soul-searing kiss. Eliza kissed him back, caught up in memories she'd long ago buried. And when his knee parted her legs and he hiked her dress up slowly, the heat of his palm scorched her thigh. His fingers slid over her skin, inching higher until he teased the silken edge of her panties.

Wrapped in his embrace, devoured by his kiss, Eliza moaned deep in her throat. Her lower body pulsed in anticipation, waiting for a touch that would shatter her balanced world.

But Reese broke off the kiss, removed his hand from that highly sensitive area and lowered the hem of her dress. He took a step back, yet his smoldering gaze never left hers.

Disappointment registered, and she stood there, fully aroused, staring into unreadable eyes. No emotion flickered through, no regret or apology or frustration, none of the things Eliza felt right now, just that damnable blank stare. She watched him take a deep breath, grab his jacket and head for the door. "I have to go."

Eliza couldn't muster a response. She continued to watch him until finally he turned and smiled quickly, granting her a peek at one dimple that had always sent her heart humming. "Thanks for dinner."

She stood there, rooted to the spot until long after she heard Reese's car speed off.

"So is she off the hook?" Garrett asked as Reese rested his head against the bed pillow in his hotel room and clicked off the basketball game on television.

He spoke clearly into the phone. "Hell, no, she's not off the hook. She's very much *on* the hook."

"She found a woman in your bed. Most wives wouldn't look too kindly on that."

"Yeah, too bad I wasn't anywhere near that bed to reap the rewards."

Garrett paused for a long moment, then said, "Man, this really has thrown you, hasn't it?"

"Damn straight. She accused me of cheating on her, little brother. She should've known me better than that."

"Reese, you knew each other for all of—what?— three months. That's hardly enough time to—"

"To get married?"

"I didn't say that."

"It's what you and Pops thought. I know that. We got hitched exactly twenty-four days after we met. And less than ten weeks later the marriage was history."

"It doesn't matter what either of us thought at the time. What matters is what you're thinking now."

Reese lifted up from the bed, swung his legs out and braced his elbows on his knees, holding the phone tight against his ear. "I'm gonna finish this."

Garrett's frustrated sigh put Reese on edge. His brother had a history with women, but no woman had ever tied him down. He'd never allowed himself to get that close. Now Garrett was getting a taste of his own medicine with a woman who wouldn't look at him twice. Maybe Garrett was finally softening up to the idea of marriage. Whereas Reese had been there, done that—and it'd been a bitter pill to swallow.

"So how's Leanne?" he asked.

"Don't change the subject," Garrett snapped.

Reese smiled. Leanne was their top-notch geologist, a woman with brains and amazing good looks—and she didn't know that Garrett existed. At least that's the impression she'd always given. She'd been on their team from almost the beginning and had been invaluable to the company. Together, all three of them had made a fortune in the oil business. "Look, I know you have my best interests at heart, but don't worry about me. I know what I'm doing."

"That's exactly what worries me," Garrett said. "You can be…"

"Watch it, little bro."

"Tenacious. That's all I was going to say. You're damn tenacious when you go after something."

"Thanks. I'll take that as a compliment," Reese said, his sour mood lifting a bit.

"Tenacious *and* a giant pain in the ass."

Reese smiled.

"So you're coming home tomorrow?"

"Nice try. No, I'm staying in Sioux Falls for a little longer. As soon as I know my plans, I'll contact you."

"Don't forget you've got a company to run. And the damn decorator has left a dozen messages for you. Apparently she needs final approval before going ahead with the plans you've discussed. I'll thank you next time for not making me your middleman. I don't do plantation shutters versus pleated shades. Hell, half the time I don't know what that woman is talking about."

Reese grinned at Garrett's obvious frustration. He felt the same way. He'd wanted his house built to his specifications, but he didn't realize how much planning and thought went into furnishing and decorating it. He'd put that aspect of his new home on the back burner, but now he had some decisions to make about furnishing it to his liking. "I'll call her in the morning. You won't have to deal with her much longer. And, Garrett, thanks. I appreciate you holding down the fort while I'm away."

"You're welcome, but you're still a pain in the ass."

"One of my better qualities these days. Oh, and be sure to say hello to Leanne for me," he managed to get in before the connection died. He grinned when he heard a string of muttered curses from his brother on the other end.

Reese didn't know how he felt about Garrett falling for someone in the company. It could destroy their working relationship. But still, he wanted to see his brother happy, and if that meant him taking a chance, then so be it. Garrett, though, had yet to make his move.

Putting Garrett's love life out of his mind, he concentrated on his own, and the vision of a hot and passionate Eliza Fortune Parker slipped into his mind.

She'd hardly been off his mind lately.

She still reacted to him the same way she always had—with eager enthusiasm. Even though Reese knew she didn't want him anywhere near her or her precious family estate, her response to his advances told a different story. And Reese found he wanted to continue turning the pages to finish this book.

She was still his wife, damn it.

He'd have to do something about that soon.

Reese clicked on the television set again, lay down on the bed and tried to concentrate on a tied game with two teams racing down the clock, but he found himself staring blankly at the screen and thinking only of Eliza.

He'd once thought she'd left because he wasn't good enough for her, but he'd been mistaken. She hadn't run off just because of his lack of money. Hell, no. She saw him as a rodeo rider with no future, who had *cheated* on her.

He shoved aside the burning ache in his gut but held

on to his anger and whispered into the lonely hotel room, "Damn you, Eliza."

"I just don't know, Diana," Eliza said as she turned in a complete circle, taking yet another look at the cut glass, crystal and porcelain vases in the upscale boutique called Message on a Bottle. "I can't decide what's best for Gina and Case."

Diana—her friend, onetime college roommate and soon-to-be addition to the family as Max Fortune's wife—cast her a dubious look. "Hey, roomie, I've never known you to be indecisive. Especially when it comes to decorating. So what's up?"

Eliza stifled a groan. She'd asked Diana to tag along to help her pick out the centerpiece for Case and Gina's welcome-home celebration. Normally, Eliza needed no help when it came to setting a table, but she'd had trouble concentrating since Reese had shown up on her doorstep the other night. He'd overwhelmed her with his accusations, then stunned her even more with a kiss that had quickly escalated from simmering kindling to a raging fire within minutes.

A kiss that might have led to a wild tangling between the gossamer fabrics in her studio if Reese hadn't backed off. Lord, she'd barely been able think when his lips first touched hers. Her mind had taken flight and her traitorous body hadn't helped matters, either. She'd fallen into his touch, aching for his hands on her breasts, and then when he'd slid his hand up her thigh, she'd wanted him to go farther, the yearning in her deep and consuming. She'd wanted him to touch her until she splintered apart, one piece at a time.

Eliza shuddered at the notion.

She'd never thought she'd lay eyes on Reese again, much less have a heated confrontation with him. She'd spent the last two nights trying to justify what she'd seen in their hotel room six years ago. Reese's explanation had fully surprised her—he'd been merely helping a friend sober up. Nothing had happened.

After what she'd been through with Warren, she'd immediately jumped to conclusions seeing a woman in her bed. But had they been wrong conclusions? Her stomach was in knots. She hadn't eaten or slept much, thinking about Reese and whether or not she should have trusted him. Had he been innocent of any wrongdoing? Had she still been reeling from Warren's betrayal that she'd immediately seen the same in Reese without really thinking it through?

Still, finding a beautiful woman in her bed the minute she left town was pretty damning evidence, wasn't it? But if what Reese confessed was true, then Eliza had unwittingly thrown away the last six years of her life. *Their* life.

Her stomach squeezed tight, the pain searing through at the thought she might have destroyed everything because of her own insecurities. Still, Eliza clung to that one shred of doubt in her mind, that she might not have been wrong. What was fact and what was fiction? And did any of this really matter? She hadn't heard from Reese in two days. Maybe he'd already left town.

"Eliza," Diana said more forcefully, bringing Eliza's head up. "Are you okay today?"

"Oh…yes, I'm f-fine," she stuttered, trying to pull herself together. No sense alarming her friend. "I want this dinner to be perfect for Case and Gina."

Diana cast her a reassuring look. "It will be, Eliza. Everything you do is *perfect*."

If her friend only knew how imperfect her life really was, she'd be shocked. She had a secret husband, for one. A man who thought she'd left him because of his poor lifestyle—a man who may have been entirely innocent of her accusations of betrayal. A man she had loved with the whole of her heart yet couldn't reveal their relationship to anyone.

Having Diana here with her today helped direct her mind back to the dinner celebration tonight and off Reese Parker, his revelations and bold behavior the other night.

"I'm glad you were able to come along today," Eliza said. "You're good for my ego."

"It's the truth," Diana replied. "And I mean every word."

"Thank you," Eliza said, quite humbled, yet today she felt anything but perfect.

"It's great that we got a chance to become close again. If you hadn't suggested I come to live in Sioux Falls a few years ago, that might never have happened."

Eliza tossed aside her misgivings for the moment to smile at her friend. "As a bonus, you snagged yourself a gorgeous fiancé."

"There is that," she replied. "I would never have met up with Max again if it weren't for you."

"So now I'm a matchmaker?"

"You get some of the credit, yes."

Eliza was pleased how things had worked out for Diana and Max, though she knew she wouldn't have the same sort of happy ending in her life.

She glanced down at the twin overlapping hearts made of pewter that she held in her hand. Engraved with Case's and Gina's names and their wedding date, she'd have the proprietor set the plaque onto whatever vase they chose—the specialty of the boutique. A glorious array of fresh flowers would serve as the centerpiece for tonight's celebration as well as a welcome-home present for the two of them from the entire family.

But she couldn't seem to concentrate. Nothing struck her eye. Usually when on a mission like this, she knew exactly what she wanted and how to acquire it. Where had her professional acumen gone?

Never mind—she knew. But she couldn't divulge her secret to Diana. Though they'd been good friends and sorority sisters at Wellesley University, she would soon become a Fortune. Eliza wouldn't put a family member in the precarious position of keeping her secret.

She watched Diana stroll over to a display of tall, tapered, diamond-cut crystal vases. Diana ran her finger along one intricate vase, then peered up to meet her eyes.

Putting Reese completely out of her mind, Eliza walked over to the display table. "I think you've found it." She lifted the vase and examined it carefully. "We'll take this one," she said to Diana. "It'll be…"

"*Perfect*," they chorused.

Nash Fortune smiled with warmth at his son and new daughter-in-law, raising his champagne glass in a toast.

"Let's welcome home the newlyweds in true Fortune style," he said as the family circled the couple in the great room and lifted their glasses. "May Case and Gina always know happiness and love." Then Eliza's father cast a loving glance at his wife, Patricia. "My wish for you both is a loving relationship filled with honesty and trust."

Patricia's smile was tentative, her lips trembling, her eyes blinking away tears. Nash took his wife's hand, and for a moment Eliza noted distress in his eyes right before he grinned. "And maybe a grandchild or two."

"We'll get right on that, Dad," Case said and everyone laughed. Everyone but Patricia. She seemed a million miles away.

"You do that, son."

Then the room ignited with conversation. When the Fortune family got together, it wasn't a quiet affair. Glasses clinked, voices mingled and laughter filled the room. Family gatherings weren't always so joyous, though. Most times it was a meeting of minds behind the Fortune empire and a way to connect the business dots camouflaged as a family function. But today was all about Case and his new wife. Eliza found herself relaxing with the newlyweds and Diana and Max, her brother, Creed, her half sister, Skylar, and her parents. Maya was on her way to the celebration and Blake had refused the invitation. A good thing, too, because Blake held no fondness for either Case or Creed, the half brothers always butting heads.

So for the first time since Reese had shown up at the charity auction, Eliza could let down her guard.

Twenty minutes later, the family sat down for their

meal in the dining room. Ivy had outdone herself with a sumptuous display of seafood—oysters, crab cakes, baked halibut and lobster tails drenched in drawn butter. Vegetables and side dishes complemented the meal, as well as four different kinds of breads and muffins. Eliza's floral arrangement centered the oblong table, standing tall enough to allow everyone's eyes to meet without obstruction.

"Oh, the flowers and vase are lovely," Gina said instantly, noting the inscription. "This has to be your doing, Eliza."

"Yeah, thanks, sis," Case said, glancing at their names and wedding date engraved on the vase. "At least this way I'll never forget our anniversary."

Gina smiled at Case and in a teasing tone said, "Yes, it'll help jog my memory, too."

Case grabbed hold of Gina's hand, bringing it to his lips for a quick kiss. "I have other ways to jog your memory, sweetheart."

Nash smiled and turned to Patricia. "Maybe we're not too far off from those grandkids."

"What? Oh…yes. Grandkids. That would be…nice." Patricia forced a smile.

"I'm happy you like it," Eliza said, "but I can't take full credit. Diana actually picked it out. She did a wonderful job."

Eliza spoke to Case and Gina, but it was Patricia's distracted behavior tonight that held her attention. Eliza knew something about keeping up a pretense and wondered if Patricia was upset or hiding something terribly important. She'd never seen her so…troubled.

And a minute later the doorbell chimed. "I bet that's Maya. I'll let her in," her father said, rising to answer the door.

If anyone could shake Patricia out of her doldrums, it would be her only daughter, Maya. It seemed that Eliza's father was anxious to please his wife, something he'd done ever since they'd first married thirteen years ago.

When Nash returned to the dining room, all eyes lifted. "Well, it wasn't Maya at the door, but we do have another guest. Eliza, this young man came to see you tonight, and I invited him to join us for dinner. Why don't you introduce him to the family?"

Startled, Eliza's gaze darted from her father to the tall, good-looking man standing beside him wearing Armani and an easy smile.

Reese.

Her heart slammed against her chest and her mind raced with questions. Why was he here? Had he given away their secret? Was he planning to? A piece of bread she'd been chewing stuck in her throat. She forced herself to swallow it down. Trapped amid a family showing more than slight interest, Eliza had no choice but to make the introductions.

Slowly, with feigned composure, she took a breath and rose on shaky legs to look him straight in the eye. She prayed that he wouldn't ruin the evening. "Everyone, I'd like you to meet Reese…Parkman."

"Parker," Reese corrected, his dark eyes narrowing on her.

"Eliza, why don't you show Mr. Parker to his seat," her father said.

Eliza hesitated, darting a glance around the room to all the family members she'd lied to over the years. Oh, God. This couldn't be happening.

"If it wouldn't be too much trouble, ma'am," Reese said casually.

Sinking fast with no one to throw her a rope, Eliza managed to say, "Of course…no trouble at all."

As if Reese Parker, her secret husband, the man who could turn her world upside down, didn't know how much his appearance here tonight would cause her nothing *but* trouble.

Four

"You say you're from Montana?" Nash asked Reese after all the introductions and handshakes were made. Reese settled back in his seat, with Creed Fortune to his right and Max Fortune to his left, Eliza seating him on the opposite side of the table from her. But from his vantage point, he could look directly into her eyes. Eyes that so far refused to meet his.

"Yes, sir. Born and raised." He sipped wine.

"The oil business must be pretty good these days," Nash said matter-of-factly. "You made a hefty contribution to Eliza's fund-raiser the other night, which was very kind."

Reese shrugged. "I have a soft spot for keeping the Old West alive. It was my way of helping the museum."

Nash glanced at Eliza, and when she didn't respond,

he continued, "My daddy, Charles Fortune, made the bulk of his wealth as a wildcatter back in 1929. It's a tough business. A man's got to have a lot of stamina to stick it out."

"And some financial support," Creed added.

Reese agreed. "That's true. I didn't have much of the latter, but I guess I'm stubborn enough when I want something. I worked my way through the rodeo circuit as a bareback bronc rider, winning some competitions and scraping by. I poured everything I had into wildcatting. The standing joke was that I couldn't find oil in a gas station."

Nash Fortune eyed him carefully. "But you proved them wrong."

Reese nodded, then glanced at Eliza, who had suddenly lifted her eyes to meet his. "You could say that I proved myself *right*."

The men at the table nodded in understanding.

Eliza shuffled in her seat and looked away, the food on her plate untouched. Clearly, she didn't want him here. Reese could take satisfaction in that, watching color rise in her cheeks and her chest heave with quiet indignation. She wore sparkling blue sapphires in her ears and around her neck, bringing out the deep blue in her eyes. Her blond hair was twisted up into some sort of elegant knot, with those long bangs softly caressing her brows. She'd dressed modestly tonight; the conservative silk blouse unbuttoned at the throat left the rest up to the imagination. And Reese did imagine undoing each one of the those buttons until he could slip his hands inside and...

"Didn't you spend a summer in Montana, Eliza?" Creed asked innocently, his gaze fixed on his sister.

She froze for a moment and those pretty blue eyes widened with a fear only Reese might have noticed. She sipped wine before answering. "Yes…I did. One summer." She cleared her throat delicately, then added, "I didn't stay in one place long, though. I, uh, did some traveling from place to place."

"It's big-sky country. People don't usually bump into each other unless it's intentional," Reese stated. Then, setting his gaze on Eliza, he added, "But trust me, if I met Eliza in Montana, *I wouldn't have forgotten.*"

Eliza shifted her focus to him, her expression bordering on dread.

Silence ensued as Nash raised an eyebrow at his daughter. The other family members stared at her, too—with more interest than she'd like, he guessed—before fixing their stares back on him. But Reese only watched Eliza. And he didn't find the wildly erotic, carefree woman he'd married that summer seated across from him. Instead she seemed subdued, unsure and, most of all, inhibited. Not at all the same woman he'd known.

Case broke the silence. "Well, Eliza might not have met you before, but you sure as hell look familiar to me. Though, I can't recall ever meeting you."

Reese stifled a sharp response. Hell, yes, they'd met. The day he'd come here to retrieve his wife, six years ago. He'd been tossed off the property by an overprotective brother who'd wanted "no damn drunken cowboy" lurking on his property. Hell, the man had offered to have him thrown in jail. Reese hadn't divulged any information. He hadn't told Case he had a perfect right to be there since he was married to his sister. No, Reese hadn't given away Eliza's wretched secret. Instead he'd gotten the Fortune message, loud and clear.

Reese smiled. "I guess I have that kind of face."

Even from across the table, he noticed Eliza exhaling her breath slowly in somewhat relief.

"So what brings you to Sioux Falls?" Nash asked, but Reese got the distinct impression the man wanted to know what he was doing knocking on his door, looking for Eliza.

"I'm here on business." Personal business, he didn't add. "Looking to acquire some horses for the stables I plan to build on my property just outside of Bozeman. I've got an eight-thousand-square-foot home sitting on a hundred and fifty acres of land. When Eliza cooked me dinner the other night, she mentioned that she knew something about interior design. I thought maybe she could help me out a little."

Eliza's expression turned from barely contained surprise to out-and-out astonishment.

"Eliza's done nice work on this home, but—" Nash began, until his wife laid a hand on his arm, halting his next thought.

"Eliza is very talented," Patricia said quietly, speaking up for the first time since Reese had met her. "She has an eye for color and design. As a teenager, she was always rearranging things and making them look better."

Eliza peered at her stepmother with gratitude in her eyes.

Gina added, "I've already requested that she do up the baby nursery when the time comes."

All heads turned her way. "I said *when* the time comes. No need to get excited. I'm not keeping any secrets."

Creed Fortune twisted his mouth, his tone dry. "Heaven forbid a Fortune keeps a secret."

Patricia's face paled almost as much as Eliza's. The rest of the Fortunes kept their mouths clamped shut with that remark, and Reese wondered what other secrets were contained in this room.

But when a pretty, dark-haired young woman walked into the dining room, all attention turned to her.

"Hello, everyone. Sorry I missed dinner." She walked over to give Patricia a kiss on the cheek. "Hi, Mom."

She was greeted with pleasantries from everyone but Creed. Reese had heard his sharp intake of breath when she'd walked in.

"Maya? Oh, hello, dear." Patricia took her daughter's hand.

Nash rose immediately. "Sit with your mother, Maya. I'll just get another—"

"No, there's no need. I'm not staying long. I just dropped by to say hello and welcome Gina and Case home from their honeymoon."

"You're not staying?" Nash asked, unable to mask his disappointment. "Your mother's been looking forward to seeing you. We all have."

Maya blinked, then doubt crept into her eyes. "I can't this time."

"Well, before you go, let me introduce you to our guest. Reese Parker, this is Patricia's daughter, Maya. Maya, Reese."

Reese rose and acknowledged her. "Nice to meet you."

Maya responded politely, but her gaze drifted over to Creed and the two exchanged glances.

"Maya, how's Brad these days? We haven't seen him in a while," Eliza asked.

"He's fine. Brad's out of town until tomorrow night. He's—"

"He's never around unless he wants something," Creed said curtly.

"That's not true!" Maya's dark brown eyes burned with denial.

Creed almost came out of his chair. "He's using you, Maya. When will you open your eyes? He wants to put his hands on Fortune money. He's already put his hands on yo—"

"Creed!" Eliza's voice rose to an uneven pitch. "Stop right there."

Maya's face flamed and tears filled her eyes. "Shut up, Creed. You don't know what you're talking about."

"Settle down. Both of you," Nash said in the same way he might have scolded them when they were children, the father overseeing his son and stepdaughter. "Creed, you're out of line."

Patricia rose from her seat and spoke directly to Creed. "You've upset Maya."

"She needs upsetting, Patricia. She needs to see what that boyfriend of hers—"

"Enough!" Maya said, stomping her foot. Then her

voice wobbled when she said, "I won't h-hear a-another word. Sorry, Mom…but I…can't stay." She burst into tears and ran from the room.

Eliza tossed her napkin down and glared at her brother. "That was productive." She rose from the table and spoke to Patricia in a soothing soft voice. "I'll go talk to her."

"Talk some sense into her, will you?" Creed remarked.

Patricia frowned at Creed, then looked at her husband. "I'm going upstairs. This is all too much for me." She glanced at Reese, then the others. "I'm terribly sorry. Please excuse me."

Nash blinked and then flung his napkin down, waiting until his wife was out of the room before confronting his son. "What's gotten into you, Creed?"

Reese rose then, ready to make his escape. "This is a family matter and I'm intruding. Please tell Eliza I'll wait for her outside. Thank you for dinner."

Nash apologized and walked him to the front door.

Once outside, Reese grabbed hold of fresh South Dakota air thanking God he wasn't born into a large family.

Eliza wrapped her arms around her middle and walked outside, ready to head off another disaster. She'd spoken with Maya and had managed to calm her down a little. She'd encouraged her younger stepsister to go upstairs and spend some time with her mother. Eliza didn't know what was going on with Patricia, but Maya had always been able to put joy in her mother's eyes. They both needed each other tonight.

And Eliza wondered, if she'd had her own mother right now, would she be able to comfort her, as well? What Eliza needed right now was a warm heart, a good ear and caring arms surrounding her with unconditional love—a mother's love. Sadly Eliza would never know that kind of love.

She found Reese waiting for her. He stood leaning up against his car, that long, lean, incredibly fit body turned away from her, his jacket tossed aside. She walked around the car to face him from a distance as moonlight shadowed his features. "Well, that's my family."

Reese looked into her eyes. "Man, is it always like that?"

Eliza shrugged. She didn't owe Reese an explanation, yet she wanted to give him one anyway. "No, not always. But there are a lot of personalities to deal with. Ego, pride and mulishness add to the mix. But there's love, too. Sometimes it gets hidden between all the turmoil, but it's tucked in there and we all know it."

Reese nodded, but she doubted he really understood.

When she shivered from the March breezes blowing by, Reese approached her and laid his jacket over her shoulders.

She hugged the lapels, closing the jacket to keep her warm as the scent of pine and Reese enveloped her. She'd always loved the scent of him, his raw, earthy power and the maleness that defined him. "What are you doing here?"

"Besides having dinner with my…wife?"

"Shhh. Keep your voice down."

"No one can hear me out here, Eliza. If you weren't so bent on keeping your marital status a secret, you wouldn't walk around worrying yourself to death that you might disappoint someone in the family. Clearly they are too wrapped up in themselves to care about your one digression."

That's not true, she wanted to say. But what good would arguing the point do? She couldn't reveal Reese as her husband and didn't know if she'd even want to. "Why did you show up here?" she asked again.

Reese jammed his hands in his trousers and leaned back against his car. He stared up into a cool, cloudless night sky. She watched his throat work as he formulated the words. "My father died last month."

"Oh! I'm so sorry. He was…kind to me and a nice man."

"He liked you," he said in a rare unguarded moment. His smile was quick, revealing that one sexy dimple that set her equilibrium on tilt. "I promised him I'd get my life in order."

"How do you plan on doing that?" she asked, still reeling from the news of his father's death.

"There's only one way," he said, then turned the full force of his focus on her. His eyes probed hers for a moment, his look resolute. "Divorce. I have the papers in my hotel room."

Eliza blinked and stifled the surprised "oh" she wanted to exclaim. Of course she knew eventually something had to be done regarding their marriage, but she'd put off the inevitable in her mind until the thought had become fleeting and distant. But now she had to deal in reality. Reese was here. And he wanted a divorce. "Okay."

"Okay?" A fierce emotion passed over Reese's expression before he nodded. "Can you get away tonight?"

He was eager to be rid of her. Eliza wondered if there was a woman or two in his life, and the thought troubled her much more than it should. "The evening's ruined. I won't be missed."

Ironically, Reese had taken pleasure in giving her family reason to believe he was interested in her, when in fact, the true motive for his arrival tonight was to liberate himself from her entirely. "Just give me a minute to grab my purse and jacket."

"Take your time," he said to her back as she headed toward the house. "I've waited six years…I can wait a few more minutes."

She stood with her back against his penthouse door, jittery as a schoolgirl with her first crush. The pop of a champagne cork made her jump as she watched Reese behind the bar working a bottle, pouring overflowing bubbles into two tall flutes. "Champagne?"

Reese's face held no emotion. "I couldn't afford to begin our marriage this way."

"So we'll toast the end of our marriage, is that it?"

"Something like that." He motioned for her to come farther into the room. "I don't bite, darlin'."

"That's not how I remember it," she blurted, then a warmth flamed her face. Eliza rarely blushed, but the memory of Reese—that mouth, those teeth—flashed quickly in her mind.

Reese's head shot up and their eyes met. He smiled, a genuine, full-out sexy-as-sin smile with that dimple peeking out, and Eliza's whole body went hot.

"Yeah, I guess you're right." He walked over to her and handed her a glass. "To getting our lives back." He sipped from his glass, then strode to the window to stare out at the Sioux Falls skyline.

Eliza stepped farther into the large, elegant room, making note of the decor almost unconsciously, while fully aware of Reese and the new kind of power he held. Money could do that—it could change a man. And Reese seemed different in so many ways. She would never have pictured him in a luxurious penthouse suite, for one, with money to burn and a lifestyle he might have only dreamed about. But he'd done it. He'd made a success of his life despite the hardships and the heartaches he'd endured. That's if what he'd told her was true. If he had been faithful to her during that brief time in their life.

"Since this may be," she began, chewing on her lower lip, "the last time we see each other, please let me say that I'm happy for you, Reese. You accomplished what you set out to accomplish."

Reese whipped around from the window. "Did I?"

Eliza blinked and cast him a curious look. "Didn't you?"

He stared at her for a long moment, a tick in his jaw pacing out a slow beat. "Success in my professional life, failure in my personal life. I think that's fifty-fifty."

"You're not a failure."

He snorted before gulping down his drink. "Darlin', we both failed, didn't we?"

Her champagne went down just as harsh as his words. It'd been a trying night, and now as she faced Reese on rubbery legs, she hated to admit the truth. "I suppose." She sat down on the chintz sofa and leaned back against a pretty pillow before her legs could give way. "Do you think we can keep this—I mean…the divorce—quiet?"

"Sure. Why not?" he said gruffly.

Eliza winced inwardly. "It's just that—"

"Damn it, don't bother explaining again. I get it. I always have. Since we married in Montana, it shouldn't be a problem. No one here has to know."

With shaky hands, Eliza set her glass down on the marble coffee table then clumsily knocked it over onto some papers that were sprawled out. "Oh, I'm so sorry." The champagne washed away some of the print. "These aren't the—"

"No," he answered, bringing over a bar towel to blot the papers dry. "Don't worry about it." He grabbed up the papers and looked them over. "I have another copy."

"What are they?" she asked curiously.

"The layout of my house," he said absently. "The designer is giving my brother a hard time back home. She needs to get started on a few rooms, and I can't make up my mind."

"Oh, yes," Eliza said, recalling the lie Reese told the family about his visit to her tonight. "The house you'd wanted me to help you with."

Reese looked over the top of the papers to stare at her. "I had to think fast on my feet."

Eliza smiled. "You were sitting down so that would make you fast on your…"

Reese lifted a brow. "God, I thought you'd lost your sense of humor."

"I haven't had much to laugh about lately." Eliza let go of her smile. She didn't realize it until just now, but there was more truth in her words than she'd like to acknowledge.

He frowned at that, then sat down right next to her, so close that the musky pine scent of him stirred her senses. "Since you're here, do you want to take a look?"

"I'd never pass up a chance," she said as she slid the papers from his hands to hers, "to take a look at designs." She studied the papers, room upon room, and the designer's ideas that were marked on the layouts. When she was through, she shook her head. She knew Reese. Well, she'd known Reese Parker, and what the designer had in mind was completely wrong.

"What?" he said, genuinely interested.

"Does the designer know you, at all?"

"No, but she came highly recommended."

"And did you discuss what you wanted for the house?"

Reese nodded. "Yeah, but not in any great detail. That's her job, isn't it?"

Eliza took a deep breath. "A good designer has to know the person she's dealing with. She has to get a feel for what you want. I doubt you want white marble for a fireplace, Reese. Or alabaster walls or a wet bar made of beveled glass." Then doubt crept in and Eliza wondered if Reese had changed more than she'd thought. Maybe he did want a modern house with trendy designs. "Or maybe you do?"

"I don't," he said emphatically. His face was just inches from hers, and when he turned, the force of his gaze on her, those dark brown eyes held her transfixed. "Tell me what you'd do," he said softly.

Eliza hesitated for a long moment. Could she afford to give him her ideas, to expose herself so openly and feel the undeniable temptation of work she craved, while trying to ignore the forbidden temptation Reese posed to her? He was the husband she couldn't claim, after all. Shouldn't she just fold up the layouts and leave?

She should.

But the work—it was far too strong an enticement.

So for the next thirty minutes she sat with Reese and they discussed his ideas and hers. They drank champagne to the last drop and, with heads together, became fully immersed in designing Reese's new home.

Once they'd discussed every room and there was nothing more to say, Eliza rose, feeling tipsy and too excited for her own good. She and Reese had come up with some great ideas together, but she wouldn't deceive herself—she'd never see her designs come to fruition.

"You'd better take me home now," she said. She grabbed her purse and jacket, then turned toward the door.

"Eliza, come back here," Reese commanded gently.

She swiveled around to find him standing by the sofa, his shirtsleeves rolled up to his elbows, his tie gone, his dark eyes gleaming and his tone reminiscent of the man she'd once loved. He looked sexy and dangerous, and before she could stop herself, she moved closer to him. "That's right, we forgot about the divorce pap—"

His lips came down on hers hard, obliterating her last words, and as he pulled her into his embrace, he also obliterated all rational thoughts she might have had. The kiss went long and deep, champagne mingling with warm lips and hot bodies and the feel of Reese's erection pressing on her ignited a fire inside her.

And when their lips finally broke apart the question must have still been in her eyes, because Reese quickly responded, "There's time for that, darlin'."

He took her hand then and, as he lowered himself down on the sofa, one tug had her falling into his lap. He pulled the knot of her hair loose, and pins went flying right before his lips met hers again. He held her close with one hand, while the other played with the strands of her hair, lacing his fingers through until he cupped her head and dipped her low. She fell back against the sofa cushion, and he followed her down, kissing her again, his lips and tongue taking pleasure and giving it fully in return.

He slid his hand down to her blouse, and buttons flew open. She felt the cool air caress her skin before hot fingers skimmed over the lace of her bra. Underneath, her nipples hardened, awaiting his touch, and when he finally pushed aside the material, he didn't disappoint. His fingers teased and tempted and he whispered in her ear what he wanted from her. The commands, the way he spoke to her, the way he touched her sent every nerve ending tingling.

"I have to be inside you," he whispered urgently.

Yes, she wanted that, too. So much. "We can't," she said, surprising herself.

"We are, baby."

"It's been six years, Reese," she breathed out.

"Making up for lost time." He nibbled on her throat.

Eliza ached from the pleasure, from having Reese want her, from feeling desirable again. She pushed his chest just hard enough for him to lift up and look deeply into her eyes. "There hasn't been anyone…else. Not in six years." She slid her eyes closed for a moment, then faced him again. "Can you say the same?"

Reese stared at her, his dark eyes burning like black coals. He shook his head briskly. "You have no right asking me that, Eliza. Not when you walked out on me without looking back."

Reese untangled his body from hers. He sat up on the sofa and slammed his body back against the cushion. Eliza rose from her prone position to sit next to him. With trembling fingers, she buttoned her blouse and tried to finger-comb her unruly hair.

"Is there someone else?" she asked quietly, setting her pride aside.

Reese remained silent.

Searing pain worked its way into her stomach, though she fought it tooth and nail. She'd put the past behind her, and now that Reese had returned, he'd managed to wedge his way in, causing her more anxiety and hurt.

She stood and grabbed hold of her jacket and purse, then headed to the door. She should have walked out before. If she had, the grim reality that she may have pushed a loving husband into another woman's arms might not be haunting her thoughts. But it was there, along with the rest of the confusion Reese Parker's appearance had brought about. And there wasn't much she could do about any of it.

Not after the pain they'd caused each other.

Not after the lies she'd told.

Not after winning the battle to give up on Reese years ago.

"I'll take a taxi home."

But before she reached the door, he was there, jamming his arms into his jacket and opening the door for her. "I'll drive you."

Five

Reese slowed the car to a stop before reaching the gates of the Fortune estate. He put the car in Park, set one arm on the steering wheel and turned to look at Eliza. She'd been quiet on the ride home. No sense making small talk. They'd both been too wrapped up in their own thoughts. In the four hours he'd spent with her tonight, he'd known a wealth of emotions, the last being fury at his estranged wife. Had she truly expected him to answer her question? Had she wanted to hear the truth? Had she expected him to live the life of a monk after she'd walked out on him?

He still wanted her; he couldn't deny it. But he'd never get over her mistrust in him. He'd been looking forward to a future with her, having babies, growing old. But she'd thrown it all away. And, damn it, before she signed those legal papers terminating their sorry marriage, Reese had to be through with her in his mind, his heart and his body.

Then he'd truly be free.

"Things got a little crazy back there," he said.

Eliza put her head down. "It always did when we got together, but I thought after six years that might have changed."

"Guess we found out it didn't."

When she nodded, her blond hair fell onto her face, and Reese reached over to gently brush it away. She looked up at him with a tentative smile. "I'll sign the divorce papers whenever you want. Did you bring them with you?"

Reese lifted his arms in a gesture of futility. "It wasn't the first thing on my mind."

She lifted her chin, and he noted the pretty blue sparkle in her eyes and her hair in wild disarray around her face. "What was?"

"Stripping you naked. Getting laid. Having incredible sex. Take your pick, darlin'."

She gasped, and her sharp intake of breath echoed through the silence. "We can't go back, Reese."

"Don't want to."

"Then what *do* you want from me?"

"I guess I didn't know until tonight." He scratched his head and went for broke. "I want you to come to Montana with me."

"What? I can't do th—"

"It's a business proposition. I want you to take a look at my house. I want you to see it firsthand and tell

me how to make it a home. You must have said it yourself a dozen times tonight—that you wished you could
see the place in person."

"Yes, but I didn't mean it literally."

"You have good ideas. You know me better than anyone else I might hire. I'm not asking you to do the work."

No, he didn't want to commit himself to hiring her
on as his designer, but he wanted her to see his house.
Not only for her design ideas but because with every
dollar he made, every oil rig that blew, every time he'd
proven himself a success, he thought of her. And now he
wanted her to see the full extent of what she'd thrown
away.

"Just come and take a look. I can have a plane waiting at sunup and you'll be home before sundown. This
house means a lot to me, Eliza. I don't want to make
any mistakes."

"It would be very…awkward, Reese. If you have
a—"

"Damn it, Eliza. I'm not building this house for anyone but me. There's a cottage on the property that's
finished. My father and I lived there together for a short
time. The place was going to be his. But now he's gone.
I'm not asking you to design something for another
woman. Hell, I don't know a woman who would stand
for that, do you?"

"No…no. But I don't know…" Yet as she spoke
the words, a light flickered in her eyes. Through the
hazy moonlight shining inside the Jaguar, Reese
could see that he'd sparked her interest. No one at the
Fortune house seemed to take her work seriously. It

hadn't taken him long to figure that out. Now, he offered her something she'd always wanted, and she'd be foolish to turn him down.

"I'm asking for just one day. C'mon, Eliza. Where's that free-spirited woman I met six years ago? Don't think too hard, just do it."

Eliza stared out the window for a long time. Reese was about to argue another round with her, but she turned suddenly with determination written on her face. "What time tomorrow?"

"I'll pick you up at seven."

"I'll be ready."

"Fine."

Satisfied, Reese started the engine, but Eliza put a hand out. "Don't drive me inside the gates. I want to walk. I need to clear my head."

Reese slid out of the car and opened the door for her. After she wished him a good night, Reese watched her walk away.

Tomorrow, he planned on making her clear head dizzy again.

"You're up early, Eliza," her father said, sipping coffee by the breakfast table. He eyed her up and down, making mental notes of her appearance.

She wore comfortable clothes today—jeans, a black V-neck sweater and a pair of boots, usual apparel for some women, but not for Eliza. Not since she'd spent the summer following Reese around the rodeo, getting her hands dirty on corral fences, trailer hitches and barbecue grills. And her father had noticed. Though he'd retired to spend more time with Patricia, his mind was as sharp as a tack and he hardly missed a thing.

Except, of course, the secret marriage she'd kept from the entire family. She could be deceptive when necessary and she'd hated every minute of fooling him and everyone else she'd cared about. The whole darn situation had escalated without conscious thought, and now, six years later, it was too late to untwist the lies.

"I have an appointment. Don't worry if I'm not home until late tonight." Eliza poured herself a cup of French roast, grabbed a croissant and swiveled around to make a quick exit. No sense adding to the deception.

"What kind of appointment?"

Trapped, Eliza decided not to lie. The truth wouldn't hurt in this case. She turned with the coffee cup to her lips, adding casually. "Just a design project. I'm going to take a look at someone's house and—"

"Dressed like that?" He shook his head. "You're off to Montana. It's Parker's house, isn't it?"

Sharp as a tack.

Okay, she thought, at least Reese had given her a way out of this. "Yes, no big surprise. He'd mentioned it yesterday at dinner."

"He's flying you there?"

She nodded. "Private jet."

Her father opened the *Tribune* and nodded. "It's about time you had a man in your life."

"Dad!" She nearly spilled coffee onto the floor. What could she say without telling more lies? At the moment, Reese was the man in her life, but not in the way her father assumed. "I'm hardly eighteen, going out on a date. It's business."

He lowered the newspaper and peered over at her. "I won't worry if you don't make it home tonight."

"Oh, I'll be here. It's just a day trip."

"If you say so. You're a big girl," he said as she walked over to him to plant a quick guilt-ridden kiss on his cheek, praying the lies would end soon.

"See you *tonight,* Dad," she made a point of saying.

Reese was prompt picking her up. She met him outside and didn't wait for him to get out of the car to open her door. She grabbed the handle and watched him slide his body over to open the door from the inside. With a push, it opened and Eliza took her seat. The fresh scent of shampoo and soap and pine struck her instantly, the heady mix permeating the interior of the car. Eliza tried to ignore how that scent affected her, but she couldn't quite disregard the way Reese looked this morning.

In beat-up boots, faded jeans and a tan chambray shirt, he hardly appeared the smooth oil executive with his own private jet, but rather he reminded her of the ruggedly sexy cowboy she'd met at a rodeo one sizzling hot summer day. His big silver belt buckle set across a trim rippled abdomen—a trophy of a championship win—caught the early morning light and her full attention. "Good morning," she said stiffly, wanting to keep a professional distance.

Reese's gaze traveled over her suede jacket to the *V* of her neckline, lingering there for a moment before he lifted his eyes to hers. She silently cursed her vivid memory—a flash of his hands and mouth on her skin and the way she'd come alive from his touch last night.

"You came prepared."

She glanced at the briefcase she held on her lap. "Just some samples, colors, ideas I jotted down."

He took off and they drove toward the airport, the radio filling the silence, a sweet country ballad that lulled her nerves.

"I like the look," he said, keeping his eyes on the road. And Eliza felt as though they'd gone back in time, when they'd dressed this way every single day.

When they reached the airport, Reese guided her onto the Gulfstream 200, and she took a seat on a cream-colored leather chair. "Get settled in," he said. "I'll check with the pilot. We should be taking off soon."

Reese disappeared into the cockpit and Eliza released her breath. What was she doing? Going back to Montana would only stir up old feelings. Feelings she'd put to rest long ago. Yet she had to admit she was curious about Reese, his home and his life. The final temptation came with seeing the layout of his very unique home. There was so much potential—empty walls and uncovered windows that needed just the right touch to make the house a home.

When Reese returned with a smile on his face, chuckling from something the pilot said, Eliza might have melted in a puddle. She remembered that hearty laugh, the richness in his dark eyes when something amused him and that darn dimple peeking out.

"Buckle up," he said, the smile still on his face. "We'll be taking off in two minutes."

"Okay," she said.

Reese sat across from her, latching his belt. Once they were in the air, he said, "I've got some reports to go over." He pointed to the window. "Enjoy the view. We'll be in Montana before you know it."

He got up to sit behind a table that also served as his desk, and Eliza did enjoy the view, both the one below her and one the sitting a few feet away, deep in concentration.

Today he seemed all business, whereas last night he'd hardly been in a business-minded mood at all. She couldn't quite figure him out. He'd seemed so intent on divorcing her, but now she didn't know what to think.

So much had changed in the last six years, but when she'd been in his arms last night, it seemed as if nothing had changed at all.

They arrived at Gallatin Field in Bozeman before nine. Reese ushered her off the plane and into his car, this time not an elegant Jag but a Yukon, with all the bells, whistles and buttons one could imagine. "Button up—there's a chill in the air."

Reese reached into the backseat, coming up with a tan Stetson hat. He plunked it onto her head, and even though he tried, he couldn't conceal a grin. "Bet you haven't worn one of these for a while."

Eliza laughed. "Not true," she said as they began the drive. "I headed a fund-raiser for a children's hospital once. We all dressed up like this and had lasso lessons, sang country songs, square-danced."

"Where, inside a ballroom?" he asked in a mocking tone.

"No, not inside a ballroom," she bantered back. "At Burt Candlewood's ranch. He'd lost his son to a rare disease," she said, unable to hide the emotion in her voice. The memory of that family's grief struck Eliza anew. She'd always wanted children. Adored them, really. She couldn't imagine the pain of losing your own child. "We raised a good deal of money that day."

Reese took his eyes off the road for a moment, his gaze studying her, before he nodded and turned his attention onto the highway again.

Eliza wrapped her arms around her middle, the descending cold temperature sending a chill through her body as they drove on.

"I've got warmer clothes at the cottage," Reese said.

"I should have known better. The weather can change quickly this time of year."

Twenty minutes later, Reese pulled to a stop on a hilly rise. From there, Eliza followed the direction of his gaze. Twin columns of stately blue spruce trees edged the road leading to the main house. The house, though, stole all of her breath, with its trilevel splendor. New England cottage stone framed the large paned windows. Timber beams braced the second story with a mix of stone and cedar shakes. As Reese drove forward onto a pebbled circular driveway, Eliza gasped in awe when the entry of the house came into view. "Oh...wow."

Oh, wow? That's all she could manage to say about a house that she would die to focus her talent on? Strategically placed flagstone steps led to a split entryway where doors to the left and right allowed entrance to the house. The second story sat above a hollowed-out area below known as an outdoor living room, complete with a rock fireplace. Eliza had only seen this done once before. Already she envisioned filling that space with an array of sturdy outdoor furniture.

"Come on, I'll give you the nickel tour," he said, and Eliza bounded out of the SUV.

"I've never seen such an architectural design done like this for a single-family dwelling. This is amazing, Reese," she said as he came around the SUV, but Eliza had already taken off toward the outdoor living room. She whirled around, taking it all in.

"This sold me on the house. This *and* the view." Reese pointed through the living space to a spot beyond, and Eliza strode over to where the living space converged onto a log-railed terrace. From that point, a small lake came into view, the clouded morning sun shedding a stingy amount of light onto the water. Eliza could only imagine the lake, surrounded by tall pines and mountains, when the sun cast its full wrath of light onto the waters.

Her heart thudded in her chest. The view was breathtaking. "I saw the layouts, but nothing compares to seeing it in person."

"Want to see the inside?" Reese asked.

Eliza tore her gaze away from the stunning view and nodded, following Reese inside the house.

"There's seventeen rooms," he said as they went inside.

Eliza let her gaze flow around the three rooms she

could see from her vantage point—the great room that faced the back view of the lake and surroundings, an area for dining, also facing the lake, and beyond that the eating area of the kitchen. All open, all wide, glorious windows, all spectacular spaces that held amazing promise if done correctly.

She glanced first at the unfinished fireplace and hearth. "I see stacked slate here, all the way to the high beamed ceiling. A solid carved mantel…dark pine. And bookcases on both sides. Wood flooring in this room, maybe throughout the entire first floor. What other rooms are on this floor?"

"There's a wine cellar just off the kitchen, a more formal living room and the master bedroom."

"And upstairs?" she said, looking at the staircase that separated the living space from the eating areas.

"Well…" Reese said with a look of deep concentration. "There's a recreation room, a gym, home office and steps up from there, two attic bedrooms—what they call sky bedrooms—and a sitting room that overlooks the lake and joins the wings of the house."

Eliza had been pretty good at reading home plans and layouts and she'd gotten a feel about this house from what she'd seen in Reese's hotel room last night, but being here and seeing the potential this house had boggled her mind.

She itched to get her hands on it.

The challenge would be tremendous and one she'd love to take on…and if it were anyone else's home, she'd be secretly dreaming up ways to get the commission.

But this was her soon-to-be ex-husband's house. The

complications were too numerous to even consider. Besides which, Reese hadn't asked her. He'd only wanted her opinion.

And that also baffled her.

Why would he *want* her opinion about anything when he'd been so incredibly angry with her?

"Let's go up," she said.

"After you." Reese gestured for her to take the stairs.

And twenty minutes later Eliza had mentally filled the entire second floor with furniture, artwork and window treatments. She took the short steps up to the third level to view two attic bedrooms with slanted low ceilings and stopped up short, feeling Reese's presence behind her. "These would be the children's rooms," she said quietly.

Reese made a sound in his throat. "Don't think so."

She whirled around too quickly and nearly bumped his chest. "I thought you wanted children," she said without thinking.

Reese stared down into her eyes, and for a long moment he didn't say a word. Then finally he said, "*Wanted* is the correct word."

As in past tense.

Reese had wanted children; they both had. And when they'd been together they'd daydreamed about having them and how their world would change.

Eliza turned around to glance at the attic bedrooms that may never hear a child's laughter. "I still want them," she admitted, unable to choke back her wistful tone.

But when she turned around, Reese had moved down the hallway to the sitting room.

After Eliza had seen every room in the house, she

gazed out the kitchen window, staring at the skyline, where the treetops met the Montana sky. It truly was big-sky country, beautiful and wide and remote. Eliza felt it all, and suddenly loneliness as vast and simple as the land itself claimed her. She let out a breathy sigh. "You have the bare bones of a gorgeous home, Reese."

He stood behind her, and she took in the scent of him, all crispness and pine, and yearned for things she hadn't dared in a very long time.

"I know."

"And a lot of decisions to make."

"A lot."

"You can afford the best decorators in the world. So why am I here?" she asked.

He wrapped his arms around her, pressing her back to his chest. But that move also placed her rear end in between his hips, the taut, firm length of him meshing with her.

She squeezed her eyes shut.

"I wanted to get you alone," he said, shoving her hair aside to nibble on her throat.

She arched into the soft, tender kisses. "But…you're angry with me."

"Furious."

He continued kissing her throat while the hands that wrapped around her waist climbed higher, to spread out just under her breasts.

She held her breath. "We're getting divorced."

"That's a fact."

His thumbs lifted to flick the crest of her breasts, the tiny act causing a riot to her system.

A loud thunderous clap brought both their heads up. Menacing black clouds moved in quickly, the sky now dark with the threat of a storm.

"Damn it," Reese said, breaking away from her. "It's gonna be a soaker! Grab your things. We'll make a run for it."

But before Eliza could grasp what was happening, Reese had tossed her jacket to her, slapped the Stetson on her head, picked up her briefcase and slid his hand in hers. "Let's go."

"Where?" she asked as he tugged her to the back door of the house.

"The cottage." And they made a dash toward the structure Eliza hadn't noticed before. The quaint one-level cottage nestled behind the house and closer to the lake was at least half a football field away.

Reese held her hand tight and she pushed herself to keep pace. The air outside hit her with chilling force, so much colder now than when they'd first arrived. Overhead the clouds opened up, bursting with sound and might, drenching them with blinding, merciless rain.

And in an instant the rain became hailstones, hitting them hard, then pinging onto the ground. Once they finally made it to the cottage, Reese guided her inside and released her hand, heading for the fireplace. "At least we have electricity in here. I'll turn on the heat in a sec, but a fire will warm us up faster. We should probably get out of these wet clothes."

Eliza blinked, watching him throw logs into the fireplace. "Even the weather cooperates with you, Reese."

Reese turned around and the dimple peeked out from

his crooked smile. "I can't take credit for the storm, darlin', but I don't think I could've planned this any better," he said without apology. "Looks like snow's on the way."

Snow?

Eliza knew what that meant.

"You're gonna have to stay the night."

Six

Reese built the fire up until the small living room glowed with golden firelight and heat sliced through the cold air. On bended knee, he glanced at Eliza shivering by the hearth, her hands jutting out toward the warmth.

"I can't stay here tonight," she said. "I have to get home."

"I doubt anyone's flying out anywhere today. Take off your wet clothes, Eliza. You're chilled to the bone."

She shuddered. "I'm...fine. The fire will dry me."

Reese stood. "Suit yourself." He took his jacket off, then unbuttoned his shirt and tossed it aside. "I'm not gonna freeze my butt off just because you decided to get modest on me."

With that, he stretched his T-shirt over his head and

flung that, too. When he went for his belt buckle, Eliza gasped, "Reese!"

"What?" he said, ready to yank off the belt. He watched Eliza's blue eyes round on his chest before lifting up to face him.

"Do you…uh, have anything else for me to wear?"

He nodded. "I'll find you something. Hang on. I'll be right back."

"You have women's clothes here?" she asked just before he stepped out the door.

"Wait and see," he replied without missing stride.

And when he returned with a black velour robe and one of his flannel shirts, Eliza lifted one blond brow.

"My father lived here with me. What'd you think?"

Eliza took the offered clothes without commenting. "I'll just use your bathroom to put these on."

"No, change in here. It's warmer. I'll make coffee. And we'll see about drying your clothes."

Ten minutes later Reese returned to the fire wearing a dry pair of jeans and a shirt, holding two mugs of steaming hot coffee. Eliza sat with her legs folded under her, cuddled up in his robe. Her hair was still slightly damp, spread out over the collar, catching firelight. "It's snowing."

"Hmm. A good day to be inside." He handed her the mug, then sat beside her in front of the fire.

"Thanks," she said, her face downcast. "I guess I'm not getting out today."

"Is that what you really want?"

Her blue eyes widened for a sec, before she took a deep breath. "I'm not sure what I want."

She stood then, and Reese made note of bright

purple painted toenails peeking out from his robe, so unlike the prissy socialite and so reminiscent of the woman he'd married.

He sipped his coffee, watching her roam around the room. "How long did your father live here?"

"About six months. He liked it here, didn't want any part of the big house."

"It's cozy," she said. "But very masculine. Big beams. Stone fireplace. Lots of wood everywhere. But there's charm here, too. Must have been hard when he died."

"Can't deny that."

"Did you have help when you packed up his things?"

Reese swallowed and didn't respond.

She looked down at him. "You haven't?"

He rubbed the back of his neck. "Not yet."

"There's time," she said gently. "My father said that when my mother died, he couldn't face packing up anything of hers. Everything remained as it was for a very long time, until finally two of his best friends came over and told him it was time. They helped him get through it."

Reese sipped more of his coffee. He wasn't sure he was ready for that.

"If you could come up with some boxes, I wouldn't mind helping," she said. "I mean, we might have all day with nothing else to—"

"Let me think about it," he said, touched by her offer to help. But he'd be damned doing any such thing with her. Not when she looked the way she did, naked underneath his robe, her hair shimmering in the firelight and her purple toenails driving him crazy.

"Okay," she said softly. Then she wandered over to

the bookshelves and lifted up one of his championship rodeo buckles. "I remember when you won this," she whispered before setting it back in place.

He rose to stand beside her. "I remember how we celebrated. In the cab of my truck. Couldn't wait to get home. We were all over each other."

She slid her eyes closed and took a long breath. When she opened them, blue flames of desire seared into his.

He untied her robe and slipped his hands inside, splaying them around her waist. "You always did look great wearing my shirts."

"Reese," she said, a warning note in her voice.

"Damn it, we're still married." He brought his lips down on hers, taking her in a long, heady kiss. She made little throaty sounds that stirred him up, and he deepened the kiss until both were breathless and turned on when it ended. "You're my wife."

"Not for long," she whispered.

"For now." And he kissed her again, tucking his hands around her backside, bringing her flush with his body. "Don't deny what you want, Eliza. We both know I'm gonna lay you down by that fire and make love to you." For hours, into the night, until he could put her out of his mind for good.

He was in lust with his wife. Once he satisfied that craving, he would finally move on, leaving her behind—the way she did him six years ago.

Eliza couldn't deny she wanted him. There hadn't been anyone else in all this time, and Reese was here, wanting her, making her body tingle and her heartbeat quicken. So when he took her hand, she followed him and together they lay down by the fire, the plush robe under her serving as their bed. Reese wasted no time unbuttoning the shirt she wore and spreading the material, exposing every inch of her.

He rose up on his knees between her legs, a look of admiration in his eyes, and on a deep breath he said, "Just as sexy as I remember."

She felt exposed and vulnerable for a moment, but his expression never wavered. Desire burned deep in his eyes as he slowly unbuttoned his shirt, exposing a darkly tanned, muscled torso. Eliza watched, unguarded now, unable to tear her gaze away. He removed his belt and buckle and, keeping his jeans on, pressed his body over hers. His lips met hers and she breathed him in, his all-male scent, delighted that he'd remembered how she liked the rough slide of his jeans on her body.

He kissed her deeply, mating his tongue with hers in an openmouthed, hot, lusty frenzy. His lips moved over her, touching her everywhere and he made love to the whole of her body first, making her ache so deeply that she felt the pain of it down to her core.

But it was his words, whispered seductively in her ear, commanding her touch and telling her in more than sensual terms what he wanted to do and how he would do it, that affected her most. Those lusty words echoed in her mind, and Reese's quiet declarations turned her body to searing lava, an eruption that readied to flow. She was hot, melting, primed for him to take her, Reese's brand of foreplay never failing to saturate her with sizzling heat.

She reached for the snap of his jeans, lowered the zipper and touched where he wanted to be touched, where she *longed* to touch.

"Still magic," he rasped out as she continued to stroke him until both needed more. He moved her hands aside and joined their bodies in a long-awaited reunion. Skin to skin now, rough to smooth, he moved over her, with her, inside her, until the years faded away and she was with him wholly now, completely.

"Let go, baby," he commanded gently. "Hold nothing back."

And Eliza flew, her body releasing with overpowering force. She clenched and moaned with pleasure over and over until she trembled with completion.

She knew Reese held back, his stamina and endurance something deliciously wicked. And they made love again and again, until the raging fire in the hearth died down to serene simmering embers.

If the third time's the charm, then Eliza had been thoroughly, unmistakably, unbelievably charmed.

All three times.

Exhausted, spent and fully satisfied, she cuddled against Reese and fell fast asleep.

Eliza sat on the sofa facing the fire, glancing at Reese as he slept. Outside, falling snow made a pretty picture, frosting the leaves with white flakes and dusting the landscape with loose powder. The cold winter scene outside distinctly contrasted with the cozy temperatures inside the cottage.

She wore her clothes, soft and warm from the dryer,

as she worked up her own sketches of Reese's home. Now that she'd seen the rooms firsthand, she had a better understanding of how each room should flow into the next with colors, textures and style.

The house was unique, in a class all its own—not unlike Reese, who would soon move in and set roots down for the first time in his life.

He'd changed quite a bit in six years, she'd recognized, but he still had the ability to flame her body. Her long, dry drought was finally over, and she'd made up her mind to live in the moment, to simply enjoy rather than think of any repercussions.

"Don't think I'm through with you yet," he'd whispered gently right before they'd fallen asleep in each other's arms. Eliza had slept with a smile on her face, grateful that Reese was an insatiable lover.

As long as she didn't fall in love with him again, she'd be fine.

They'd been careful. Reese had taken the proper precautions. They were still married, so why shouldn't she enjoy a healthy, thoroughly satisfying sexual interlude?

With her husband.

Reese's low voice startled her. "You look busy."

"You're awake."

"Barely," he said, rolling onto his back to stare at the rough beam ceiling. "What time is it?"

"Four."

His chest was bare, and he'd slept with his jeans riding low on his hips, the snap opened enough for her to view his navel and then some. He rolled onto his side, his hand bracing his head, to study her. "What are you working on?"

She snapped her briefcase closed. "Designs. I'll show you later. Do you have anything to eat in this house?"

Reese chuckled. "Sex always did make you hungry," he said, then added more wistfully, "I forgot that." He rose and stretched, pulling his muscles taut, lifting his arms up high in the air. Then he turned to toss a few logs on the fire before adding, "You got dressed."

"I can't roam around all day in your…shirt."

He shot her a no-nonsense look. "Why not?"

"I really am hungry, Reese."

"I noticed." His mouth twitched.

"For *food* this time."

Rising, he strode over to her, bent down and kissed her lightly on the lips. "Okay, let's see what's cooking in the kitchen."

It was so casual a kiss, so off-the-cuff, so reminiscent of their life together back when things were carefree and easy, that Eliza froze. She sat ramrod stiff, chastising herself for thinking the unthinkable.

She *couldn't* fall in love with him again. They were getting a divorce. They'd moved on, leading separate lives now. She wouldn't even think about the out-and-out lies she'd told her family.

"You coming?" he called out.

She shoved the briefcase and those thoughts aside and walked into the kitchen. "Neither one of us can cook worth a darn. Too bad it's snowing…oh, you have an indoor grill."

Reese pulled two steaks out of the refrigerator. He grabbed two beers, a package of frozen vegetables and some sourdough bread and set them on the table. "Between the two of us, we can rig something up."

Eliza's stomach growled. "If you can manage not to burn the steaks, I'll do the rest."

"I never burn the steaks," he said in a serious tone.

"You always burn the steaks."

"We never had steak," he said defiantly.

Eliza stopped for a moment, then conceded the point. "You always burned the *burgers.*"

With a quick nod, Reese admitted, "That's better."

They ate partially burned steaks with overcooked and underseasoned veggies, but at least the bread was fresh and the beer cold. After the meal, Eliza pulled out her drawings and they sat comfortably on the sofa, going over her ideas.

Reese sipped from his second beer, watching her eyes skim over the layouts he had stashed here in the cottage. She'd marked them up with her design ideas, and he had to admit they were good.

"The windows downstairs that look out onto the lake shouldn't be covered. The view is breathtaking. You wouldn't want to hide that, unless of course you want—"

"I don't," he interrupted. "I agree. Keep them uncovered."

She smiled and nodded. "I see deep hues of golds and browns in the living rooms. The great room with a stacked stone fireplace should have built-in shelves on each side—pine would work nicely. And the floor should be all wood, with some woven carpets to break it up. I've written it all down."

"Okay," he agreed. Damn if he couldn't picture the rooms taking shape the way she described them.

She nodded again and continued to work through the drawings. "In the sky bedrooms I see blue. Blue walls and whitewashed wood trim all over. There's this great color called Blue Bliss—I think it'd be perfect."

"Okay," he said, continuing to watch her. She really loved this work, yet she spent her time on fund-raising. Not that helping charities wasn't noble, but he knew she wasn't doing what was in her heart. Reese thought it had something to do with her family and their attitude toward her craft. They supported her home projects, but never believed she'd make a success of herself if she branched out in the world. That was part of Eliza's problem, he thought. She didn't have enough faith in herself. And she certainly hadn't placed any faith in their marriage.

Her eyes glowed with passion now and Reese hid a satisfied grin. He'd seen that same look on her face hours ago, when they'd exhausted each other. He liked that Eliza liked having sex. It had sure made being married to her a hell of a lot of fun. But having sex and making love were two different things. They'd had wild, uninhibited, mind-blowing sex today, a release of pent-up tension for her and total frustration for him. Tonight, he planned on taking her to his bed and making slow, easy, lazy love to her. He wanted to draw out the pleasure for as long as he could. For both of them.

He'd half hoped that taking her to bed wouldn't

have been as good, as thrilling as it once was, but it had been that and more. It hadn't been exactly the same but even better.

Which would make saying goodbye to her that much harder. But there was no doubt in his mind that they had to part ways. Still furious with her, still pissed off at how easily she'd thrown away their marriage, thinking that he'd been unfaithful to her, Reese couldn't find the forgiveness he needed. He'd clung to his fury too long to let a roll or two in the sack change his mind.

Yet, as he watched her work so diligently, with her head down and all that glossy blond hair falling across her shoulders, he couldn't deny that he wanted her. When he'd fallen in love with her, it'd been a hard fall. He'd had to pick himself up by the bootstraps to get on with his life when she'd left him. And he had. There was no turning back.

"So what do you want to do in the master bedroom?" she asked.

That question grabbed his attention. "Get naked again?"

She blushed, her pretty face going all rosy. "Reese, be serious. I'm talking about your new master bedroom."

"I *am* being serious."

She glanced down at the designs in her lap. "But… we have more to do."

He stood and gathered up the layouts, tossing them onto the sofa, then reached for her hand. He tugged her up so that she stood toe-to-toe with him. "I'm glad you agree."

Bending his head, he kissed her soundly on the lips.

When she gazed into his eyes with dewy softness, Reese lifted her up into his arms. "Let's go check out my bedroom. See if you can make any improvements in there."

Reese lowered her down onto his bed and took his time with her, creating a slow, tortuous buildup of desire. Eliza wove her hands in his short sandy locks, explored his shoulders and his back while he kissed her, caressed her skin, nibbled on her body, making her moan with easy, unhurried pleasure.

He moistened her breasts with his tongue until she ached, then slid his hands down to her belly, making circles in slow motion until he reached farther down to cup her womanhood. She arched up quickly.

"Relax, baby," he whispered in her ear. "You won't be sorry."

And she did relax, letting her body succumb to all the things Reese did to her, all the things he whispered in her ear.

They moved erotically, in rhythm with each other. And when he rolled onto his back, Eliza took him in her hand, then her mouth and wrung out the pleasure for him the way he had for her.

And, once protected, Reese rasped, "Show me how it's done." Eliza felt no shame, completely wrapped up in the moment as she recalled this command—their private little joke from Reese's rodeo days.

Eliza climbed atop and took him in, moving on him with undulations that created a lusty, sexy ride for both. She reveled in the pleasure on his face as she rode the wave, and when he took control, guiding her with his hands and hips, she moved quicker now, sensations heightened, meeting his powerful thrusts until both shuddered with striking force.

Minutes later, cradled in Reese's arms, she spoke from her heart. "I never minded burgers, Reese."

Reese's chest heaved and he blew out that breath slowly. "I shouldn't have married you, Eliza. I was outclassed and I knew it. I couldn't provide you with what you needed."

"Reese," she said, turning to look into his eyes, "it was never about money."

It was about love, and they had that. They'd fallen in love quickly, madly and had been crazy about each other. When she believed he'd been unfaithful, the wound to her heart had been devastating. She'd been injured beyond belief and had to go home to Sioux Falls and pretend everything was right in her life. Whenever someone had caught her with a distant, remote look on her face, they'd simply blamed Warren Keyes and the scandal of their broken engagement. But Warren had been the last thing on her mind. She'd been filled with Reese Parker and she'd lost him.

"We had burgers in the kitchen, but *steak* in the bedroom," she added.

Reese shoved up from the bed and peered down at her. "Yeah, the sex was hot. Still is. But you couldn't bring yourself to tell your family about me. Then or now."

He stood up and nailed her with a hard look. "And then you walked out on me thinking I'd cheated on you. Guess you never really knew me, Eliza."

She watched him walk into the bathroom, heard the

shower turn on and knew he would wash away what had happened between them just now and cling to his righteous anger.

That night, Reese held Eliza close, breathing in her scent, reminded of her gentle moves and little sounds she made as she slept. He managed to shove all thoughts of her betrayal out of his mind so that he could get a decent night's sleep. As it turned out, he'd never slept better.

Morning dawned, and with the storm over, the sun breaking through lingering clouds, Reese rose quietly, leaving Eliza in his bed. He dressed and entered the room in the back of the cottage he'd converted into a temporary office to make some business calls.

After two long-winded conversations that sapped his energy, he hung up the phone, leaned back in his chair and stared out the window. He'd never liked the business end of the oil business. It made him antsy and impatient. He'd much rather be out in the field, working with his experienced crew—the roughnecks who knew everything there was to know about drilling oil—seeing firsthand when a well blew, streaming rich black crude. And though he hadn't enjoyed becoming a suit, he'd loved every second of his success, building a company from the ground up, employing dozens of workers, being in control of his life.

He'd never give up that control again.

Eliza's bright laughter broke through his thoughts. Suppressing a smile, he walked down the hallway toward the sound to see what his soon-to-be ex was doing.

He found her in the kitchen.

In another man's arms.

The jar to his system staggered him momentarily.

Until he realized she was dancing with his brother, Garrett.

Dancing?

"Hey, look who decided to crawl out of his hole this morning." Garrett stopped long enough to slant him a big smile.

Reese leaned against the doorjamb, arms crossed, irritated at the jealous sweep of emotion that invaded him. "Hands off, little brother."

Garrett's smile never faded, but he did release Eliza, lifting his hands in the air, palms up in old Western-movie-style. "I was only showing the lady the two-step."

"I was just telling Garrett I've got a fund-raiser coming up this spring and I needed a refresher course in—"

"What are you doing here?" Reese asked his brother, none too pleased seeing the rosy glow of joy on Eliza's face, a glow his *brother* had put there. This time the stab he felt pissed him off big-time.

"Just checking on your property, bro. After the snowstorm, I thought I'd see if the house was still standing." He winked at Eliza and she grinned. "Little did I know I'd find my sister-in-law here."

She had showered and dressed. Eggs were frying in a pan and coffee brewed in the pot. Reese pushed away from the door and entered the kitchen, grabbing a mug and pouring a cup of coffee. "We're going over the terms of our divorce."

Garrett lifted his brows.

Color drained from Eliza's face.

Reese sipped his coffee.

"And I thought you brought Eliza here to give you ideas about the house." Garrett glanced at her and she sent him a shaky smile.

"Is that what you thought?" He spoke to Garrett and then winced inwardly seeing Eliza turn quickly away. In that fleeting moment, he noted her every emotion—hurt, anger, betrayal and dawning realization—register on her face. Reese sucked in a deep breath. "Fire the decorator. She's all wrong. I'll find someone else."

Garrett shook his head. "You hired her. You're gonna have to let her go."

Reese nodded, conceding the point. "You're right."

"He hates it when I'm right," Garrett said to Eliza. She was busy scrambling eggs. She glanced up and their eyes met for an instant. She stabbed at the eggs, the spatula making mincemeat of them, and Reese figured she'd imagined the eggs were his head as she smashed his brains into tiny pieces.

Hell, he'd wanted to get his revenge. He'd wanted to tempt her with this house, show her what she'd thrown away, injure her the way she had him…and he'd succeeded. But he wasn't ready to let her go.

"It's time I got going," Garrett said.

"Me, too," Eliza said, piercing Reese with a look. "I want to go home."

"Done," he said. "My pilot is on standby."

"Then, if you'll excuse me, I have a phone call to

make." With that, Eliza breezed past him and left him alone with Garrett.

Garrett poked a fork into the eggs, sampling them. "You sure you know what you're doing, Reese?"

Reese narrowed his eyes. "I always know what I'm doing."

His brother chewed for a moment, then set his fork down and shot him a look. Hell, he hated when Garrett got serious. "So you're through punishing her?"

"Sleeping with my wife would hardly be considered… punishment. Didn't get a single complaint last night." Reese finished off his coffee.

"That's not what I meant and you know it." Garrett lowered his voice, glancing toward the hallway. "She said she offered to help you pack up Pops's things."

"She told you that between dances?"

"We had a little conversation about Pops, yeah. It was damn nice of her, Reese. She's a keeper. And if you're too stubborn to see it, then quit messing with her. Let her go."

"When I'm ready."

"Oh, you're ready, brother. In fact, if she has anything to say about it, right about now…you're *toast*."

Seven

"I can't thank you enough, Eliza," Diana said as they folded up Diana's summer clothes to ship off to Australia. "This is hardly as easy as packing up my stuff from Wellesley."

Eliza smiled, remembering her college days with Diana. Her beautiful bedroom was ten times the size of their room in the sorority house. "You mean when all we had was half a closetful of clothes, our books and some videos?"

"Don't forget the posters of Bon Jovi. We *both* had plenty of those."

"I remember. I think I still have them somewhere," Eliza said, trying to keep her focus. She'd offered to help Diana pack up her house, boxing up some things for Max to take with him to Australia. But in truth,

Eliza's heart wasn't in it. She'd been distracted ever since Reese put her on his private jet alone, sending her back to Sioux Falls, three days ago. He'd claimed he was needed in Montana and had provided her with the plane trip, a limo to take her home and a long good-bye kiss.

Or kiss-off.

She'd had one glorious day and night with Reese, before it had all fallen apart. Now she was angrier than she'd ever been—at herself…and at Reese. She'd fallen into his trap. She realized that now. Reese had wanted to tempt her with that stunning house, his success, the man he'd become. She'd seen it all…and she could envision a life with him again. But then suddenly he'd pulled the rug out from under her and had given her the brush-off.

She fully expected to receive the divorce papers by messenger now, the final blow to a marriage that should never have occurred. It was a mistake to have gotten involved with him again. She should have insisted on signing the divorce papers as soon as he'd shown up on her doorstep. Now, she realized, as the ache in the pit of her stomach would testify, she still had feelings for him. If she didn't, husband or not, she would never have slept with him again. That whole day had been magical. At least *she'd* thought so. But for Reese it had only been a game. She didn't know what he truly wanted from her. At one time he'd been a person she could trust and rely on. She'd had so few people in her life that she could really depend on, and Diana, her dear friend who would be leaving for Australia soon, was one of them.

"Oh, look, I still have the ticket stub for the... Hey, Eliza, what's wrong?" Diana asked softly. "You've been staring off into space since you got here this morning."

Eliza wouldn't lie. Not to Diana. She was sick of lying to her friends. "I know. I'm sorry." She folded up the box she'd just filled with summer shorts and tank tops and turned to her friend. "Remember when I told you that I've been keeping a secret for a long time?"

Diana's gray-green eyes widened with surprise. "I do, but you never told me what it was about."

"Well, it's about Reese Parker."

"The gorgeous guy who came to dinner the other night?"

Eliza nodded. "We have a past."

"Oh, well...he did seem to have a connection to you. But, honestly, I thought he was someone you'd just met. I caught him looking at you a few times during dinner. And I thought, oh, boy, this guy's interested in Eliza."

Eliza sighed and sat down on Diana's bed. She picked up a ruffled pillow and hugged it to her chest. "It's a long story, but basically my life's in limbo right now. I spent some time with him again...and, well, I thought we were through. Now I'm not sure what to think."

"He lives in Montana?"

She nodded.

"That shouldn't be a problem. Look how I met Max. And now I'm getting married and moving to Australia. Montana seems doable."

"It's not where he lives that's the problem. It seems neither one of us can move on from what happened in our past. We're both...angry. I'm not sure I can trust him."

"Wow—sounds familiar."

Eliza smiled and took her friend's hand. She couldn't help but envy Diana for the way her life had worked out. She'd had her problems with Max, but they'd been resolved and now Diana had a wonderful life ahead of her. Eliza felt that maybe her chance with Reese had come and gone six years ago. "I'm happy for you. You know that. Max is wonderful and you're going to have a great life with him. But for me, I'm afraid to hope for that kind of happiness. I have a good life. I don't want you to think I'm whining, but there's always been something missing."

"Because you never knew your mother?"

"Yes, that's part of it. I think I'd be able to confide in my mother the way some moms and daughters talk. I really miss that. Patricia seems so moody lately, but we've never been very close anyway. My father and brothers love me, I know that. But I've never felt as close to another human being as I was with Reese. We spent one whole summer together right after my break-up with Warren. It was the best time in my life. And then everything fell apart."

"Wow. You were in love with him."

"Deeply."

"What are you going to do?" Diana asked with sympathy in her eyes.

"I'm going to concentrate on the Children's Center fund-raiser coming up next month. I've got loads of work to do and I'm hoping to put Reese Parker completely out of my mind."

She grabbed another box and starting filling it with

yearbooks, photo albums and CDs. "But first I'm going to pack you up and get you ready for your trip. And then you're taking me out to lunch."

Diana chuckled. "That was the deal."

"Yes, and there's no backing out on a deal."

Eliza had never backed out on a commitment in her life. Ending her marriage would be a first.

And it meant losing Reese all over again.

Reese glanced down at the papers piling up on his desk and frowned. He'd been swamped with work and had yet to get away from his three-story office building any earlier than ten o'clock at night in the last few days. He had reports to read, permits to file and Leanne's latest geology survey waiting for him to go over. Garrett sat facing him with an expectant look, waiting for an answer about whether to abandon Well #13, the directional drilling project that had run into costly problems.

When his secretary buzzed in, Reese pushed the intercom button, grunting at her, "What?"

"Sorry to interrupt, Reese, but I've got another decorator lined up. She'll meet you at your house at five this afternoon."

Reese ran a hand through his hair. Hell, he didn't want to see another damn decorator. None of the three he'd already met with had been right. He couldn't trust them with his house. "Can't make it."

"How about—"

"No. Put them all on hold for now, Sally. It's a waste of my time. I don't like any of them. It'll just have to wait."

"Okay, let me know when you have time."

"I will," he said, and as an apology for his foul mood he added with more civility, "Thank you, Sally. I appreciate it."

"Sure, boss."

Then he faced Garrett. "So the whipstocking didn't pan out? I think we should abandon the well. No sense pouring good money after bad. But before we do, let's check with Leanne, okay?"

Garrett nodded, his eyes going just a little bright at the mention of their geologist's name. Garrett had it bad for the brown-eyed brunette who had just as much brains as good looks, even behind those black-rimmed eyeglasses she wore. She'd been a godsend to them both, her intelligence matching up with Garrett's hands-on approach and Reese's good instincts. Together they made a great team and a whole lot of money. But Garrett, never one to be shy, was out of his element with her.

"Okay. But I'm with you. No sense throwing more money into that well. We've had too many problems as it is. And speaking of problems, I take it you're not getting anywhere with your house?"

"No." Reese didn't want to delve too deeply into his reasons for turning down four decorators already. None compared to Eliza. He hadn't gotten her off his mind for more than a few minutes at a time during his very busy days. He had more thinking to do and didn't want to discuss her with anyone, not even his brother.

Garrett sat there smiling and nodding his head.

Reese ignored him and looked down at the reports on his desk. "Anything else?"

"Yeah, something else. She got under your skin, didn't she?"

Reese wouldn't feign ignorance. He knew what his brother was getting at. "Like a thorn."

"So you're still bleeding?"

"No! I'm not bleeding, Garrett." Reese let out an impatient sigh.

"Are you or are you not getting a divorce?" Garrett asked.

"None of your damn business."

"My brother's happiness is my business," Garrett bantered back easily. "And I think you still care about her."

The truth was that Reese had been having second thoughts about Eliza. All he'd wanted for six years was to get even with her, to pay her back for the heartache she'd caused him. He'd accomplished what he'd set out to do, but being with her again had been…incredible. He'd been with women in the past and there hadn't been a one that measured up to her. All short-term casual affairs that meant nothing to him. But Eliza had meant something. At one time she'd been everything to him.

He'd struggled these past few days with his need for revenge. When he'd kissed her goodbye the other day at the airport, she'd been rightfully angry with him. He'd deliberately hurt her and she'd known it. The brush-off had been complete. But as he'd stood on the tarmac watching the plane take off, taking Eliza away from him for good, he'd wondered if he'd done the right thing.

She'd explained her reasons for leaving him six years

ago, and deep down Reese knew that Eliza had known very little love in her life. She'd *never* known complete unconditional binding love, so maybe she hadn't been able to recognize it when she'd experienced it with him. She hadn't trusted him. She should have, but could he overlook that now? Could he even begin to forgive her?

She'd been caught between a stepmother who hadn't shown her great affection, an indifferent father and two brothers who had their own lives to live. Her family was a mess, in his estimation. The powerful Fortunes were hardly the picture-perfect family the press would have people believe. They had problems, hardships, secrets and scandals.

The more he thought about her, the more he realized he had to make sure before letting her go. He had to see her one more time.

But he sure as hell wouldn't give his brother the satisfaction of being right. "Let it be, Garrett. I'm not in the mood."

Garrett scoffed. "You're fooling your—"

Leanne walked in, glancing down at the files she was holding. "Sorry to interrupt, boys, but I need a minute of your time."

Reese rose from his chair, shoving files into his briefcase as inspiration struck. One way to keep Garrett out of his hair was to put him in the hot seat. "You know what, Leanne, you can discuss anything you need to with Garrett. You two…work together. I'm beat. I'm taking this work home. You both know how to reach me in case of an emergency."

He walked out with the satisfying image of two very stunned expressions in his wake.

"Thanks for getting me away from work today, Nic. I haven't had a girls' day out in quite some time. Lunch and a shopping spree really helped." Eliza climbed the steps to her house, carrying three shopping bags full of new clothes, lingerie and shoes. She'd gone all out and a little wild with Roberto Cavalli, Dolce & Gabbana and Prada today.

"You've earned a little indulgence, Eliza. It's been a heck of a week for you," Nicole said, removing her Christian Dior sunglasses as they entered the sunlit foyer. "And I'm not just speaking about the Children's Center fund-raiser you're organizing. You've been on a roller-coaster ride this week." Then, lowering her voice and speaking near Eliza's ear, she added, "With your blockhead of a husband."

Eliza chuckled. No one who'd ever seen Reese or spent any time with him would ever consider him a blockhead. Yet she'd come up with a few choice descriptive words for him lately, as well. "I can't think about him, Nic," she said. "It's too darn confusing."

But she had thought about him every single day. And at night, while trying to sleep, his image would appear and she'd recall that one blissful snowcapped day they'd spent in Montana. For a short time, Reese had let down his guard, showing her the man he'd once been, the man she had once loved so desperately.

He'd been sweet and strong when they'd made love as though the past six bitter years had simply faded away.

Eliza smiled at the memory of being in his arms and feeling his power and tenderness, his fierce desire and his unshielded passion. Nothing had ever been better.

But he'd hurt her and she still reeled from that unexpected rejection. Even one week later, Eliza felt the cold slap of his calculated rebuff.

She should feel relieved that he was gone once again from her life. Her secret marriage was safe and would soon end. But she had a niggling feeling that he wasn't through with her yet. And that she wouldn't like what else he had planned for her.

"Confusing or not, you're holding up better than I would under the circumstances."

"Looks like you two girls did some damage today." Nash Fortune walked into the foyer, looking over Eliza's shopping bags.

"Hi, Dad."

"Hello, Mr. Fortune," Nic said. "Nice to see you."

"It's always good to see you, Nicole. So what have you two been doing besides emptying out the boutiques?"

Nic laughed. "That just about covers it. That and a gourmet lunch at the Culver Hotel."

"Eliza, I can't recall the last time you've been on a shopping spree," her dad said, wearing a curious expression.

"I twisted her arm," Nic offered, "and she twisted mine. I've got *five* shopping bags sitting in my car."

Nash looked at Nicole with a smile and a shake of his head, then directed his attention to Eliza, raising an eyebrow. "Does all this shopping have anything to do with Reese Parker?"

Eliza glanced at her friend and then, on a swallow, returned the question. "Why would you think that?"

She'd had enough experience with lying to throw the ball back in her father's court, so to speak. The less she revealed, the better. But she was darn curious to know what her father meant. He hadn't questioned her about her trip to Montana other than asking how her return flight had been after the snowstorm.

"Take a look in the kitchen, honey."

Puzzled, Eliza walked through the foyer and into the great room that led to the kitchen, with Nicole and her father right behind her. Once she stepped into the kitchen, she gasped. "Oh, these are…lovely." She turned back to her father. "Are you saying these are for me?"

Nash pursed his lips. "Patricia doesn't care for tulips. You know she loves roses."

"Right," Eliza said, staring at a huge bouquet of pink, lavender and white tulips sitting tall and pretty in a simple glass vase. With impending dread shoving through her sense of pure delight, she asked, "You didn't read the card, did you, Dad?"

Nash shot her a you-know-me-better-than-that look. "No. But a man can assume, can't he? He flew you to Montana, honey. It doesn't take a rocket scient—"

"That was business, Dad," she interrupted as she touched the firm, smooth petal of one of the flowers.

Her father scoffed gently, with an incredulous note in his voice. "Are you saying he's actually going to hire you?"

Eliza's stomach churned, both from her father's lack of faith in her and from Reese's obvious attempt to throw temptation at her with a house any decorator would love to get their hands on. Obviously neither of them thought her worthy of the challenge.

She managed a slight shrug in answer.

"Must be three dozen there," Nic said, changing the subject. "They are gorgeous."

"Mmm," Eliza said, removing the card nestled between the tall stems. Tulips had special meaning for her, and damn Reese for remembering. For making her think about the mare named Tulip and that one wild, sensual ride they'd both taken that day in the saddle.

From then on, tulips had been her favorite flower.

It had been their private little joke.

Eliza hated to open the card, but not doing so would only cast more suspicion. She read the card silently. *Remember?* it said. She'd been right—this had been Reese's doing. But the rest of the note caused her more alarm. *Dinner at seven tonight. I'll pick you up.*

She closed the card carefully. "It's just a thank-you for helping him the other day," she fibbed, hating herself for lying and Reese for putting her into this position.

Her father nodded with a dubious expression and bid the girls farewell. "I'll see you later, girls. Eliza, we won't be home for dinner tonight. I think I've just thought up a way to surprise Patricia. And you can thank Parker for that."

Eliza managed a small smile. She hated that her father even knew Reese's name. "Okay, Dad. Have a nice time."

"Goodbye, Mr. Fortune."

As soon as Nash left the kitchen, Nicole lifted wide

eyes to her. "Well? Don't keep me in suspense. What does the note say?"

Eliza handed her the note and she read it aloud. "Remember?" Nicole peered at her waiting for an explanation.

"Don't ask. It's too personal. But he wants to have dinner with me?"

Nicole glanced at the note again. "He's not giving you a choice. This isn't an invitation but a command."

"Yeah, I noticed that. The old Reese wouldn't have been so demanding. He'd have asked me out sweetly and I would have melted from his charm."

"Maybe he's ready to have you sign the divorce papers now."

Eliza pursed her lips. "He doesn't have to deliver them in person. We've, uh, said all there is to say."

Nicole cast her a serious look. "Have you really?"

"Yes, I think so. I can't…do this. I'm not going out with him tonight."

"God, Lizzie. That white Escada outfit you bought today would be perfect."

Eliza rolled her eyes. "Traitor."

"Well, it would be. Don't deny you didn't have a man in mind when you bought that."

"I must have *lost* my mind to let you talk me into it."

"You look great in it."

"Maybe, but I'm not wearing it tonight. If he wants me to sign the divorce papers, I'll do it right here."

"In the house? That's risky."

Eliza let go a pent-up sigh. "I'm tired of lying to everyone, Nic. I just want this to be over. Hopefully I can finally make Reese understand that."

"Are you saying you're over him?"

Eliza's heart sped up thinking of him being back here in Sioux Falls. Thinking of the way it had been with them in the past. Thinking of how they'd spent that one magical night in Montana last week. Was she over Reese? She had to stop lying to herself, as well. "No, I'll never be over him. I love him so much it hurts."

Eight

Early that evening, Eliza changed her clothes, removing her black dress slacks and cashmere sweater in favor of faded blue jeans and a flannel shirt, thinking this the perfect form of rebellion. She would not go out with Reese tonight. She'd stay in, be comfortable in her clothes and work up the designs she had in mind for revamping her bedroom while inside her studio.

When Peggy O'Hare came in a few minutes before seven, Eliza was truly surprised at the hour. She'd finally relaxed enough this afternoon to fully immerse herself in her work, almost forgetting about Reese.

"Sorry to bother you, Eliza. But Mr. Reese Parker is here to see you. I asked him to wait in the great room. Would you care to see him?"

Eliza tidied up her notes and stood. She decided to treat Reese's appearance here tonight in a businesslike manner. They had legal issues to resolve and that was the crux of it. "Yes, I'll be down in a minute. Thanks, Peg."

The aging housekeeper nodded and then smiled. She'd known Eliza since her birth, being a loyal employee and something of a grandmother figure to Eliza, as well. "He's a handsome one," she said. "And quite a bit nicer than that Warren fellow." Peggy wrinkled her nose. "I never liked him."

"Come to think about it, neither did I," Eliza said with a small smile, realizing the great truth in that.

"I'll tell Mr. Parker you'll be down shortly. You'll need a minute to change your clothes."

"No, I won't," Eliza blurted. "I'm coming right down."

Peggy narrowed her eyes but only nodded before exiting the room. She knew Eliza well. On any other occasion, Eliza would never receive a guest in her house without looking her best. But Peggy was never one to pry, thank goodness. It was one reason the entire family trusted her and treated her with respect.

Eager to get this over with, Eliza headed down the grand staircase, finding Reese waiting for her at the base of the stairs. Wearing jeans and a black Western shirt with studded snap buttons, he looked impeccable, gorgeous and just like the old Reese, the one she'd fallen head over heels in love with. He smiled and that darn dimple popped out, making her heart soar. She nearly stumbled on the steps.

Seeing him again affected her more than she wanted to admit.

Good God, he held his black felt Stetson in his hand. She'd always been a sucker for that hat.

"Hello, Eliza," he drawled, the low timbre of his voice setting her nerves on edge.

She reached the bottom stair and took a deep breath. "Reese."

"You got my note?"

Eliza nodded. "Yes. And the flowers," she said without thanking him. "But I'm not going out with you tonight." Or any other night, she thought. She had to make a clean break. Thankfully luck was with her again. The house was seemingly quiet, her father and Patricia out, and heaven knew where everyone else had gone. She could say whatever she needed to without fear.

Reese shot her a quick smile. "Yes, you are."

"No, Reese. Let's just end this now. Did you bring the divorce papers?"

"No."

"No?" Exasperated, Eliza shook her head at him. "Well, you should have. What's going on, Reese? Why are you doing this?"

"I'm taking you out on a date. No great mystery there."

"A date?" Eliza had just about lost all of her patience. She'd never been through a divorce before, but she was reasonably certain you didn't date the husband you'd planned on shedding from your life. "You can't be serious, Reese. What do you really want with me?"

Reese gazed into her eyes, gripped her hips, splaying his hands wide and tugged her closer. He lowered his mouth to hers and claimed her lips in a slow, sensual kiss that knocked Eliza for a loop. She indulged in the familiar taste of him and nestled against his body, breathing in the scent of fresh pine and all man. He consumed her heart and soul, but she couldn't allow it. She had to stop him from destroying what sanity she had left. When she pulled back, he followed, refusing to break off the kiss.

He cupped her head with one hand, while the other kept her close. He dipped his tongue and tasted her, and Eliza's resistance slowly faded away.

When he finally broke away, he stared into her eyes.

"I'm not dressed for a date," she said, and the weak excuse had sounded better in her head.

He glanced at her attire with a leisurely perusal, those dark eyes missing nothing. "You're dressed perfect."

"I can't date you, Reese," she tried again.

"Oh, so you don't really want to learn the two-step?"

"What?" Sharp surprise elevated her voice to a squeak.

He planted a quick kiss on her mouth and laced their hands. "Come on," he said, tugging her along. "I have a warm coat for you in the car. You need your purse or anything?"

Dumbfounded, Eliza shook her head. "No."

Reese seemed to have everything she needed.

"Okay, then I hope those are your dancing shoes, sweetheart."

Eliza glanced down at her Nike Shox. "They'll do," she found herself saying.

Reese escorted her outside, and the chill hit her, immediately knocking sense into her brain.

But it was too late. Reese plopped his Stetson on his

head, then wrapped her inside a suede coat lined with
lambswool and ushered her inside his car, heating her
body and…warming her heart.

Reese sat back in his seat, sipping Jack Daniel's and
Coke, lazily watching Eliza work the dance floor with
the instructor he'd hired for the hour. They had the
small, trendy honky-tonk to themselves, a three-piece
band, full service at the bar and a dining room for the
entire evening. As soon as the hour was up, Reese
planned on dominating all of Eliza's time.

She had moves. And he liked them all. Even in those
plain clothes, the perfection of her curvy body was evident in the flare of her hips in those jeans and the press
of plaid against her full breasts. She swayed in rhythm,
learning how to shift her weight and rotate around the
dance floor with the instructor named Denny Thorpe as
her guide.

Reese ached to get her alone again and he didn't
know if it annoyed or pleased him that he reacted to her
in such a primal way.

She laughed, throwing her head back, apologizing to
Denny when she accidentally kicked his shin. Her eyes
sparkled blue fire and her face was flushed.

Reese shifted in his seat, uncomfortable with the
heat rush invading his groin, and took another swallow
of liquor.

When the band stopped playing, Denny released
Eliza's hand and faced Reese, the flickering lights
traveling the dance floor dotting them with color. "You
want a turn now, Mr. Parker?"

"I'll take my turn…later," he said, peering at Eliza. Her face flushed even deeper. "Are you two through?"

Eliza nodded with a breathless smile. "Oh, I think I'm definitely through," she said, looking at Denny. "Thanks for the instruction. It was fun. And I'll contact you about my fund-raiser, okay?"

"Sure. No problem," he said, his spiked hair and tattoos a definite contrast to the posters of Tim and Faith, Toby Keith and Rascal Flatts on the walls at Country Incorporated. Denny didn't look as though he would enjoy country twang, but he'd come highly recommended and had done a great job. "Well, if there's nothing else, I'll be going."

"Thank you," Reese said, standing and tucking a fifty-dollar tip into Denny's hand. "There's nothing else."

And when he left the room, Reese escorted Eliza to her seat. She flopped down ungraciously. "Wow, that was…exhausting."

"You'll get your second wind after dinner."

Eliza pushed her bangs out of her eyes and redid her ponytail, tying up the ends that had fallen down. She glanced at the band, playing a catchy tune, and the team of bartenders and waitresses who were standing by, enjoying the music. "I still can't believe you rented this whole place out."

Reese took his seat, as well. "You said you needed to learn the two-step. You looked good out there."

"Denny's a good instructor. I'm pretty clumsy on the dance floor. I think his shin is still smarting."

Reese smiled, enjoying the carefree banter. He'd been so doggone consumed with revenge that he hadn't taken the time to really enjoy anything in the past. And now he planned on enjoying Eliza, wispy bangs, baby blues, mind-numbing tight jeans and all. "You're mind's always working, isn't it? You suckered that guy in for one of your charity events."

Contrite, Eliza replied, "He offered."

Reese raised his brows.

"Okay, I sort of guilted him into it, but it's for a good cause. While the Sioux Falls' Gentlemen's Club is having a Texas Hold 'Em tournament, the Ladies' Auxiliary will learn the two-step from Denny and a few of his friends."

"And this is to raise money for?"

"The Children's Center. We supply critically ill children with…hope," she said, then added, "last year we built a playground for the kids, provided means of transportation for the families and sent twenty children to Disney World. It was quite a year."

"Would you miss it if you didn't have that in your life anymore?"

Eliza glanced off for a moment, then returned to him with an honest reply. "I'll always volunteer. I've been doing this too long not to. I want to help, but no, I wouldn't miss organizing the events. It's what I do and I do it well. People know that. They're always coming to me and sometimes, Reese, I wish I could just… disappear."

"Then you should."

Eliza chuckled. "It's not that simple."

No, nothing in their lives was simple right now, but Reese never let anyone prod him into doing something that his gut told him not to do. He just wasn't made that way. But for Eliza it was different. She needed that work to fill a void in her life. And to some degree it did fulfill her. Reese couldn't help wondering if Eliza had been searching for something her whole life. Love, maybe? To be accepted and loved for herself? Her lack of faith and trust in him might have had to do with the way she'd been raised—with a silver spoon right out of the dishwasher, instead of one rubbed with love and polished to a shine.

Reese let the subject drop and focused on the meal the waitress had just set before them.

They dined on thinly sliced steak slathered in barbecue sauce, corn on the cob, peanut coleslaw and biscuits. Eliza drank lemonade, while Reese sipped his whiskey and Coke. Eliza nibbled on her food delicately—once a lady, as they say. She'd always been a class act, refined and mannerly.

Except in the bedroom.

There, Eliza threw refinement and inhibition to the wind. She was a wildcat, responsive and sensitive to his every touch. Reese itched to take her to bed again.

She was the only woman he wanted in his bed. He wondered if it were even possible to regain what they once had. So much time had gone by, and hard, angry feelings had been harbored on both ends for all of that time.

Eliza played with the remaining food on her plate, moving her fork around. When she finally glanced up, he noted indecision in her eyes. "So why are we on this date? And don't say it's because I needed to learn the two-step."

Reese leaned back in his seat and studied her, deciding to grant her the truth. Maybe it was time for both of them to come clean. "Were you ever going to tell your family about our marriage, Eliza?"

Her blue eyes went wide with shock. She leaned back in her seat slowly, setting her napkin on the table with care. "Is *that* what this is all about?"

Reese shook his head. "No, this is about revenge. I came back here…to hurt you."

Eliza's back went stiff. Her eyes filled with moisture. "I know," she said, then added softly, "you succeeded."

Reese took a long pull of oxygen. "I'm used to getting what I want, Eliza. And I wanted you to see my success. To see what you missed out on. I wanted to make you sorry for walking out on me."

"I've been sorry," she said, her voice not much more than a squeak, then added quietly, "but you've been… cruel." She rose from her seat, her stance firm, and spoke without hesitation. "I want those divorce papers now, Reese. The game is over."

Reese shook his head and said calmly, "Sit down, Eliza."

"Why? Why should I let you—"

"You wanted the truth and I gave it to you. This isn't a game."

She scoffed, her eyes going bright with indignation, "No, this is a divorce."

"Is that what you really want—a divorce?" he asked, uncertain of her answer. He'd give her the damn divorce if she really wanted it. But he wasn't going to let her waltz out of his life again.

Eliza blinked, appearing deep in thought, then slowly lowered herself to her chair. When she looked at him, her eyes beseeched his. "Is that what *you* really want?"

A slow, sexy ballad played softly in the background, the band forgoing the lyrics to simply let the music tell the story. Reese rose and took her hand. "What I want is to dance with my wife."

Eliza's eyes blazed. "And Reese always gets what he wants?"

"I don't know…you tell me," he said, changing course and smiling down at her, stroking his thumb over her hand gently. "Will you dance with me?"

"It's not two-stepping music," she said cautiously, her resolve and anger ebbing. He felt the release of tension under his palm.

"You should know by now—I'm not a two-stepping kind of man."

Eliza stared into his eyes, watching him closely as if making up her mind.

"Come on. I want to hold you in my arms." Reese tugged her hand and she rose willingly.

He guided her onto the dance floor and wrapped his arms around her, bringing her close enough to share body heat. "You smell good, Eliza." He nuzzled her throat, breathing more of her in, then tightened his hold on her. "Feel good in my arms."

She resisted for a second, then set her head on his shoulder and they swayed slightly back and forth to the rhythm of the music. "I'm not going to sleep with you tonight," she announced quietly.

Reese had to smile. "I know. I want to take you out again tomorrow night."

Eliza sighed into his chest and waited half a beat before answering. "Okay."

Not sleeping with Reese last night had taken its toll on Eliza. She'd been angry and hurt with him and his brutal truths. But afterward, he'd been respectful of her wishes, understanding her gentle fury at his deception. He'd been a perfect gentleman, taking her home, planting a quick, chaste good-night kiss on her lips at her door before driving off.

For some odd reason, Eliza felt she'd won a round with him. And she'd realized that Reese had been right in clearing the air between them. She wanted honesty.

She got honesty.

But tonight was different. She couldn't wait to see him. She couldn't wait to see what the promise of a night free of lies and deception would bring.

She'd thought about him all night. And this morning, while at the Children's Center committee meeting, she'd been told that an anonymous donor had pledged an obscene amount of money for a new children's playground in Sioux Falls. The donor refused any recognition whatsoever. But Eliza knew. It had to be Reese. Money didn't drop out of the blue like that. In all her years in fund-raising, she'd never had someone donate without being given their due credit. Corporations wanted the good press a hefty donation would bring; private donors liked having their names associated with the project.

But just to be sure, she'd pried the information out of the treasurer, a good friend who owed her a big favor.

Eliza hadn't been shocked when she'd seen the name on the pledge sheet. She'd been…humbled.

And so pleased she could hardly keep from jumping his bones when he picked her up looking gorgeous dressed in a black tuxedo.

As they entered the elevator to his penthouse, Eliza felt his eyes on her, watching her every move with a hot gleam. She felt daring tonight, donning her new Ralph Lauren cream halter dress, scooped low in front, decorated with enough gold sequins to make King Tut jealous. The only jewelry she wore was long, delicate chandelier earrings that nearly touched her shoulders.

Reese had taken off her coat in the lobby of the hotel and raked her over with a dangerous look that had sent hot shivers down to her gold-mesh-sandal-encased toes and back.

"You trying to kill me, darlin'?" he asked, eyeing her breasts that nearly scooped out of the scoop neck.

Eliza smiled coyly, glad they were alone in the elevator. "Only a little."

Reese raised a brow. "As long as we're being honest," he said, moving closer and taking her in his arms, "I've always wanted to do this." He lifted her chin with one finger, while the fingers of his other hand wreaked havoc on her cleavage. He lowered his head, brushing his lips to her mouth first, then nibbled lower, down her chin, her throat, until he cut a moist, hot path to her breasts. He fondled one, dipping his hand inside the stretchy material, rocking Eliza back on her heels and against the elevator wall, while his mouth devoured the other, just above the cut of the very low, sweeping neckline.

She rested her head back, giving him full access and breathed out, "You've never done this?"

"Not in an elevator. Not with you," he said between kisses. When the elevator stopped on the fifteenth floor, he groaned, then righted the material on her dress, kissed her quickly and took her hand.

They exited the elevator and walked only a short distance to the penthouse's double-door entrance. Before allowing her inside, he moved her against the door, pressing his body to hers and trapping her with two hands braced on the door. "Here's the deal. If you say no to me tonight, I'll respect that, but you'll be contributing to my slow and painful demise."

When he kissed her, his mouth competed with his granite-hard erection for her attention. It was quite a contest, one she enjoyed completely. He'd made his point and Eliza relished the heady sensation of being given a choice. Reese didn't demand and she liked seeing him with his guard down for a change.

He smiled at her, that dimple peeking out again, heating her blood, and Eliza figured she'd have to be made of stone to deny him anything tonight.

Reese was sure she'd worn that dress to torture him. She was succeeding. Conservative, demure Eliza, went for bold and sexy tonight. With candlelight flickering across the room, she stood facing him, eyeing the elegantly dressed table set for two. The soft light cast her in a golden glow, complementing the highlights in her upswept hair, the rosy hue on her face, the long, slender cut of that dress and legs that brought his view down to sexy, gilded mile-high heels.

He envisioned her wearing nothing *but* those heels, all tall, tan and temptingly naked. Reese wanted her again. Bad. But he wanted something more from her.

Her trust.

Even now, as her gaze roamed the penthouse suite, taking in crystal vases of tulips and tapered candles glowing, with soft music playing, he noted wariness in her eyes. Her mind seemed to be clicking away, wondering if she could place her faith in him.

He couldn't blame her. He'd set out to hurt her and he had. But his plan had backfired. He couldn't walk away from her as he'd intended.

Lucky for him, he'd recognized what was most important to him, revenge being the furthest thing from his mind. Now he planned on helping Eliza heal from wounds he'd inflicted and from older, deeper wounds he'd had no part in exacting.

He wanted to be alone with her tonight, yet he'd intended on taking it slowly. He'd planned on keeping his hands off. He'd planned on enjoying time with her innocently. That's what second dates should be all about—learning about each other, gaining a certain attainable trust. Not rushing things.

Until he'd gotten a look at her in those clothes.

Reese was no fool. She'd dressed for seduction tonight.

Who was he to deny her?

"Are you hungry?" he asked, glancing down at the dome lids covering a savory meal.

Eliza tilted her head to one side and approached him. "That depends."

"On?"

"What you're serving." Her scent wafted in the air, fresh and exotic all at the same time.

Reese popped the champagne cork, keeping his gaze fastened on her. He poured two flutes and handed her one, their fingers brushing from the slight contact. "Champagne for now. Anything you want for later."

"Mmm," she said, sipping her drink and sliding her eyes closed, the look on her face so damn sensual that Reese's blood pressure shot up. "Sounds…good."

Reese narrowed his eyes. "You're a tease, Eliza."

Slowly she opened her eyes. "You liked that about me once."

He sipped his champagne. "I *love* that about you now."

The flute in her hand visibly shook. She lowered the glass down and stared at him, searching for the truth. "I can't do this again, Reese. Not unless you're serious."

Reese set his champagne glass down. "I told you once—this isn't a game. I'm serious."

Eliza bit down on her lower lip, then shook her bangs from her eyes. "So we're seriously dating?"

Reese grinned. "You're putting a label on something that doesn't need one, darlin'."

"*I* need one."

"Okay," he said, picking up the flute again. "Let's drink to seriously dating each other."

Eliza lifted her flute and, with a soft clink, sealed the deal.

"Now that we've settled that, do you want to sit down and have dinner?" he asked.

"As opposed to?"

Reese undid his tie, removed his tux jacket, tossing them both on the wing chair beside the sofa as he gazed at her with heat smoldering in his eyes. He undid all the buttons on his shirt, letting the shirt hang against bronzed skin and a hard body. He took her hand, planted a kiss on her palm, then slid it down to his belt buckle, flattening her fingers to his painful erection. He shot her a daring look. "Making love by the skyline, destroying the sheets on my bed, steaming up the hot tub."

She batted her eyes and smiled seductively. "All of the above?"

He smiled. "Done."

Nine

Reese led Eliza over to the elegant sliding doors that looked out to a balcony. Stars twinkled overhead, challenging the city lights for brilliance. Between the two, the sky sparkled like diamonds.

"It's a good night to be inside, looking out," Reese said, standing behind her. He nuzzled her neck with his nose, then planted hot, moist kisses there. Eliza's breath caught in her throat. "It's a good night to be inside…*you*."

Every night was a good night for that, she thought wickedly.

Reese untied the straps of her halter, exposing her shoulders. He kissed the nape of her neck again, then moved on to the bared skin of her collarbone. Slowly he slid the straps farther down until the material was held up solely by the round curves of her breasts. With a gentle tug, Reese pulled her free of the rest of the dress. It slid down her body smoothly and heaped into a puddle of gold sequins.

Reese cupped her breasts from behind, his hands firm and possessive as he flicked her nipples with his thumbs. Eliza slid her eyes closed and rested her head back against his chest. "Reese," she said breathlessly, "we're in front of the window."

And she was naked but for her heels and lacy thong.

"No one can see us way up here, darlin'. Enjoy the view," he said, then spun her around to stare into her eyes. "I know I am."

His mouth came down on hers, devouring her with hot, lusty strokes of his tongue and softly murmured commands. He spun her around again, bringing her fully up against him, and held her tight, with one hand gripping her hips, the other threading underneath her thong and sinking into her soft feminine curls.

"Oh." She slid her eyes closed again and moaned from the intense pleasure Reese created with his fingers. Behind her, he was rock-hard, rubbing into her and reminding her of the fulfillment yet to come.

He stroked her with finesse, finding all the right places. She swayed her body, unable to control the rocking sensations hitting her full force.

He kissed her throat and whispered in her ear, "I'm gonna watch you explode, darlin'." She popped her eyes open, seeing him in the reflection of the glass-paned sliding doors.

Seeing them both in the reflection, the erotic picture

they made and Reese's intense look, she'd never been more aroused. Exposed in front of the door, she knew that no one could see her through the darkness and height and yet she'd never felt so completely free.

Eliza lifted both arms up above her head to work her fingers through his hair, holding on tight, her breaths coming harder now. She made little throaty sounds, and Reese encouraged her with sexy, erotic words. "You're almost there, baby. You're so damn beautiful when you co—"

"Reese, Reese," she moaned as blasting heat and electric tingles racked her body. She swayed, she moved, she stilled. And the explosion shook her, consuming her, the release leaving her with a heady thrill of completion.

Reese held her from behind, letting her come down slowly, kissing her throat, patiently waiting.

She turned in his arms. She still wanted him. She wanted more. She pulsed with the need to have him fill her. "Let's go destroy your sheets," she whispered.

"That's my girl." Reese lifted her up and carried her to the bedroom.

Eliza smiled thinking that there was no doubt about it. She *was* Reese Parker's girl.

Reese laid her down on his bed, looking at the perfect picture she made there with tousled hair fanning out, bared to him but for the creamy lace thong and those killer heels. It was where she belonged—in his bed, with him, forever. He'd come to that realization some time ago but refused to allow the thought to become reality. He'd been blinded by his need for payback, retribution, revenge. But now he'd seen her in her element, seeing the real Eliza for the first time. She wasn't just the bold, sexy woman he'd met one summer day in Montana. No, she was vulnerable and sensitive and compassionate. Extremely intelligent and competent. Caring. She had talent that she was afraid to pursue, dreams she put on hold. She wanted what most people wanted—to be loved fully and completely.

Reese had given her that kind of love before and it had gone bad. But he was willing to try again, willing to put the past behind him.

He'd fallen in love with her again.

He watched her wiggle out of her thong, gliding it down her body.

"Don't you dare take off those heels."

A low rumbling chuckle came out of her throat. "You mean these?" She lifted one leg, pointing her toes at him.

"Yes, damn it."

He cast off his shirt quickly and reached for his belt buckle, but Eliza covered his hand with hers. "Let me."

Reese dropped his hands to his side.

She rose up on her knees, unfastened his belt, unzipped his pants and reached in, taking him into her hands. Reese slammed his eyes shut, his hands going into her hair, threading through as she stroked him tenderly. When she shifted gears, taking him into her mouth, he flinched— the hot, moist pressure nearly doing him in. After a minute of intense pleasure, Reese stopped her. "Enough."

Eliza understood. They knew each other so well. She lay back down, her eyes fastened on him.

He shed the rest of his clothes and covered her

with his body, spreading her legs and finding her wet heat. He thrust inside her, claiming her with powerful, potent, overwhelming need. He moved. She moved. They rocked together, the heels of those sandals scraping his back.

It happened fast from then on, hurried, wild. Reese poured everything he had into her until both met with a fierce overwhelming climax.

He came down to kiss her again and again. She kissed him back just as readily and something changed between them then. Something strong and urgent. And he sensed the moment when Eliza found her trust in him.

She smiled, her eyes filled with a soft glow.

Reese took hold of her hand and kissed it, then locked their fingers together. He'd forgotten to use protection. It had happened so fast, the need so urgent. Or had it been a deliberate act? Had he purposely shoved those thoughts away? Reese had always wanted children with Eliza.

They still had issues. Eliza was lying to her family about him. She'd been omitting the truth for six years. He'd leave it up to her how to resolve that problem.

He was due back in Montana tomorrow. He had a business to run. There'd been a small fire at one of the oil wells. Luckily it had been contained before it had spread, but two of his crew had been injured. He'd just learned of it this afternoon and needed to find out the details. Breaking this date with Eliza hadn't been an option. They were on fragile ground here, and he'd set out to earn her trust and heal past wounds. She was too important to him now. But Reese had to return to

Bozeman. He owed those injured workers a visit and he needed to see a report on the fire.

He rolled on his side, resting on his elbow to look at her. She had her eyes closed, a look of sated tranquility on her face. She caught him watching her and smiled. "What?"

"You look…happy."

She bit her lower lip and nodded. "I am." Then she rolled on her side and her beautiful full breasts jiggled from the movement. "Are you?"

Reese nearly snorted. "I'm in bed with a gorgeous woman, about to make love to her again. Oh…I'm happy."

Eliza rode her fingers across his chest. "Again?"

"Or we can have dinner now? Hot tub? Whatever you want. Reese Parker aims to please."

She giggled. "Oh, you're pleasing me."

Reese took her into his arms, curling her body into his. He breathed in her scent, that exotic mix of female smells that drove him crazy. "Stay with me tonight. I want to wake up with you in my arms."

Eliza hesitated a moment, and Reese realized she was planning her next lie to her family. She was a grown woman with a life of her own, but she lived in the family home. They'd know that she'd stayed out all night. There would probably be questions. Reese read all that in the tentative look on her face.

She sighed heavily and closed her eyes, then reopened them with a steady look. "I'll stay the night."

The next morning Eliza heard the steady hum of water running in the shower and then a squeak in the plumbing when the faucet was turned off. She opened her eyes and watched Reese as he entered the bedroom. Smelling clean, his hair tousled and still damp from his shower, she followed his fluid movements as he dressed into a pair of dark slacks and a fresh white shirt. His gaze met hers as he buttoned up his shirt. "Stay in bed. Sleep. It's early and I kept you up late last night."

Eliza smiled warmly, vivid memories flooding in as to exactly how Reese had kept her up last night. She stretched, her arms going up over her head, and the sheet dropped down a bit, uncovering her nude body.

Reese groaned, sat down on the bed and kissed her gently on the lips as he covered her up again. "Don't tempt me. I have an early flight out." He set the key card on the dresser next to her. "Stay as long as you like. I'll be back Friday night."

As much as Reese's tone indicated he'd rather be in bed with her, his expression was all business. He'd already dismissed her, his mind focused on his company and what he had to do this week. It was crazy, but she missed him already. She glanced at the key card he trusted her with and felt that they were finally making progress. "I'll see you Friday night, then?"

He nodded. "For our third date."

She grinned. "It'd be kind of hard to top last night."

Reese reached out and twirled a strand of her hair around his fingers. "If you don't mind being seen around town with me, I'll be sure to make our next date just as memorable."

Eliza sighed, then took a big swallow, reminded of all the lies she'd told her family about her relationship with Reese. If she and Reese were seen around town together, the news would get back to them. The family would know that they were dating, and even though her father had alluded to it, she'd denied anything was going on again and again. Eliza knew her days and lies were numbered. She wanted to tell her family the truth. If only she could bring herself to do it. But her father had been distracted lately and Patricia had never seemed more unapproachable. The thought of owning up to her secret six-year marriage weighed heavily on her. "Reese, I need a little more time," she said softly.

He gazed deep into her eyes. "I came back for you, Eliza."

"I…know." And she was glad of it now.

"No, you don't understand. Six years ago. I came here to see you after you walked out on me."

"What?" Eliza lifted the covers nearly to her chin and bolted up in bed. "When?"

"A few days after getting your note. You burned me bad and I was pissed and hurt and confused. I stewed on it and once I'd calmed a little, I knew that I couldn't let you just walk out of my life so easily. So I came here looking for…I don't know. A fight, I guess. Something. I had to know what happened."

"What did happen? I…we…never saw each other."

"Your brother Case tossed me off your property. Wouldn't let me in the house."

Stunned, Eliza could barely make sense of this. "Why not?"

Reese snorted, then laughed wryly. "He didn't want a drunken cowboy anywhere near his sister. She'd had enough of a bad time lately, he said and then threatened to call the police." Reese continued to twirl her hair, watching it twine around his finger rather than witness the pained expression on her face.

"I'm sorry. If Case had known who you were… maybe—"

"He was protecting his sister. I got that. But even then, I didn't reveal your secret. I've waited six years, darlin'. I suppose I can wait a little longer for you."

Eliza never loved Reese more than at that moment. No longer demanding and imposing, he'd opened up his heart and quietly given her the time she needed. "Thank you for coming after me," she said, her eyes filling with tears, thinking if Case had only allowed Reese entrance to her home the last six years might have been spent differently. But that was water under the bridge and she wouldn't dwell on the past. Still, it gladdened her heart that he had cared enough to come after her and confirmed that she wasn't making another mistake with Reese. "And thank you for giving me the time I need now."

He tugged her hair, letting it go completely, then brushed a sweet kiss across her mouth. "Friday night."

Eliza lingered in his bed long after he'd gone. Sated from a night of lovemaking and thrilled to have Reese back in her life, especially now that he'd confessed to coming after her, she'd never felt more certain about him. Or more content.

As tentative as their relationship was right now, Eliza knew that they were headed on the right path. And it no longer frightened her. She'd given up on her mistrust of Reese, letting down the barriers that had kept them apart.

She stayed in his penthouse suite most of the morning, showering and dressing lazily, then she called a taxi. During the ride home, she decided on telling her father that she was dating Reese Parker. If questioned further, she'd own up to spending the night with him last night, as if Nash wouldn't have already assumed that from seeing her return home in evening clothes.

With bravado, Eliza entered her home, fully prepared to shed some minor truths regarding her relationship with Reese. However, she found the house empty but for Ivy, who was preparing tonight's dinner, and Peggy, who was busy polishing silver in the dining room.

"Hi, Peg," she said, taking a seat in the dining room with elbows braced on the table and hands holding up her chin, just as she had as a little girl. Eliza had always loved to watch Peggy's regimented process of shining up the silver.

"Morning, Eliza." Then with a raised eyebrow she said, "Or should I say good afternoon, dear girl."

Eliza laughed.

"I see you've got a few wrinkles on your dress," she said lightly. "I'll have it dry-cleaned for you."

Eliza blushed. "Thanks."

"I like seeing the smile in your eyes. It's been too long."

"Are my eyes smiling now?" she asked Peggy, remembering that she'd say that very thing whenever Eliza was extremely happy.

"As bright as when you found the most Easter eggs during the hunt or when your father surprised you with your first car. Or the day you showed me your Wellesley diploma."

Eliza shrugged. "I guess…I'm happy."

Peggy wiped the knife clean of polish, stroking the blade back and forth with a soft cloth as Eliza looked on. "That Reese Parker is a nice man."

This time Eliza wouldn't argue. Eliza felt it deep down in her bones. "Yes, I think so, too."

Peggy shot her a knowing glance. "Next time maybe you'll think to bring a change of clothes."

"*Thinking* didn't have much to do with it, Peg."

This time Peggy blushed, turning the aging housekeeper's face rosy red. "Ah, that man is lucky to have you, Eliza. I hope he realizes that."

"Yes, I hope so, too," she said, wondering if she and Reese had a real chance at happiness the second time around.

Ten

Reese sat in the wingback chair in his penthouse suite, going over ground surveys for three new drilling sites with Leanne. She sat on the sofa with papers, reports and financial statements spread out on the marble cocktail table. Leanne's dark eyeglasses kept slipping down and she kept setting them in place with the slightest touch of her finger.

Reese chuckled and she lifted her eyes.

"You're a good sport for agreeing to this," he said.

"I've never been to Sioux Falls before. Not that I've seen much of the town since we landed this morning."

"I've kept you pretty busy, I know. But it's important to me, Leanne. I need to be here right now."

She nodded, eying him with a question on her lips, but luckily she thought better of it. Reese appreciated that. He'd kept his marriage and his life private for a long time. Now wasn't the time to open up to her or anyone else, for that matter. Not until his relationship with Eliza was resolved.

He'd gone back to Montana for two days and decided enough was enough. He wanted to see Eliza tonight, a full twenty-four hours sooner than she expected him. He'd called her every day since leaving her in this suite the other morning, but had been too tied up with work to spend any real time on the phone with her. Then he'd decided the hell with it. He was the boss. If he wanted to be in Sioux Falls with Eliza, he'd just bring his work along with him.

And his associate, Leanne Finnegan.

An hour later, Leanne lifted her head, tilting it from side to side, then rubbed the tension out of her neck.

Reese watched her, noting how pretty she was. Beautiful, really, and probably the perfect match for his brother.

He tossed his papers down. "Quitting time," he said. "And not a moment too soon, I see. Are your eyes crossing yet?"

Leanne grinned. "I'll live, Reese."

"God, I hope so."

Leanne set her own survey reports down on the cocktail table and, sitting up straight in her seat, she took off her glasses. Then, in an efficient move, she removed the pins from her hair, and dark, silky waves poured over her shoulders. "Mind if I ask you something?" she said quietly, scooting her way along the sofa to get closer to him.

Reese leaned back in his chair. "Not at all. What's on your mind?"

Leanne took a deep breath. "Do you think I'm attractive?"

Surprised, Reese hid his stunned expression and kept his voice even. "I'd say you're beautiful, Leanne. Why?"

She seemed edgier than he'd ever seen her. She bit her lip, and when she sighed, Reese noted the rise and fall of her breasts. Even though she wore a no-nonsense pin-striped business suit, any man with eyes in his head would know that she had a gorgeous body.

She kept her dark eyes fastened to his. "What if I told you I'm attracted to someone I work with?"

"Uh, well…that would be okay," he said, his nerves jumbling a bit and wariness creeping in. "As long as it didn't interfere with your performance…at work, I mean." Suddenly he felt like Dr. Phil. And he certainly didn't like the way she was staring at him as though he could make or break her with his replies.

"So you wouldn't think it unprofessional? Because I'd have to make the first move. He doesn't seem to know I exist."

He watched her move even closer to him, her eyes vivid, clear and intense. Reese rubbed his temple, keeping his panic down. Hell, if Leanne was interested in him, he'd missed all the signs. Heaven help him, he'd never want to hurt her. Or lose her. She was the best geologist in the business. Had he given her the wrong idea, asking her to join him here in Sioux Falls? "Leanne, you're not giving yourself enough credit. Any man would know—"

She touched his arm, stopping his next thought. "Not just any man, Reese."

Reese froze. Her fingers slid across his shirt.

"Your brother."

His dread evaporated instantly and he was filled with astounding relief. The irony almost killing him, he barely contained his composure. "Garrett?"

She nodded. "Is he seeing someone?"

Only you, in his dreams, Reese almost blurted out.

"No, he's not seeing anyone. In fact, Leanne, I'd say this is a great time to let him know how you feel."

"Really? And it would be okay with you?"

Reese smiled. "More than okay with me." He winked. "Don't worry. Somehow I think Garrett won't mind one bit."

Leanne sank back on the sofa looking more than mildly relieved. "Thank you, Reese. You won't say anything, right?"

"My lips are sealed," he said, thinking that Garrett was one lucky son of a gun, to have the woman of his dreams make a play for him without any secrets, lies or deception. Reese was elated to be off the hook, and now his brother would come to know some happiness in his life. Hell, he'd been pining away for Leanne for months now, too damn intimated by his own feelings to make a move. "Come on, let's get this work together. Then we'll grab a quick dinner."

"Sounds good to me," she said, gathering up all the papers she'd brought and setting them inside her briefcase. With a click of the case, she turned to add, "All ready. I'm starving. Do you know where we can get some good hometown cooking?"

"Actually, I know this little honky-tonk." Reese

helped her on with her coat and they smiled at each other before he put a hand to her back and guided her to the door.

Reese reached for the knob just as the door opened from the other side with a decided click.

Eliza stood on the threshold.

With wide assessing eyes, she stood ramrod still for one moment, her gaze darting from him to Leanne and back, taking in his hand on Leanne's back and the smiles on their faces. Eliza's mouth dropped open. There was no mistaking her thoughts. Everything was revealed to him, from the pained look on her face to the hot, angry tears welling in her eyes.

She stepped back just as he reached out to her. "Eliza, wait…"

She shook her head and kept backing away. "Don't, Reese. Just don't. I get it now," she said, with near hysterical laughter.

"Damn it, Eliza. This isn't what it—"

"I've been such a fool," she declared, "and now your revenge is finally complete!"

Before he had a second to formulate just the right words, she turned on her heel and ran straight to the elevator, climbing in. The door slid closed before Reese had a chance to catch her, but in that one instant he noted heated accusation in her eyes and sheer devastation on her face.

Reese leaned heavily on the doorjamb and closed his eyes. Eliza could have waited for his explanation. She could have heard him out. Instead, she chose to believe the worst about him. She didn't trust him. She never had. And he feared that maybe she never would. Sadly Reese also realized that Eliza had no faith in herself or what they meant to each other.

Leanne touched his arm. "Reese, I'm so sorry. Did I do—"

He shook his head and cast her a solemn look. "It's not your fault, Leanne. Mistakes were made a long time ago. And now we're both paying the price."

"I didn't know you were involved with anyone, Reese. By the look on your face, I'd say it was pretty serious."

"*Intense* is the correct word."

"Who is she?" Leanne asked, then waved off the question. "Never mind. It's not my business."

Reese sighed heavily. Hell, Leanne had confided in him about Garrett, so why not confide in her about Eliza? Right now, with his heart heavy, he could use a friend. "She's my...wife."

The only woman I've ever loved.

Eliza drove home frenzied, the pain almost unbearable. She parked the car outside the front door of her home and hurried inside, bumping into Patricia and her father in the foyer.

"Eliza, what's wrong?" Patricia asked, a deep frown on her face. This was one time Eliza didn't need or want Patricia's concern. At any other time she would have relished it, but now she just wanted to be left alone.

"Nothing," she said, lying once again. "I'm not feeling well." She bypassed her father and headed for the staircase.

"Eliza," her father called out.

"I'll…be…fine, Dad," she said, climbing the stairs quickly, heading to her room. She slammed her bedroom door and then leaned heavily against it, relieved to finally be alone, away from more lies, hurt and deception.

Her tears fell rapidly, freely, streaming down her face. She wouldn't have to pretend to anyone that everything was all right. Here, in the sanctity of her bedroom, she could cry her eyes out and let her heart bleed for a love that shouldn't have ever happened. She sank down to the floor, confused, hurt and angry.

Reese couldn't have planned it any better, could he? He'd led her to believe he was sincere, wanting a fresh start, and she'd fallen for it and him—again. Seeing him with another woman, one who'd made him smile, one who had looked at him with such blatant admiration, had nearly destroyed her. Had he been in Sioux Falls all along? Maybe he hadn't left that morning, at all. Maybe he'd planned on duping her longer, but her showing up unexpectedly certainly couldn't have been planned. She asked herself once again, what kind of game was Reese playing?

Her cell phone rang.

Eliza wouldn't look at the number on the screen.

She couldn't talk to anyone right now.

She lifted it out of her purse and shut it off.

Then she dug into her purse again, pulling out the envelope and the note she'd written to Reese, the note she couldn't wait to have him read, the reason she'd gone to his penthouse this evening in the first place.

Through a waterfall of tears, she skimmed the writing with disgust.

Dear Reese,

I've finally realized that the lying and deception must stop. It's not fair to you or to me. By the
time you read this, I will have told my family the
truth about our marriage and the lies I've told for
six years. I can only hope they will understand
when I apologize. I love you, Reese. I always
have. We both deserve to have our marriage out
in the open, free of secrets. I will see you soon and
hopefully we can put the past behind us once and
for all.

Your wife,
Eliza

Eliza ripped up the note and tossed it away, but the sad
ache in her belly remained. She'd never known such pain.

She lay down on her bed, rehashing the time she'd
spent with Reese, looking for clues, trying to figure out
why she hadn't seen this coming. Was she that big a fool?

Reese hadn't looked guilty when she'd found him
with another woman. He'd only looked surprised. She'd
caught him red-handed. Or had she?

For the first time in her life, Eliza really reexamined
what she'd seen, both six years ago in that hotel room
and tonight. Could Reese possibly have been innocent?
On both accounts? Had she walked in on something tonight that could easily be explained?

Eliza shoved her eyes closed, the turmoil of the past
few weeks taking a heavy toll on her body and her
mind. She needed to rest, to clear her head.

She couldn't think anymore.

She slept until a soft knocking on her door roused her.

"Eliza, it's me, Nicole."

"Nic?" Drowsy and disoriented, Eliza sat up in bed. "What are you doing here?" Once the events of the past few hours rushed in, Eliza regained some composure. She realized the time. She hadn't slept all night but only a few hours. She got up and opened the door.

Nic stood in the doorway holding a big Louis Vuitton bag. "Your dad called me. He's worried about you."

"Oh," she said, moving aside to let her friend in. "That's not like him."

"Well, forgive me, but you look like hell. I can understand why he'd worry. What happened?"

Eliza sat down on her bed and Nic followed. "*Reese* happened." Then she glanced at her bag. "What'd you bring?"

Nic smiled. "Pajama party." She lifted out two pairs of pajamas decorated with red cherries and green stems, a bottle of wine and two crystal glasses.

Eliza's mood lightened temporarily. Through their teen years, they'd always managed to console each other with a sleepover and lots of good honest talk. The wine came as an added feature in their adulthood. "How'd you know?"

Nic took hold of her hand. "Like you said, Reese happened. We'll get in our pajamas later. Right now let's have a glass of wine and talk, okay?"

Eliza nodded. Nicole was the only person she trusted with her thoughts, doubts, fears and mistakes. "You pour the wine. I'll pour out my heart."

"That bad?" Nicole asked, a look of deep concern on her face.

"Nic, I'm either the biggest fool in the world or I've made another huge mistake in judgment. Maybe both."

Nicole opened the bottle of wine and poured two glasses, handing her one. "I'm listening."

Eliza began, "Well, I don't how it could get much worse...."

"This isn't the worst thing in the world, Nash."

Eliza woke to the sound of her stepmother's elevated voice coming from right outside her bedroom door. She opened her eyes, squinting at the daylight pouring inside her window. Glancing at the clock, she realized the late morning hour. She'd overslept.

"Give her a chance to explain," she heard Patricia say.

"She lied to all of us," Nash said to his wife. "You know how I feel about liars. Eliza, wake up."

Her father's stern voice jarred her into action. She sat up in bed, rubbing her forehead and the fuzziness away. She and Nicole had overindulged a little last night, the numbing power of a great Chardonnay finally ebbing.

"We've been waiting for you to get up for an hour," her father called out from outside her door.

Eliza's brows furrowed in confusion when she saw the *Tribune* newspaper sliding under her door.

"Get dressed, Eliza. And come downstairs. You have some explaining to do."

She hadn't heard that tone from her father since, as a young girl, she'd taken a feisty mare out for a ride without permission. The horse had tossed her off as she rounded the corner of the stables, right in front of her father's eyes.

"I'll be down, Dad. Give me a minute." She rose immediately and picked up the newspaper left under her door, the headlines glaring and unmistakable no matter how many times she blinked her eyes. "Oh, no!"

Fortune Heiress's Summer Fling and Secret Marriage Revealed!

Eliza's heart slammed against her chest.

She continued to read the words that burned a hole in the pit of her stomach.

> *Eliza Fortune, chairperson and benefactor to many South Dakota charity organizations, hid her secret six-year Montana marriage to former rodeo champion Reese Parker from family and friends. Apparently her wild summer fling ended badly, and now Mrs. Reese Parker is being sued for divorce.*

Eliza finished reading the article that portrayed her as a fickle, insecure, spoiled woman who rebounded after her broken engagement with mayoral candidate Warren Keyes, duping both her family and close friends by hiding her marriage to a onetime down-on-his-luck rodeo rider. The article went on to describe Reese as a prosperous oilman who'd made his way up the ranks despite his estranged marriage to the Fortune heiress, wanting out of the union at any cost.

Eliza's head throbbed. She'd never meant to hurt her family. She'd decided to tell them the truth despite what had happened last night with Reese. But someone had beaten her to it. And she suspected she knew who'd leaked this story to the press.

Trina Watters, Nash's ex-wife and her half-brother Blake's, biological mother. The woman had been accused of causing trouble for both Case and Gina and Max and Diana. A bitter woman, she seemed to find some sort of delight and satisfaction at hurting Nash and his family.

Eliza finger-combed her hair, changed into a pair of black slacks and a warm beige cashmere sweater, set her feet into suede loafers and went downstairs. During the night, after a good long, revealing talk with Nicole, she'd come to some important decisions that would affect her entire life.

Today she planned on making things right and finally, once and for all, taking charge of her life.

Her bravado faded somewhat when she entered the great room to find Case, Creed and her father staring at her from their allotted seats around the room as though she'd stolen the Hope diamond.

The only friendly face was Patricia's. Eliza appreciated her support, even if she had been remote lately. "Good morning."

Male voices grumbled their greeting.

"Sit down, Eliza," Patricia said with kindness. "I've poured you a cup of coffee. Ivy set out some pastries. Would you care for one?"

Eliza sat down to face her family, with Patricia seated next to Nash on the sofa and her brothers in wingback chairs on either side of them. "No, thanks, Patricia. I'm not…" She glanced at her father's expectant face, then at her two older brothers. "I don't have an appetite."

The room was quiet, and Eliza knew she had an audience and her family's full attention. "I'm sorry for all this. Truly. I can't tell you how much I hated lying to all of you. I hope you can forgive me, but most of what the article said is true. I left here six years ago after finding Warren in bed with his campaign manager. It was a hard time in my life. I went to Montana to escape the scrutiny and all the press. You all know the reasons I didn't reveal the truth about Warren to the press. I was trying to protect the family and our good name. Trying not to cause a scandal. A broken engagement is surely less seedy than the real reason I walked out on him.

"When I went to Montana, the last thing I expected was to start another relationship. But I did. I fell deeply in love with a kind, sweet-natured rodeo rider. Reese. I realized then what love really was—at least I thought I did. Reese and I had a wonderful summer together. We married quickly."

Nash's intake of breath resounded in the quiet room.

Eliza's expression implored her father. "I'm sorry I didn't tell you. I wanted…some time. Some privacy. And then, shortly after, my marriage to Reese fell apart."

"What happened, Eliza?" her father asked.

"It was a big misunderstanding. I jumped to wrong conclusions. I guess I'd still been smarting from Warren's betrayal. But I didn't realize it at that time. I walked out on Reese and came home."

"You couldn't have loved him much," Case said pointedly.

Eliza shook her head. "Oh, quite the opposite, big brother. It killed me to walk out on him. We'd been so happy. I came home feeling like a failure. Twice I'd been hurt. Twice I felt I'd been betrayed. I didn't want another scandal. I realized how the press would spin the story. I worried about our family's reputation and…my own. My charity work would have suffered. But I'd been wrong about Reese. Yes, he came here for a divorce. But since we've spent time together, I realized that I still love him with my whole heart. And if he'll take me back, I want our marriage to work."

"Why wouldn't he take you back? He certainly hasn't been acting like a man with divorce on his mind," Nash said.

Eliza wrinkled her nose and decided to keep the details of her last encounter with Reese private and the fact that he'd come here initially with revenge on his mind. "Uh, well, there might have been another misunderstanding. But I've learned my lesson. I'm not about to let go of the man I love. Not this time."

Eliza glanced at her brothers, who seemed to have eased the tight expressions on their faces. Then she glanced at Patricia. She nodded in understanding, her eyes soft and beckoning Nash to do the same.

"If you'd have told us the truth six years ago, we would have worked it all out as a family," her father said quietly.

Patricia spoke up. "Eliza thought she was protecting us."

"Plus, I felt so humiliated, Dad. I couldn't put our family through another one of my messes, just months after my broken engagement."

Nash nodded. "I can understand that, honey." Then he took Patricia's hand. "I wish you hadn't lied to us, but I forgive you."

Patricia stiffened visibly but cast her a soft smile. "There's nothing to forgive. You only did what you thought was right."

Eliza let out a heavy sigh, relieved that her secret was finally out in the open. "Thank you—all of you—for listening. And not judging me."

"We love you, Eliza," her father said, "and want you to be happy. I like Reese."

"You do?"

"He's a self-made man. And he married my daughter."

"But someone's out to hurt our family, Dad. Leaking that story to the *Tribune* smells of Trina's handiwork," Case said with an angry gleam in his eyes.

"I think it was her, too, Dad. I'm going to talk to Blake and see if he can do something about her." Eliza finally sipped her coffee, her stomach unclenching now. Though the thought of accusing Blake's mother wasn't a welcome one, Eliza had always been able to talk to him. Unlike her brothers, who never gave Blake a chance.

Creed snorted. "Blake has no control over her."

"You aren't being fair to him," Eliza said. "Neither one of you has ever given him the benefit of the doubt."

Case and Creed remained silent.

"He's over at Skylar's now. See if you can talk some sense into him," her father said.

"I'm going to, Dad. And thank you for understanding about me and Reese."

Nash rose and walked over to her. He took her hand and she lifted her face up to meet his smile. "You have my blessing, honey. Patricia and I only want you to be happy."

Eliza glanced at Patricia, who also smiled. Something was going on between her father and Patricia, but Eliza couldn't quite put her finger on it. Yet she relished her family's forgiveness and made a promise to herself to do her best to make things right between her and Reese.

Nic had really helped her realize one very important thing last night: Eliza had never fought for her marriage. She'd never stuck around long enough to listen to Reese and hear his explanations. She'd readily made wrong assumptions about him and their marriage. Five unanswered cell phone calls from Reese last night had her believing in him again. He'd cared. He'd called. He'd wanted to work things out. Eliza had to believe that now.

But she'd also come to one other conclusion last night.

It had taken a three-hour-long conversation with Nicole sparked with honesty and courage, enough for her to face a real truth: Eliza had never felt worthy of love. She'd never felt completely, unconditionally loved by another human being. When Reese offered her that, she'd been too frightened to accept it. She'd found a way to sabotage her marriage, leaving Reese before he might leave her.

As ridiculous as it seemed, Eliza felt the truth of that revelation in her heart. She'd been scared of accepting true love from the one man who deserved her faith and trust.

Eliza was ready to give Reese that, now.

If only he'd accept it and take her back.

But first she had to deal with her brother, Blake. And see if he could put a stop to Trina's hurtful meddling.

Eleven

"Aw, hell," Reese said, glancing at his watch. "It's lunchtime already. And I promised to get you back home before noon today. I've dominated enough of your time."

Leanne smiled and offered more graciously than he deserved, "We had to finish up our work here, Reese. Besides, I don't have any pressing plans in Montana or anywhere else this weekend."

"Unfortunately neither do I." Everywhere he looked in his penthouse suite, he was reminded of Eliza and the night they'd shared here. The passion they'd experienced had blown his mind, but it had been so much more. They'd forged a bond of trust that night. They'd really connected, tearing down all the walls that had separated them. Reese had begun to think that they could put the past behind them and look toward the future.

He couldn't begin to imagine how the manure hit the fan in the Fortune household this morning. After reading the *Tribune*'s society page, he could only stare angrily, seeing the harsh words printed about Eliza, wondering how she was coping with all of this. Protective instincts streamed in. But he couldn't do a damn thing to help her unless she wanted him to. At least the truth was finally out in the open.

"You could go see her," Leanne said softly.

He shook his head. "She won't answer my calls." Besides, how could he possibly convince her that she could trust him? He'd been falsely accused twice now and his pride and ego had taken a hit.

"She'll have a change of heart, Reese."

When a loud knocking resounded against the front door, Leanne glanced at him with a gleam in her eyes. Reese wasn't that much of an optimist. But when he answered the door, the last person he'd expected to find was standing in the doorway, glowered at him. "Garrett?"

Garrett moved past him, took one glance at Leanne settled back against the sofa and turned on Reese again with an arch of his brow. "Am I interrupting?"

"No." Reese shut the door, narrowing his eyes. "What are you doing here? Is something wrong?"

Garrett wore his no-nonsense look, the one Reese recalled from their youth, the kind he would have when he thought he'd been robbed by an umpire's bad call at home plate. "You tell me, big brother."

"Garrett," Reese said, walking past him to take his seat again. "It's been a long couple of days. What do you want?"

Garrett's gaze flowed over Leanne, raking her over from top to bottom, a hot, angry glint in his eyes. "Where are you staying?"

Leanne's pretty brown eyes fluttered. "Where am I...what?"

"Staying. Are you sleeping—"

"Uh, Garrett?" Reese finally understood his brother's appearance here. "Be careful. You wouldn't want to use up the small amount of charm God gave you all at once. I don't think Leanne could take it."

Leanne rose from her seat and glared at Garrett. "Are you insinuating that your brother and I...we..." Clearly livid, Leanne couldn't get the words out. She looked at Reese.

Reese snorted and lifted up from his seat. "Garrett, relax. I asked Leanne to work with me here in Sioux Falls so that I could make amends with my wife. Leanne's room is two floors down."

Garrett's jaw unclenched.

"Didn't you get my message?" Reese asked his brother.

"I thought I did, loud and clear."

And you came running, Reese thought. Well, that was one way to unwittingly force Garrett to make his move with Leanne. "Then you weren't listening hard enough. You know, my wife is sure good at handing out accusations. I'm glad my brother has more sense."

Garrett eyed him for a moment, swallowed down, then nodded.

"Don't explain anything to him, Reese. It's none of his business." Leanne's eyes sharpened on Garrett's.

"Oh, I think it is," Reese offered, scratching his head and wondering why the two people he loved most in the world would think the worst about him. Love, betrayal and years of ruthlessness might have something to do with it.

"In fact, you two deserve some privacy."

When Leanne began to protest, Garrett walked over to face her, a smile teasing his lips. "Reese is right. I'd like to speak with you privately. You deserve an apology. I had no right coming here thinking what I was thinking. It's just that…hell," he confessed, softening his tone, "you make me crazy, Leanne."

"There's that charm coming through again." Reese reached for his coat from the closet.

But Leanne's eyes warmed instantly. "*Crazy?* In a good way?"

Garrett smiled wide. "In a *very* good way."

Reese opened the front door. "I'm going for a walk." And a strong Jack and Coke. Garrett was on his own now, and Reese figured if his brother didn't blow it, Leanne might soon become a permanent member of the Parker clan. Now if he could only figure out what to do about Eliza, both Parker men might find this trip to South Dakota worthwhile.

Eliza took a long, hot shower, taking equal time drying off and primping, then styled her blonde locks into soft shoulder-length waves. She dressed in deep shades of red, a bold color and look for her. But what she hoped to do today with Reese was bolder than anything she'd planned in her life. She donned a crimson double-breasted coat—the retro look reminiscent of the sixties—over a tight-fitting red knit dress, with tall black leather boots adding to the whole package of a woman on a mission.

Hopefully not an impossible one.

First she had to deal with Blake. With the late afternoon sun giving way to gloomy clouds, she headed outside and walked the distance to Skylar's homey little cottage, passing the stables along the way. Her father had been right. Seeing Blake's car outside, she knew Blake was paying a visit to his sister. Unfortunately his visits never seemed to extend to the main house. Blake hadn't felt welcome there, though Eliza had done everything in her power to let him know he was just as much a part of the family as his three older siblings. But Blake and Sky had been born of Trina Watters, and though Nash had tried, he never truly convinced his youngest son that he'd belonged in the Fortune family. Her father had built the cottage for Skylar when she graduated college, hoping to keep her close, enticing her with being near the stables and her beloved horses.

With Blake, it had been different.

There was no enticement that could keep him from the sharp edge of bitterness that seemed to consume him. Case and Creed never helped matters, either. They were always coming down hard on Blake. Today Eliza would try her hand at putting a stop to Trina's meddling. Then she'd be free to deal with her husband. Having her family's blessing helped boost her resolve, but with or without it, Eliza wanted a future with Reese.

Blake was closing the front door to Skylar's home when he spotted her standing by his car. Eliza was glad for the timing. She hated the thought of including Skylar in this. Her younger half sister kept to herself mostly, spending her time caring for the horses. So far, she had been untouched by the family's feuding, and Eliza was happy to keep it that way.

"Blake, do you have a minute? We need to talk."

Blake nodded and glanced back at Skylar's front door with a guarded look. "Not here, though. Let's take a walk."

Obviously he wanted to keep their conversation away from Skylar, too.

"We could go into the main house."

Blake scoffed. "No, thanks." He moved along the winding path that led away from the cottage and the lushly sculpted grounds. Eliza kept pace as they headed toward the stables. Once they were a good distance from the cottage, he asked, "What's on your mind?"

Eliza cut to the chase. "You saw the *Tribune* this morning? I take it your visit with Sky today had something to do with that."

He kept walking but slowed his pace. "I read the article, Eliza."

She stopped her stride as they reached the large white-plank double doors of the stables and gazed up at him. He was tall and lean and just as handsome as the other Fortune men. "It's true. All of it. And I'm sorry for lying to you. I've made amends with Dad. I hope you'll forgive me, too."

"I have a feeling you're not here only to apologize."

Blake had always been so darn serious and to the point. She laid a hand on his arm. From underneath his bulky tan leather jacket, she felt his muscles tense. "You're right. I suspect your mother leaked the news, Blake. She's caused trouble for the family in the past, for Case and Gina and then Max and Diana. It's hurtful and it's got to stop. I don't know how she's doing it other than to think she's been spying on us somehow."

Blake closed his eyes briefly. "Damn it. I know. I'm the one who should be apologizing. She's hurt you now, too. What can I do to help?"

Eliza lifted her lips in a small smile. "Talk to her. Make her see that she's not getting anywhere by all of this. And, Blake, you and Case and Creed shouldn't fight all the time. It's hard on the family to see you at odds. Do you think that you can let go of some of your anger?"

He shrugged and didn't bother with denials. "It's been with me a long time."

"Isn't it time to let it go? We're family. Hurting one another isn't going to solve anything. What your mother is doing is proof of that."

Blake pursed his lips and let go a labored sigh. "I'll think about it."

"Thanks—for letting me apologize and for trying to talk sense into Trina. I want you to know that I don't blame you for any of this. It's not your fa—"

"Damn right it's his fault." Case burst out of the stables abruptly and spoke with vehemence, interrupting their conversation.

"Case." Eliza warned her brother with a long, hard stare. She had to admit he looked menacing, dressed in black from head to toe, grasping a leather riding whip.

"Trina's bad news, Eliza. We all know it. And Blake is just sitting back, watching her hurt us. I've been her victim and now so have you."

"Blake's not to blame," Eliza defended.

Blake set his hand on her arm, his fingers gently digging in. "Don't defend me, Eliza. I don't need it. I don't need one damn thing from the Fortunes."

"Great," Case said with a snarl, tapping the riding crop onto his other hand. "Then why don't you take that damn mother of yours and get out. The farther the better. She'd better not try to pull anything else or—"

"Or what, Case?" Blake's tone became lethal. "Your threats don't scare me."

"It's not a threat, baby *brother*," Case said with disgust. "It's a damn fact."

Eliza stood by, watching her brothers argue, unable to intervene. Neither of the two bullheaded men would listen to her.

"Take your bad-ass threats and shove them, Case." Then Blake cast Eliza a cold look. "You see what I'm up against? Sorry, Eliza. I've had enough."

Blake turned on his heel and headed for his car. Eliza watched him until he revved up his engine and zoomed away, leaving Fortune property in the dust.

Shaking her head, she left Case where he stood, too darn upset to say anything to him.

She only hoped her next stop would go more smoothly. Her life—her happiness—depended on it.

Eliza stood outside the penthouse suite holding her breath and bolstering her courage. No matter what she found on the other side of the door, she thought decidedly, she would speak her mind and let Reese know her true feelings. She might be making a huge mistake, but her gut, her heart and her head, believed differently.

She owed her marriage this much, realizing far too late that she had thrown away too many years of happiness. She had unwittingly shifted Warren's betrayal onto Reese without giving him the benefit of any doubt. She hadn't even entertained the possibility that he'd been faithful, and that clearly hadn't been fair to him. She'd proceeded to remove him from her life, thinking it was better to let him go before he found a reason to dump her. Recently she'd seen the folly in her thinking. She'd never fought for her marriage. She'd never fought for what she truly wanted.

Now it was time for her to make a stand and show the man she'd married what she was made of, inside and out. She'd fight for him tooth and nail, if it came to that. But Eliza hoped it wouldn't. She'd had enough conflict in her life lately, hiding her marriage from her parents and dealing with her ever-feuding family.

She raised her hand to knock on the penthouse door then remembered her key card. Boldly she slipped the card into the slot, opened the door and stepped inside.

She found the same brunette on the sofa, her eyes downcast, scouring over a mass of paperwork that draped from her lap to the sofa cushions, eyeglasses somewhat askew on her nose. The long, dark, flowing locks of hair Eliza had seen last night were now tied back in a tight knot at the back of her head.

"Are you guys back already, finished with your brotherly bonding?" she said without looking up.

"Uh, no," Eliza said, uncomfortably. It was obvious Reese wasn't here.

The woman looked up, righting the glasses on her nose with one delicate slide of her finger. Immediately she gathered the papers onto her lap, then set them aside and smiled. "Oh, Reese will be glad to see you." She stood and, as she approached, put out her hand. "I'm Leanne Finnegan."

Eliza eyed her for only a second before taking her hand. "Eliza Fortune...*Parker.* I'm Reese's wife."

God, it felt so good to say that out loud.

"I know who you are," Leanne said far too confidently, irking Eliza no end. So the woman knew she was Reese's wife and yet Eliza had no idea who this woman was making herself comfortable in Reese's hotel room. "About what you saw last night—"

"Listen, I really don't know who you are and what you're doing with my husband, but I'm here to tell you that I love Reese very much. And if you want him, you're going to have a fight on your hands. You see, I happen to know that he's worth the trouble."

"I agree, and he'll be happy to hear you say that."

"Who the hell do you think you—"

"Eliza?"

She turned at the sound of Reese's deep voice. He stood in the doorway, next to his brother Garrett. Though Garrett was a good-looking man, he didn't compare to Reese. He wore tight jeans and a funky faded T-shirt with an emblem of a bucking bronco, reminding her of the old Reese Parker, the cowboy she fell in love with six years ago. But she knew that the prosperous Montana oilman with the sleek sports cars, fancy penthouse suites and to-die-for new home was the man she loved *now*. The two had become one in her heart. She couldn't separate them. He was who he was. And she loved everything about him.

"Reese?"

"I see you've met Leanne."

Eliza held her breath. And when Reese didn't offer any explanations, she was ready to comment…until Garrett walked over to Leanne and slipped an arm around her waist. "Leanne is our geologist. Been with the company almost from its inception. She's brilliant and hard-working, beautiful and…" he said, staring into Leanne's big warm brown eyes, "my girl."

Eliza swallowed. "Your girl?"

She turned to Reese.

Standing with arms folded, leaning against the door-jamb, he smiled.

Then he pushed away from the door and walked over to Eliza, slipping his arm around her waist possessively. He brought her up against him. The solid wall of his chest felt like granite, strong and unyielding. *Depend-able*. And oh, so right. "Sorry, you won't have to fight her for me. She's taken. And so are you."

Eliza gasped. "You heard?"

"Everything, honey."

Eliza's heart beat like a drumroll, thrumming hard and fast against her chest.

Garrett grabbed Leanne's hand. "This time it's your turn for privacy, big brother. I'm taking Leanne home."

Reese nodded, keeping his eyes on Eliza.

"Nice, uh…nice meeting you," Eliza muttered, her head swimming.

But Garrett had already swept Leanne out of the suite.

Once they were alone, Reese bent his head and took her in a long soul-searing kiss.

When Eliza came up for air, she spoke with resolute clarity. "You were never unfaithful to me."

"Never, sweetheart."

Tears misted in her eyes. So much time had been lost. But she could only look to the future now. "I love you, Reese Parker."

He hugged her tight. "So I've heard."

"I've never stopped loving you," she admitted softly, pressing her face into his chest.

"Eliza," he said, pulling her away enough to look deeply into her eyes. "I loved you once, very much. I love you now even more, if that's possible. I came here looking for revenge, but instead I found what's been missing in my life. *You.*"

"Oh, Reese." She sighed with happiness, then spoke clearly and honestly from her heart. "I've made a mess of things. I didn't know how to love or be loved and I didn't understand the full scope of what it meant to trust someone fully. How could I when I didn't have faith in myself? I didn't believe myself worthy of your love. We were so happy and I didn't…trust you."

Reese hugged her tight. "Do you trust me now?"

Eliza nodded. "With my life. I do trust you, Reese."

"Enough to leave your home and family?"

"Yes, oh, yes. I want to be with you. I want us to be together."

He brushed a soft kiss to her forehead. "Then come back to Montana with me. You can start up your own design company if you'd like. And I'll be your first client. I'm officially hiring you to decorate my new home. Make it yours. And mine. Make it *ours*. But first I want you to marry me."

Eliza's mood lightened, and giddy with love, she replied with a soft chuckle, "We're already married, Reese."

"I want a real wedding, with all the trimmings. I want our families and friends there. I want us to renew our vows. Hell, we'll even invite the press so there's no doubt in anyone's mind that we were meant for each other."

"Yes," she said with joy overflowing. "I want that, too. So much, Reese."

"So you'll marry me and do up the house of your dreams?"

"Yes, I accept your proposal. I'll marry you," she answered, lifting a hand to caress his cheek. She allowed Reese's love to pour into her freely now. She would welcome it unconditionally, trust him completely and finally feel worthy to accept his devotion without doubts or fears. This time around, she had enough faith in herself for both of them.

"I'm getting the *man* of my dreams, sweetheart." She rose up to brush her lips with his in a sweet mating and the promise of a wonderful future together. "The house is an added bonus."

* * * * *

MISTRESS OF FORTUNE

by
Kathie DeNosky

KATHIE DeNOSKY

lives in her native southern Illinois with her husband and one very spoiled Jack Russell terrier. She writes highly sensual stories with a generous amount of humour. Kathie's books have appeared on the Waldenbooks bestseller list and received a Write Touch Readers' Award from WisRWA and a National Readers' Choice Award. She enjoys going to rodeos, travelling to research settings for her books and listening to country music. Readers may contact Kathie at: PO Box 2064, Herrin, Illinois 62948-5264, USA or e-mail her at kathie@kathiedenosky.com.

This book is dedicated to the authors of the FORTUNES. It was a real pleasure working with you and I hope we get to do it again soon.

One

"Good morning, this is Sasha Kilgore, public relations assistant."

"Hi, Sasha. Blake Fortune, here."

At the sound of his smooth baritone filtering through the phone into her ear, Sasha's heart skipped a beat and she had to remind herself to breathe. "Hello, Blake. What can I do for you today?"

"I need a favor, Sasha."

Every time he said her name, a tiny little flutter in the pit of her stomach reminded her that she apparently still carried the remnants of a schoolgirl's crush for the youngest of the Fortune men.

"I'll do what I can," she said, hoping she didn't sound too eager. "What do you need?"

"You."

"Me?" Her pulse raced and the room suddenly felt as if it had become a vacuum.

"I know this is late in the game to be asking about something like this, but I'm opening a new casino here in Deadwood toward the end of the month and I need your help coming up with a special PR campaign to kick things off. I want it to run though the summer to attract vacationers."

It was completely ridiculous, but she felt a little disappointed that his call wasn't of a personal nature. "Hotels and the gaming industry aren't exactly my area of expertise."

Why hadn't he consulted his own PR director? Surely he had one. After all, this would be the third casino he'd opened in the past four years and she'd heard through the office grapevine that he'd recently formed his own corporation.

"Come on, sweetheart." His use of the endearment sent a little shiver straight up her spine. "We both know you're one of the best. Otherwise you wouldn't be working for Dakota Fortune."

She felt warm all over from just the sound of his voice. "So now you're going to resort to charm and flattery?"

"Is it working?"

She laughed. "No, but it's nice to hear."

"Tell me you'll help me out here, Sasha," he said, his voice taking on the no-nonsense tone she was used to hearing from him. "My public relations director is out on family medical leave, helping his wife with their new twin girls and I'm up against a wall on this. Fortune's Gold is opening in three weeks."

"I've never seen the place and that makes it extremely difficult to come up with ideas that would work for you," she warned.

"Not a problem. Just set a day and time and I'll send my private jet to pick you up."

"I could probably research your needs on the Internet, then—"

"You'll get a better idea if you see the operation firsthand," he said obstinately.

If there was one thing about the Fortune men that she knew as surely as she knew her own name, it was that they didn't take *no* for an answer.

Sighing, she reached for her electronic planner. "The earliest I could possibly meet with you would be day after tomorrow. Would that be convenient or would the following week be better?"

"Friday's great. I'll be looking forward to seeing you. Plan on spending the weekend here in Deadwood, then we'll fly back to Sioux Falls together on Monday morning."

"That's three days."

"Your math skills are impressive."

"And your persistence is annoying."

His deep chuckle caught her off guard. To her knowledge, she hadn't heard him laugh in years and she'd come to the conclusion that his brothers, Case and Creed, had been right when they'd insisted that Blake didn't have a sense of humor. Apparently, they'd been wrong.

"Come on, Sasha. You'll be able to get an idea of what my clientele experience while they're here. That should help you come up with a more attractive promotional offer. And besides, it'll be a nice little break away from the rat race."

Oh, he was good. He knew just what to say and just how far to lower his voice to make her feel as if it really meant a lot to him for her to spend the weekend working on his promotion campaign.

"I suppose it would be nice to get away for a weekend," she said slowly. "I just wasn't aware that it would take that much time to research what you need and come up with a viable plan."

"I thought since you'll be here, you could go ahead and take a look at my other casinos and give me a fresh perspective on ways to promote those as well." He paused. "But if it's a problem…"

When his voice trailed off, she shook her head at how masterful he was at getting what he wanted. "No, no problem. I should be able to clear my calendar for the weekend." Truth to tell, she didn't have anything planned beyond cleaning her apartment and vegging out in front of the television for a Julia Roberts movie marathon on one of the cable channels.

"Then we're set. I'll have my pilot pick you up at eight on Friday morning. And, Sasha?"

"Yes."

"Thanks."

He made the word sound extremely intimate and caused the fluttering in her stomach to go absolutely berserk. But before she could get her suddenly paralyzed vocal cords to respond, he hung up.

"Who was that?"

She looked up at the sound of the familiar male voice to find Creed Fortune standing in her office doorway, looking extremely suspicious.

"It was your brother Blake," she answered cautiously.

"Half brother," Creed corrected tightly. "What did *he* want?"

It was a well-known fact that although Creed and Blake were brothers, they weren't close. Far from it. At the best of times, they were barely civil and at the worst, openly hostile.

"His PR director is on leave of absence and Blake asked me to help him work up a campaign for the opening of a new casino."

She concentrated on inputting her meeting with Blake into her planner. Why did she feel as if she were being disloyal to Creed? They had never been anything more than good friends.

"Are you going to help him?" From the disapproval in Creed's voice, Sasha could tell that he thought she should have turned Blake down.

She nodded. "I see no reason why I shouldn't help him with the grand opening of his new casino."

"I can give you a damned good reason." Creed shook his head. "The son of a bitch can't be trusted. Hell, I'd trust a rattlesnake before I put any kind of faith in Blake Fortune."

"That's a horrible thing to say about your brother, Creed." Being an only child, she'd always wanted a brother or sister and couldn't understand anyone feeling such antagonism toward their sibling. "Whether you get along with him or not, he's still part of your family."

Creed grunted. "The worst part."

Choosing her words very carefully, Sasha met his piercing gaze head-on. "You're one of my best friends, Creed, and I place a lot of value on that friendship. But don't ask me to choose sides. Whatever grievances you have with Blake are between the two of you. I have nothing to do with it."

His mouth flattened into a straight line a moment before he nodded. "All I'm saying is, watch yourself around him, Sasha. He's just like his mother. Bad news."

Hoping to lighten the moment, she grinned. "He'd probably tell me something similar about you. Now, why don't you go back to your office and do something productive while I get back to work?"

Long after Creed had left her alone, Sasha wondered what could possibly have caused the siblings to be at such odds. The two older Fortune brothers, Case and Creed, made no secret of the fact that they had no use for their younger brother. And from everything she'd seen and heard, the feeling was more than mutual. Blake had even gone so far as to leave Dakota Fortune, the multibillion-dollar corporation their grandfather had founded, to build his own empire in the South Dakota gaming industry. As far as she knew, he still maintained his shares of stock in Dakota Fortune and was a member of the board of directors, but had nothing to do with running the enterprise.

Leaning back in her leather desk chair, she stared at the entry she'd just put into her planner. It appeared the hostilities between the Fortune brothers were escalating and they expected those around them to choose sides in their battle of wills—something she had no intention of doing.

Unfortunately, she wasn't sure how she was going to avoid it. She was good friends with one brother and the other brother had always had the ability to make her feel as if the earth moved whenever he looked her way.

Sighing heavily, she shook her head as she opened the browser on her computer and keyed in a search for casinos in the Deadwood, South Dakota, area. When war broke out between Creed and Blake it could very easily destroy whoever got in the way. She needed to keep that in mind and make sure that she wasn't the one caught in the middle when it all came to a head.

Blake sat in the back of his corporate limo at the small private airfield just outside of Deadwood as he waited for his pilot to taxi his Learjet up to the tarmac. After talking with Sasha, he'd spent the past couple of days working with the contractors and decorators responsible for putting the finishing touches on his newest and most luxurious hotel casino yet.

He was determined to see that Fortune's Gold was the premier place to stay in Deadwood and a welcome addition to his newly formed Fortune Casino Corporation. Along with the Belle of Fortune, his hotel casino decorated like an 1880s riverboat, and the Lucky Fortune, a family friendly establishment where parents could drop off their kids at a supervised indoor playground while they gambled without worry, he would be able to successfully offer something to suit everyone's tastes and needs.

Mentally reviewing what still needed to be done, he concluded that he only had a couple of more details to nail down, then he'd have the rest of the weekend to concentrate on Sasha and his mission. He'd told her the truth about his PR man being on leave of absence because of his wife having a set of twin girls. He had, however, omitted that the man had only taken the time off because Blake had insisted on it. A promotional campaign for Fortune's Gold wasn't the real reason behind his calling Sasha or his wanting her to join him for the weekend in Deadwood.

When Blake had attended his oldest brother

Case's wedding reception back in February, he'd noticed that Sasha had been Creed's date. Then, thinking back on it, Blake remembered seeing her with Creed at several functions and family gatherings over the past year. It was clear there was something going on between the two of them and spoke volumes of how special Sasha was to Creed. Blake knew for a fact that his brother was notorious for never dating the same woman more than a few times before he moved on to his next conquest. But Creed obviously felt differently about Sasha and that was what Blake found more than a little interesting. And quite useful.

Sasha had been a freshman when he'd been a senior in high school. Although they hadn't been friends, Blake had a photography class with the shy auburn-haired girl and could have sworn she'd had a crush on him. To his recollection, they'd never spoken back then, but several times he'd caught her watching him, and when his gaze had locked with her pretty green eyes, Sasha had turned several shades of red and glanced away. But in recent years she'd apparently gotten over her schoolgirl crush and turned her attention toward snaring the middle of the Fortune brothers.

Blake smiled. It was past time he rectified that situation and reclaimed what was rightfully his.

When the pilot brought the jet to a halt several feet from the limo, then lowered the door, Blake got out of the car and walked over to offer Sasha his hand as she descended the built-in steps. The moment her soft, delicate palm touched his, a jolt of electric current zinged straight up his arm.

"It's good to see you again, Sasha," he said, dismissing the sensation as some kind of static electricity.

Once she was standing on the pavement beside him, he pulled her into his arms for a lingering hug. When he felt her slender body shiver against him, he concentrated on keeping his expression passive. No sense giving away his intentions before he had the opportunity to ensure their success.

"Did you have a nice, uneventful flight?"

Stepping back, Blake could tell his familiar manner confused her, just as he'd intended. Good. Throwing her off guard and keeping her there was exactly what he wanted to do.

"Y-yes, the flight was blessedly calm." The slight blush on her porcelain cheeks was an encouraging sign and he was confident his plan was going to go off without the slightest hitch.

"I'm glad. At this time of year, turbulence can be a problem."

The early April sun shone weakly through a

bank of clouds, but did little to take the chill from the stiff breeze ruffling the soft auburn curls that had escaped the tight knot of hair at the back of her head. Turning her toward the limo, Blake slipped his arm around her shoulders on the pretense of shielding her from the wind and motioned for his driver to take care of her small travel case.

"Let's get you into the car before you freeze," he said, ushering her over to the long, black sedan.

She drew her coat a little closer as they walked the short distance. "It is rather chilly."

Once they were comfortably seated inside the warmth of the limousine, it wasn't lost on him that she scooted all the way across the bench seat to the other side. He clearly made her nervous and Blake had a good idea why. There was no doubt in his mind that bastard, Creed, had warned her to be wary of him.

"We'll go on to Fortune's Gold from here," Blake said, deciding that work might get her mind off whatever poison Creed had fed her about him. "Then, after you get an idea of the type of clientele I want to attract, we'll eat lunch at Lucky Fortune, tour that facility and end the day at the Belle of Fortune." He smiled. "The Belle is where you'll be staying this weekend."

"That sounds like an excellent idea." To his

relief, she visibly relaxed and her pretty smile caused an odd feeling to grip the pit of his stomach. "I've been doing some research on Deadwood and your competition. After I tour your casinos, I'll be better able to judge if my ideas will work, but I think I already have a plan in mind that I'm sure will fit your needs."

"Great." He made sure to give her his most encouraging smile as he reached over and took her hand in his. Giving it a gentle squeeze, he added, "We'll discuss your ideas tomorrow morning, then have the rest of the weekend to relax and have fun."

Her smile disappeared immediately and she looked as if she might bolt from the car. "Fun?"

If Blake could have gotten his hands on Creed at that moment, he'd have taken great pleasure in tearing his brother limb from limb. No telling what kind of outright lies and distorted half-truths Creed had told her about him.

"I thought since you're here, you might like to try your hand at some of the gaming tables and tour a museum or two. Deadwood has several dedicated to the town's old west history." Thinking quickly, he added, "It might give you another idea or two for the packages I'd like to offer."

She looked thoughtful a moment before she nodded. "You do have a point. Adding admission to one of the museums as part of a special on room rates and meals would be very nice."

As his driver parked the car under the entryway at Fortune's Gold, Blake opened the door and climbed out of the car, holding out his hand to help Sasha to her feet. "Then it's settled," he said, careful to keep the triumph from his voice. "We'll check out a few of the sites tomorrow, then we can decide on the one that will enhance the deals I'll be offering."

When he escorted her through the front entrance of his soon-to-be open casino, he watched her reaction as she looked around at the opulent decor. He'd spared no expense in re-creating the elegance of a high-end Las Vegas establishment, while still maintaining the relaxed atmosphere Deadwood was known for.

"This is beautiful, Blake." She walked over to touch the cool black marble countertop on the registration desk. "I love your use of black, gold and cream. It's very striking and goes perfectly with the crystal chandeliers."

He hadn't counted on her enthusiasm pleasing him quite so much. "I'm hoping Fortune's Gold will attract some of the high rollers from the midwestern cities who might not have the time to make it to Vegas, but could get away for a couple of days to gamble here."

"I'm sure it will be quite popular as a weekend getaway." She continued across the lobby to descend the two steps leading down into the sunken casino area. She nodded toward a variety of slot machines and gaming tables. "I see you have all of the most popular games and gambling devices."

A loud noise on the far side of the casino, where several men were installing some of the decorative trim work, caused her to jump and Blake realized that she still wasn't completely at ease with him. Maybe if he gave her a moment or two alone to collect herself it would help. Throwing her off guard was one thing, but her being a nervous wreck would be detrimental to his plans.

"If you'll excuse me, I need to find the foreman and check to see that everything is still on schedule." He gave her his most reassuring smile. "I'll only be a few minutes."

"Of course." She motioned toward the gaming tables. "If you don't mind, I'll just wander around here to get a better feel for the place."

After talking briefly with the foreman, Blake retrieved a pass key from the main office, then went to find Sasha. When he spotted her, she was standing beside one of the many rows of slot machines and he couldn't help but notice how attractive she was. In high school, she'd been nice looking, but that had only been a hint of things to come. The pretty teenage girl had grown into a strikingly beautiful woman with a figure that could tempt the most pious of saints.

"Is everything still on target for your grand opening?" she asked, clearly disconcerted when she caught him studying her.

"So far, so good." Walking over to her, he placed his hand to the small of her back and guided her toward the elevators. "Ready to see the rooms?"

She stopped to give him a dubious look. "Is that necessary?"

He shrugged. "I thought it might give you a couple of ideas about accommodations for the package offers. I was thinking we could offer about three different options for our guests to choose from."

Looking a little uncertain, she finally smiled. "I told you, the hotel and gaming industry isn't my area of expertise. But touring the rooms does sound like an excellent idea and might help me make the offers more attractive for guests to bring spouses and children."

"PR is PR, whether it's for a casino or a corporation like Dakota Fortune," he said, stepping back for her to enter the elevator. "It's just a different market."

When the doors whispered shut, she laughed

and shook her head. "There's a little more to it than that, Blake."

Her soft voice saying his name did strange things to his insides, but he didn't give it a second thought. He was on a mission, and the success or failure of his objective depended on him keeping a cool head and not letting emotion enter into the equation. It was the way he did business and it had served him quite well over the past four years.

When the elevator doors swished open on the top floor, Blake guided Sasha down a short hall to the executive suites. He'd known in advance which one he'd be showing her and made sure the housekeeping staff had it ready for her inspection.

"This is one of the suites we'll be offering to the whales."

"Whales?"

Fitting the key card into the lock, he opened the door when the light blinked green. "That's the term used in the gaming industry for high rollers. They expect to get their rooms and meals free because they drop more than enough money in the casino to cover the costs, as well as make us a nice profit."

"In other words, it's incentive to get them to gamble in your establishment," she said, glancing around at the expertly decorated rooms.

"That's the idea," he said, nodding. "With

enough comps, they'll be happy to stay here and gamble exclusively with us instead of visiting the other casinos."

She walked slowly around the suite's living room. "This looks like something I might see on one of the television shows about Las Vegas." Turning to face him, she smiled approvingly. "I would think your whales will be quite pleased with this kind of complimentary service."

Nodding, Blake walked over to open the French doors leading to the bedroom. "That's what I'm aiming for. I want this to be *the* hotel for the wealthy when they visit Deadwood."

"I haven't seen the other hotels in town, but I think you've accomplished your goal. This is absolutely beautiful," she said, wandering into the master bathroom. She stopped suddenly and her face reflected her astonishment. "Good lord, Blake. That tub is almost large enough to swim laps." She shook her head. "I don't think I've ever seen a bathtub that large."

Walking up behind her, he placed his hands on her shoulders as they gazed down into the black marble Jacuzzi tub. "We'll offer champagne and caviar for two, in case a gentleman and his lady want an intimate bath together."

Her slender frame stiffened beneath his palms

and she quickly stepped away from him. But not before he felt a slight tremor course through her and noticed a faraway expression cross her face.

"I—I think I've seen enough to know what you'll be offering in the way of accommodations to your wealthier clientele," she said, her steps purposeful as she started for the door. "Why don't we take a look at the standard rooms?"

As he followed her across the living room, Blake smiled. Sasha was nervous all right, but in a good way. He'd bet a day's take in one of his casinos that her reaction to his touch had more to do with the fact that she was still attracted to him than from anything Creed could have told her.

When he pulled the door to the Executive Suite shut behind him, Blake watched the gentle sway of her hips as she walked down the hall to the elevator. He smiled. His plan was not only going to work beautifully, it was going to be a pleasure for both of them.

He was going to seduce Sasha right out from under Creed's nose. And there wasn't a damned thing his older brother could do to stop him.

Two

By the time Blake's driver delivered them to the entrance of the Belle of Fortune Hotel and Casino that evening, Sasha wondered what on earth she'd been thinking when she'd agreed to help him. Spending the day with him had played havoc with her equilibrium and only confirmed what she suspected after she'd talked to him earlier in the week. She was still attracted to him and, although it wasn't the same as when she'd had a crush on him in high school, the fascination was still there just the same. Trying to deny it would be utterly futile.

Unfortunately, he hadn't helped her predicament. From the moment she stepped off his private jet, it seemed as if he'd seized every available opportunity to touch her. Then, there was the matter of his leaning close whenever he spoke to her. It wasn't what he said that caused her to have a perpetual case of goose bumps shimmering over her arms, it was the way he said it. Listening to his smooth baritone as he explained his plans for building a gambling empire, his voice seemed to wrap around her like a warm cocoon. She wasn't sure how he did it, but Blake had managed to make the most mundane detail sound incredibly intimate.

As they walked across the lobby of the authentically decorated hotel, she wondered what had gotten into her. She wasn't that same starry-eyed teenager with a huge crush on the best-looking boy in school. She was a grown woman with a much broader perspective of what to look for in a man besides a handsome face.

It was true that Blake had grown into a devastatingly handsome man who could turn the head of any female possessing a pulse. With his dark-blond hair, blue eyes and sensual good looks, he could just as easily have been a movie star as a businessman.

But it wasn't just the way he looked that caught Sasha's attention. It was his commanding presence that demanded respect and the undivided attention of whomever he was addressing that made him seem larger than life. And if he was smart, he'd use that to his advantage in his promotional campaign.

"Blake, what kind of advertising budget are you planning for the opening of Fortune's Gold?" she asked thoughtfully as they waited for the elevator.

"I haven't set a limit," he said, stepping back for her to enter the car ahead of him. "I'll spend whatever it takes to kick this off the right way. Why?"

"Do you think that's wise, not setting a budget?" she asked.

Pushing the button for the top floor, he shrugged his wide shoulders and shook his head. "Money isn't an issue."

She chided herself for asking such a stupid question. Of course money wasn't an object. Blake was a Fortune, and besides his family owning the largest corporation in the western part of South Dakota—maybe the entire state—he was quite a successful businessman and multimillionaire in his own right.

"I was thinking—"

He suddenly placed his finger to her lips, stopping her. "It's past five, Sasha. The business day is over and it's time for pleasure."

"But—"

She intended to tell him that business was the only reason she'd come to Deadwood. But when he wrapped his arms around her and pulled her to him, the words stuck in her suddenly dry throat and all thoughts of a promotional campaign flew right out of her head.

"You know what they say about all work and no play, Sasha."

"Th-they make a person dull?" Her mind told her to push him away, but her body refused to cooperate.

As if in slow motion, she watched him nod his head, then smiling, lower his forehead to hers. "Remember, you're not only here on business. You're here to get away for a weekend. And I'm personally going to see to it that you relax and have a little fun while you're in town."

His smoldering blue gaze held hers until she felt as if she might melt into a puddle at his feet. Then, just when she thought he was going to kiss her, the doors swished open. Releasing her, he stepped back for her to exit the elevator ahead of him.

The tendons in her knees felt loose and rubbery as she walked out into the hall, and she found it extremely difficult to draw air into her lungs. Dear heavens, he hadn't even kissed her and she was about to lose it.

Taking first one breath, then another, she wondered if her luggage had been delivered to her room. Earlier in the day, Blake had sent his driver to take her small bag to the Belle while he'd shown her around the Lucky Fortune. Hopefully, it would be waiting for her. And if she had any sense, she'd pick it up and call for someone to take her to the airfield. Or if there weren't any outgoing flights this evening, she could find a car to rent and drive back to Sioux Falls without waiting to see what he'd do next.

"Which room is supposed to be mine?" she asked, desperately hoping she didn't sound as breathless as she felt.

"This way," Blake said, moving to her side to open a door with Riverboat Queen engraved on an ornate wood-and-brass plaque.

When she walked into the suite, Sasha marveled at the beautiful antique decor. The living area had been decorated like a nineteenth-century parlor and it appeared no detail had been overlooked. From the floral-print rug on the hardwood floor to the flocked wallpaper and wainscoting on the walls, it was meant to make the occupant feel as if they'd taken a step back in time and had boarded a real riverboat.

"Are all the rooms decorated like this?" she asked, letting curiosity get the better of her.

"No. Only the suites." He opened the door to the

bedroom. "Standard accommodations are pretty much like any other hotel room."

When she walked into the bedroom, her breath caught at the sight of the huge poster bed with a lace canopy and matching crocheted bedspread. "This is absolutely gorgeous, Blake."

A half smile curved the corners of his mouth and she could tell her comment pleased him. "When I bought the Belle some people thought I was crazy to insist the decorator use real antiques for the high-end suites. But it's been a big hit with those looking for the old West experience."

"I can understand why your guests like it," she said, spying her small suitcase. Walking over to it, she picked it up and started back across the room toward the door. "It goes along with the casino's riverboat theme and is quite charming."

His expression turned to a deep frown as he pointed to her overnight bag. "Is something wrong? Would you rather have a different suite?"

"No, this is very nice," she said, shaking her head. "But I think… That is, I…"

Her voice trailed off as she tried to think of something to say that wouldn't reveal the real reason behind her early departure. There was no way she was going to admit that the chemistry between them was about to send her into sensual shock. Opting for silence, she simply continued to stare at him.

A confident expression slowly replaced his dark scowl. "I make you nervous, don't I, Sasha?"

"D-don't be ridiculous," she stammered, wondering what had happened to the articulate, intelligent woman she'd always prided herself in being.

As he moved closer, she had to force herself not to take a step back. It would have only proven his theory right and that was something she was determined not to do.

"You want to know what I think, honey?" he asked, moving even closer.

"Not really." She did take a step back when he continued to slowly, deliberately close the distance between them.

"I think you're feeling it, the same as I am." He smiled knowingly. "And I think you want to run from it, from me."

"I don't have a clue what you're referring to, Blake."

His confident grin sent a knot to the pit of her stomach. "Liar."

She set her case down and took a step back, then another. "I don't know what you think I'm supposed to be feeling, but—"

"Don't play dumb, Sasha. It doesn't become

you." He shook his head. "We both know you're a hell of a lot smarter than that."

"All right, I'll give you that much." She felt her knees come into contact with the edge of the bed. Great. Her retreat had been stopped and he was still advancing. "But you have one thing wrong."

"What would that be?"

"I never run from anything."

At least, that was normally the case. But in this instance she wasn't certain that standing her ground would be all that smart. Especially when Creed's warning kept echoing in her ears—Blake wasn't one to be trusted.

"Really? You aren't nervous about the way I make you feel?"

Unable to make her vocal cords work, she shook her head.

He came to stand in front of her and as close as he was, if she drew in a breath—which wasn't possible at that moment—her breasts would brush the front of his sports jacket. "If that's true, Sasha, then why do you want to go back to Sioux Falls this evening? Why not stay and enjoy your weekend here?" His voice dropped when he added, "With me."

She swallowed hard as she tried to think of something to say that wouldn't refute her adamant denial. "I didn't say I was going back tonight."

"Then why did you pick up your suitcase and head for the door?" Before she could come up with a plausible excuse, he reached up to lightly chafe her lower lip with the pad of his thumb. "You aren't wanting to get back to see someone, are you?"

His light touch sent a tingling awareness skipping over every nerve in her body and she had to concentrate hard on what he'd just said. "N-no…I mean yes. That's it. There's someone I'd like to see."

His deep chuckle let her know he wasn't buying her excuse for a minute, but to her relief, he stepped away from her. "Did anyone ever tell you that you can't lie worth a damn, sweetheart?"

Drawing in some much needed air, she trembled all over as anger streaked through her. "If you'll remember, I'm here at your request for help with your promotion. Nothing more."

As they stared at each other like two prize fighters sizing up their opponent, the phone on the bedside table rang several times before she finally reached over to answer it. She had no idea who the caller could be, but whomever it was, she definitely owed them a debt of gratitude.

"H-hello?"

"Sasha, are you all right?" Creed's deep voice was a welcome sound.

"Hi, Creed. I'm fine. Why do you ask?" At the mention of his brother's name, she watched Blake's easy smile disappear and his eyes narrow dangerously.

"You sounded a little shook up when you answered the phone." She heard him release a frustrated breath. "You know I don't trust that son of a bitch. I guess I was reading something more into the tone of your voice than was there."

"I suppose so," she said, careful to keep her voice as noncommittal as possible. From the dark frown on Blake's handsome face, he wasn't happy to hear that his brother was on the other end of the line, nor did he intend to leave the room until she'd ended the phone call. "Was there something you needed, Creed?"

"Not really." From the slight hesitancy in his voice, she could imagine his sheepish grin. "I was a little worried about you and I wanted to make sure you're being treated well."

"I am."

"Good," he said, sounding a little more at ease. "Just remember, if you have any problems all you have to do is give me a call. I'll be more than happy to fly down to Deadwood and give that jerk an attitude adjustment."

"Thank you, that means a lot, Creed." She

couldn't help but smile at her friend's concern. "I'll see you Monday morning."

When she hung up the phone, Blake's expression was congenial enough, but there was a spark of anger in the depths of his blue gaze that sent a chill coursing through her. "Your boyfriend checking up on you?"

"Creed and I are good friends, but that's as far as it goes," she said, wondering why she felt the need to explain her relationship with his brother.

He stared at her for several more seconds before he spoke again. "I have a couple of things I need to take care of," he finally said. "Change into something more casual and I'll come back in about an hour to take you to dinner."

"Is that an order, Mr. Fortune?" Her irritation with his high-handedness returned tenfold.

His expression became unreadable a moment before he shook his head and pointed to her black suit. "I just figured you'd want to trade your skirt and heels for something more comfortable."

"There's no need for you to come back up here. I'll meet you downstairs in the restaurant," she said when he turned to leave.

He looked as if he intended to say something. Instead, he gave her a short nod and without another word left the room.

When Sasha heard the outer door close, she

finally released the breath she was certain she'd been holding from the moment they'd entered the suite. What on earth had she done? More importantly, why had she let Blake get to her?

She'd had every intention of leaving when they'd walked into the suite. And if she hadn't let his goading rile her, she'd be on her way to the airfield at that very moment.

But no. She couldn't leave well enough alone. He'd been so sure of himself, she'd taken up the challenge and had been determined to prove him wrong. Unfortunately, the only thing she'd accomplished was doing what he wanted her to do in the first place—to spend the weekend with him in Deadwood.

Shaking her head, she couldn't help but wonder what she'd gotten herself into. Or, more importantly, how she was going to get out of it.

The second Sasha stepped off the elevator and walked toward the entrance of the Golden Belle Restaurant, Blake watched several men in the lobby turn to stare at the auburn-haired beauty in the jade silk pantsuit. Her slender body moved with a sensual grace that he found absolutely fascinating and he took a moment to enjoy the view.

Blake was going to enjoy sharing a physical relationship with Sasha. The chemistry between them was utterly amazing. He couldn't keep his hands off her. And her reaction to his touch, her breathlessness whenever he came near her, indicated that she found him to be every bit as compelling.

But he'd have to be careful not to put too much pressure on her, too soon. He'd have to take his time and romance her in order to prove that whatever Creed had told her about him had been erroneous.

Gritting his teeth at the thought of Creed's interrupting phone call, Blake had to force himself to calm down. He'd thought that by acting like Creed, it would win her over. But it was clear she was tired of the bulldozer approach to romance.

All Blake had to do was change tactics, turn on the charm and Sasha would be his for the taking. He could be himself and old Creed would take care of the rest. Knowing his half brother the way he did, Blake was confident that Creed would keep reminding her of his suspicions, continue to make phone calls to check up on her and ultimately push her right into Blake's waiting arms.

He smiled as he watched Sasha standing by the entrance to the restaurant, obviously waiting for him. She was a captivating woman and he wasn't the only one who thought so. Apparently, the men who had turned to watch her walk across the lobby found her just as mesmerizing. One in particular caught Blake's attention when the man approached Sasha to strike up a conversation.

For reasons he didn't care to analyze, a wave of possessiveness shot through Blake and he wasted no time in moving in to stake his claim. "You're late, sweetheart." He met the interloper's curious gaze with a cold smile as he slipped his arm around Sasha's shoulders. "You'll have to excuse us. We're on our way to dinner." He nodded toward the casino. "And I'm sure you'd like to get back to the action."

The man returned Blake's stare for several silent seconds, then lifting the drink he held, he nodded a silent concession. "Have a nice dinner."

As the man descended the steps into the casino area, Sasha turned on Blake. "Are you always that rude to your guests?"

Sliding his hand down her back to cup her elbow, he steered her back toward the elevators. "Are you in the habit of encouraging men to hit on you?"

"Not that it's any of your business, but all he wanted from me was to see if I knew what time it was," she said, clearly exasperated.

Blake grunted. "Yeah, and I'm Buffalo Bill Cody."

When the elevator doors opened, she stopped dead in her tracks. "Why are we going back upstairs? I thought we were going to dinner."

"We are." He urged her forward, then pushed the button for the top floor. "I had the staff set up our dinner in my suite."

"Why?" If her expression was any indication, she was anything but happy about the arrangement and more than a little suspicious of his motives.

"I thought it would give us a chance to talk un-interrupted and catch up on old times," he said, shrugging.

She looked at him as if she thought he might be a few cards shy of a full deck. "Catch up on old times? Since I started working at Dakota Fortune, we've only spoken briefly at the office and a few times at the social functions I've attended with Creed."

His gut burned at the mention of his half brother's name, but Blake stifled the urge to curse aloud. The success of his mission depended on him keeping a cool head.

When the elevators doors opened, he guided her down the hall toward his suite. "You're forgetting that we attended the same high school."

She shook her head. "Don't feed me that line, Blake Fortune. You didn't have the slightest notion that I existed back then."

"That's where you're wrong, Sasha." Opening the door to the Admiral's Suite, Blake stood back for her to enter his private domain. "I would have had to be as blind as a damned bat not to have noticed one of the prettiest girls in school." He smiled. "And I've never had vision problems."

"Give me a break." She rolled her eyes. "We had a photography class together for one semester and in that whole time, I don't remember a single instance of you speaking to me."

Walking up to stand in front of her, he touched her soft cheek with his index finger. "Believe me, sweetheart, I found out all I could about you after that first day of class. But you were too young for me back then."

"There's only…three years difference in our ages." To his satisfaction, she sounded a little breathless and confirmed his suspicions beyond a shadow of doubt that she was still attracted to him.

Smiling, he shook his head. "I was a typical eighteen-year-old boy with a raging case of hormones. I wanted a whole lot more from a girl than sharing a few chaste kisses. And let's face it, Sasha, at fifteen that's all you were ready for."

"Why are you telling me this now, Blake?" Her confusion was reflected in her luminous green eyes and he didn't think he'd ever seen her look more desirable.

He was going to enjoy his seduction of Sasha

Kilgore. But it was time to back off a little and let her catch up.

Deciding it would be in his best interest to put a little space between them, he guided her over to the table his staff had set up by the window overlooking Deadwood's historic district below. "I told you. We're talking about old times, sweetheart." He held her chair, then seated himself on the opposite side of the small round table. "You were in the chorus weren't you?"

"Yes, but you weren't."

The flicker of the small candle on the table between them brought out the highlights of golden red in her auburn hair, fascinating him. "That doesn't mean I don't remember your singing at my graduation."

"Oh, dear," she said, her cheeks coloring a pretty pink. "You remember that?"

"It was quite an honor for a freshman to be asked to sing a solo at another class's graduation," he said, nodding.

He'd anticipated her wanting to know what he remembered about her and he'd done his homework in advance. Besides thumbing through his high-school annual, Blake had spent several hours trying to think of all the times their paths had crossed during his last year of school.

The color on her cheeks deepened. "Having to perform in front of all those people made me a nervous wreck. That's when I decided to limit my singing to the shower."

"That's a shame. You have a beautiful voice and did a wonderful job with the song." Reaching across the table, he took her hand in his. "I'd like to hear you sing again sometime, sweetheart." He smiled and before he could stop himself, he added, "My shower has great acoustics."

Her eyes widened a moment before anger filled their green depths. "I don't think so."

"Never say never, Sasha."

She pulled her hand from his and, pushing her chair back, rose to her feet. "I don't know what you're up to, Blake Fortune. But it's not going to work."

Rising to face her, he didn't think twice about taking her into his arms and drawing her to him. "I'm not up to anything more than having dinner with a beautiful woman that for years, I've wanted to get to know better."

He heard the hitch in her breath a moment before she trembled against him. "Why now? Why after all these years are you—"

"Hush, Sasha."

Before she had the chance to question him

further, Blake lowered his mouth to hers and at the first contact, he felt as if he'd been hit by a bolt of lightning. Nothing could have prepared him for his reaction to the softness of her perfect lips, yielding to the demands of his.

But it was her response that had him hard in less than two seconds flat and forgetting all about slowing things down. Resistant at first, when she melted against him, her fingers curled into the front of his shirt as if she needed to hold on to him to keep from falling at his feet.

As he tightened his arms around her and continued kissing her, a tiny moan escaped her slightly parted lips and he took advantage of her acquiescence to slip his tongue inside. Blake acquainted himself with her tender inner recesses, exploring her thoroughly, savoring the sweetness that was uniquely Sasha.

He slid his hands from her back, up along her sides to the underside of her breasts, but stopped just short of cupping the soft mounds. He sensed that too much, too soon would only scare her away. And that was the last thing he wanted to do.

Reluctant to completely break contact with her, he held her slender body close as he eased away from the kiss. Neither spoke, but he could tell that he'd accomplished two of his goals. He'd managed to stop her from arguing with him, as well as establishing the direction he intended for their friendship to go.

Three

As Sasha sat, staring at Blake across the elegantly arranged table, she had no idea what she was eating or how it tasted. After that kiss, she was lucky to remember her own name, let alone take notice of the food on her plate.

When she'd been a teenager, she'd fantasized about him holding her, kissing her. But she'd never thought the dream would come true. Nor could she have imagined eleven years ago how his kiss would affect her. It had been at least fifteen minutes since they'd sat back down for dinner and she still felt as if every cell in her body tingled.

"How is your steak?" he asked, pointing to her plate.

She stared at the filet mignon, amazed that she'd eaten almost half of it without recalling a single bite. "Uh…very good."

His pleased smile caused a little flutter deep down in the most secret part of her. "I had the new chef I hired for Fortune's Gold prepare the meal for us. I intend to include an intimate dinner for two as part of the high-end package I'll be offering and wanted your opinion on ways to improve it."

Glancing at the table, Sasha shook her head. "I can't think of anything to improve on this. The food is delicious and the use of fine china, instead of the heavier restaurant plates, is a wonderful idea. I also think the sterling-silver candle holders add an elegant touch. I'm sure this will be quite popular with honeymooning couples."

"Or lovers wanting a romantic weekend getaway," he said, lowering his voice as he placed his hand atop hers where it rested on the pristine tablecloth.

The suggestive sound of his smooth voice and the promising look in his dark-blue eyes set her pulse racing and caused a delicious little shiver to slide up her spine. Everything she thought she'd wanted at the age of fifteen was coming true. Blake Fortune had not only noticed her, it appeared that he intended to sweep her off her feet.

But she was finding it extremely difficult to believe that the object of her adolescent dreams had finally noticed her. "What do you really want from me, Blake?" she asked as she carefully placed her fork on the edge of the delicate china plate.

"I told you, sweetheart. I need your help with the ad campaign." He gave her a smile that made her feel warm all over. "And I'm using it as an excuse to get to know you better. Something I should have done a long time ago."

He seemed sincere enough, but Creed's warning that Blake couldn't be trusted continued to whisper at the back of her mind. Had her friend been right about his brother? Could Blake be up to something underhanded?

But it made no sense. What would he possibly stand to gain? She certainly couldn't give him any information about Dakota Fortune that he didn't already have access to.

The feel of his palm gently caressing the back of her hand sent the fluttering in the pit of her stomach into overdrive and ended all speculation about his possible ulterior motives. "I…um, think I'd…uh, better go back to my room," she said, extricating her hand from his. She suddenly found it extremely hard to form a coherent thought and she needed to put some distance between them in order to regain her equilibrium. "I'm really tired and I think it's time for me to call it a night."

She could tell by the expression on his handsome face that he wasn't buying her excuse for a minute, but scooting his chair away from the table, he rose to his feet and offered her his hand. "I'll walk you back to your suite."

"Th-that won't be necessary." His much larger hand enveloping hers as she stood up made her feel as if the temperature in the room had gone up a good ten degrees. "I'm pretty sure I can find my way to the other end of the hall."

Putting his arm around her shoulders, he shook his head as they walked to the door. "If there was one thing that Nash Fortune taught his boys, it was proper date etiquette."

"D-date?"

Guiding them out into the hall, he chuckled. "Whether it's business or pleasure, when a man asks a woman he has more than a passing interest in to have dinner with him, it's a date."

She shook her head as she pulled her key card from her small evening bag. "You didn't ask me to have dinner with you. It was more of a command."

He took the card from her, fitted it into the lock, then after opening the door, stood back for her to enter the suite. "Considering you were about to take off, I didn't feel that you gave me much of a choice."

Turning to face him, she asked, "In other words, as a board member of Dakota Fortune, you were pulling rank on me?"

Shrugging one shoulder, he gave her a lopsided grin and pulled her into his arms. "I hadn't thought of it that way, but whatever works."

Sasha caught her breath at the feel of his solid strength pressed against her from her breasts to her knees. "Wh-what do you think you're doing?"

"I'm going to kiss you good-night," he said, his voice so low and hypnotic that she felt as if she'd spontaneously combust at any moment. "That's usually the way a first date ends, honey."

Before she could remind him that she didn't consider their dinner a date, he lowered his head and captured her lips with his. That was when Sasha ceased thinking altogether and gave in to the temptation of once again experiencing the power of Blake's sultry kiss.

Firm and commanding, his mouth moved over hers with a masterfulness that caused her head to spin. But when he parted her lips with his tongue to slip inside, he not only robbed her of breath, he left her with nothing but the ability to respond.

Tasting of wine and pure male desire, he explored her thoroughly as he stroked and teased. Sasha wondered if she'd ever be the same again when he slid his hands from her back along her sides and up to the swell of her breasts.

Her skin tingled when he broke the kiss to nibble his way to the sensitive hollow at the base of her throat. "Y-you're taking this…farther than a simple… good-night kiss," she said, struggling to breathe.

"Do you want me to stop?"

His warm breath and the vibration of his masculine voice against her skin had Sasha feeling as if a spark ignited within her soul. But when he covered her breasts with his hands to test their weight and tease the suddenly tightened tips through the layers of her clothing, her body began to tremble and she had to force herself to concentrate on what he'd asked her.

"N-no… Y-yes."

Why was she having such a hard time gathering her thoughts? And why couldn't she tell him outright that she wanted him to stop?

"You want to know what I think, Sasha?"

"Not…really." Drawing air into her lungs was becoming decidedly more difficult with each teasing brush of his thumbs over her taut nipples. And like it or not, she really didn't want him to stop.

Moving his hands to her back to draw her more fully against him, he nuzzled the hair at her temple. "I think you need to get a good night's sleep. If we're going to visit a couple of museums and spend some time introducing you to some of the casino games, you'll need your rest." Kissing her forehead, he released her, then walked to the door. "Good night, Sasha."

As she stood there waiting for her head to quit spinning, he turned to give her a smile warm enough to melt her bones. Then, just when she thought he was going to cross the room and take her back into his arms, he walked out into the hall and quietly pulled the door shut behind him.

Staring at the closed door for several long seconds, she finally managed to breathe normally as she slipped off her pumps and slowly made her way into the bedroom. She wasn't certain her rubbery legs would support her for the short distance, let alone allow her to balance herself on a pair of high heels.

She should have left earlier in the evening as she'd intended, she thought as she changed out of her jade silk pantsuit and into her baby-doll pajamas. She was so far out of her league with Blake, they weren't even in the same ballpark.

But as she unfastened the clip holding her hair in its tight chignon, then slipped between the crisp linen sheets on the big four-poster bed, she had to be honest with herself. Although she was completely out of her element with Blake, she'd never felt more exhilarated or alive in her entire life.

Blake pulled his cell phone from his belt as he pushed the breakfast cart down the hall toward the Riverboat Queen Suite. After walking Sasha back to her room last night, he'd spent several sleepless hours rethinking his approach for getting her into his bed and came to several conclusions.

Thanks to his brother, she was clearly wary of him and more than a little confused by his interest after all this time. That was why he'd have to pull out all the stops in romancing Sasha Kilgore. It might take a little more time than he'd anticipated, which didn't set too well. But in retrospect, it would heighten the pleasure when they finally did make love.

Dialing directly into her room, he waited for Sasha to answer.

"Hello." Her voice was slightly husky from sleep and caused an unexpected rush of heat to zing through his veins.

"Good morning, sleepyhead."

"Blake?"

"None other."

"Why are you calling me at—" He heard the rustle of bed sheets and could imagine her sitting up in bed to push her hair out of her eyes and look at the clock. "Dear God, it's only six-thirty."

He laughed. "Get out of bed and open the door to your suite, Sasha."

"Why?"

"Do you always ask this many questions?"

"Do you always answer a question with a question?" she retorted.

"Just open the damned door."

"All right, but this had better be good," she grumbled, hanging up the phone.

When she flung open the door a few moments later, Blake smiled as he pushed the cart into the room. Sasha looked about as sexy as he'd ever seen a woman. Her pretty face wore the blush of sleep and her long auburn hair tumbled well past her shoulders in a wild array of soft curls.

But it was the sight of her long slender legs that sent his blood pressure soaring. Her teal silk robe was one of those short numbers that ended about mid-thigh and revealed more than it covered.

Deciding that it would be in his best interest not

to point out that particular fact, he opted for discussing her mood. "I take it you're not a morning person."

"And I take it you are." Waving her hand toward the covered plates and silver coffee carafe, she arched one perfect eyebrow. "Please tell me that's for someone else."

"Can't do that, sweetheart," he said, taking plates from the cart to place then on the small table by the window. "I thought we would have breakfast together before we head out for the day."

She frowned as she shook her head. "I never eat this early in the morning."

But she did follow him across the room and stood there looking so damned adorable, he'd have liked nothing more than to take her into the bedroom and have her for breakfast. Instead, he wisely motioned for her to sit down.

"Experts say that breakfast is the most important meal of the day."

"Those so-called experts are no doubt morning people that the rest of us would like to string up by their toes," she groused, sinking into one of the chairs. "At least, until after we've consumed several cups of coffee."

He laughed as he poured them both a mug of the

rich, dark brew. "Please, drink up. I'd like to keep my toes safe."

To his satisfaction, she picked up the cup, held it up to appreciate the aroma, then closing her eyes, smiled. "Mmm. How did you know I love mocha-flavored coffee?"

He seated himself in the chair across from her. "I haven't met a woman yet who doesn't think that anything chocolate is almost as good as making love."

Opening her eyes, she stared at him over the rim of the cup as she took a sip of the rich brew. "Oh, really. And what do you prefer?"

He grinned. "Sex, of course."

Clearly embarrassed, she shook her head. "I meant what flavor of coffee."

"I know, but you didn't phrase it that way." Changing the subject before he said something that got him into deeper trouble with her than he was already in, he removed the covers from their plates. "I didn't know how you like your eggs. I hope scrambled is to your liking."

"That's fine, and I do appreciate your thought-fulness, but—"

Before she could protest further, Blake picked up her fork, speared some of the fluffy eggs and put it into her mouth. "Now, isn't that good?"

She glared at him as she chewed, then swallow-ing, she nodded as she reached for the fork. "Yes."

He held the utensil away. "You want more?"

"Yes."

She said the word grudgingly and from the look on her face, he decided it wouldn't move them any closer to the physical relationship he wanted if he seized the opportunity to gloat. Handing her the fork, he picked up his own and for the next few minutes they ate in companionable silence.

"When do you want me to present my proposal for your ad campaign?" she asked as she poured herself another cup of coffee.

"You've already worked it up?" He didn't par-ticularly want to discuss business. He had other, more enjoyable pursuits in mind.

To his relief, she shook her head. "I have a few more things to go over, but I should have it ready by this afternoon."

"I don't think so."

"Excuse me?"

"Today is your day off." He reached out to take her hand in his. "I promised you a day of fun and that's exactly what we're going to have." He raised her palm to his lips and kissed her tender skin. "Now, go get dressed so we can get started."

"Wh-what on earth could we possibly do at

this hour of the morning?" Her voice sounded a little shaky. "The museums won't open for several more hours."

It was all he could do to keep from telling her what he wanted to do and how he'd like to spend the day with her in bed. "Sweetheart, casinos are open 24/7."

As if she suddenly realized that he still held her hand, she extricated it from his. "I've never gambled before and wouldn't even begin to know how to play any of the games."

He smiled. "It's pretty simple and it will be my pleasure to teach you." He rose to his feet, walked over to the phone on the desk and dialed room service. While he waited for one of the staff to pick up, he motioned toward the bedroom. "Get dressed while I get someone up here to clear the table."

"Is that an order or a suggestion?"

From the look on her face, he could tell that he'd better watch the way he phrased things. "I was merely suggesting that you might want to put something on." He grinned. "I love the hell out of the way you look in that little silk robe, but you might give one of my waiters a coronary when he sees your long, sexy bare legs."

Sasha's heart raced as she glanced down at her robe. She hadn't considered its length when she'd packed yesterday morning and the only male that had ever seen her in it was Melvin. Of course, besides being a big yellow cat, Melvin had been neutered several years ago and couldn't care less about females, feline or human.

But Blake was an entirely different matter. He was a virile, twenty-nine-year-old man who exuded sexual charm from every pore of his skin. Unfortunately, she'd been so irritated by being awakened at what she considered to be an ungodly hour, she hadn't given the length of her robe a second thought. But from the look on his face, he'd definitely been thinking about it. A lot.

Giving the hem a little tug in a futile effort to make it longer, she edged her way to the bedroom door. "I think I'll…uh, go change."

Her heart-rate accelerated even more when Blake winked and gave her a wicked smile. "Good idea. And make sure it's something casual and comfortable."

Nodding, she slipped into the bedroom and closing the doors, made a beeline for her suitcase. As she gathered her things for a quick shower, she tried not to put much stock in Blake's flirting. She had a feeling the man wasn't above using whatever means it took to get what he wanted. The only problem was she had no idea what Blake could possibly want from her beyond her proposal for the ad campaign.

Could it really be as he'd said? Did he really just want to get to know her better?

As she toweled herself off and dressed, she came to the conclusion that Creed's warnings about Blake had stemmed from the hard feelings between the two brothers and weren't really a reflection of Blake's character. From everything she'd seen, Blake was just as he appeared—a highly successful businessman who not only wanted her to design a promotional campaign for his casinos, he was interested in getting to know her on a more personal level.

"The man you've dreamed about half of your life has finally discovered that you exist and you're having second thoughts about becoming involved with him?" she asked herself as she twisted her unruly hair into a tight knot at the back of her head. "Are you insane?"

But as she put on her mascara, gathered her jacket and prepared to join Blake in the suite's living room, she decided that her mind wasn't what worried her. If she let herself go and gave in to his charismatic charm, it was her heart that could very well be in danger of being lost.

"Blake, this is ridiculous," Sasha laughed when he motioned for her to push a stack of poker chips into the middle of a circle on the green felted table.

After touring the town's museums chronicling Deadwood's colorful history and having a scrumptious lunch at Blake's other hotel and casino, the Lucky Fortune, they had returned to the Belle of Fortune for her to try her hand at a few games of chance. Blake had a man he'd called the pit boss set up a private table for him to teach her the various card games and she was finding that although they were fun, she'd starve to death if she had to make a living in the world of professional gambling.

Blake leaned close when the dealer shuffled, then dealt the cards. "The dealer is showing a six and has to stay on seventeen," Blake whispered closely to her ear. "You have twelve and the odds are in your favor to win the hand. Take another card."

The feel of his warm breath on her overly sensitive skin distracted her from the game. Taking a deep breath, she used every ounce of willpower she had to react normally. "Are you sure? What if the card the dealer has facing down is an ace? Then he'd have eighteen and there's the possibility I'd lose."

Blake nodded. "That's true. But that's why it's called gambling. You have to take the chance in order to come out ahead."

"But—"

He softly touched her chin with his index finger and turned her head until their gazes met. "Sweetheart, life is full of risks. Sometimes you win. Sometimes you lose. But keep in mind, there's a fifty-fifty chance that the risks you don't take could have been missed opportunities."

Her heart skipped several beats as she gazed into his amazing blue eyes. There was a challenge there and she knew beyond a shadow doubt, he was talking about her taking a chance on a whole lot more than just a hand of cards.

"I don't know," she said uncertainly.

She wasn't sure she had the courage to risk becoming involved with Blake. She could very well end up with a broken heart, as well as having her pride completely shattered.

"Take a break," he said to the dealer, standing patiently awaiting her decision on the hand of cards. As the man silently nodded and walked away, Blake turned her to face him. "Give me a chance, Sasha. Give *us* a chance."

She shook her head. "There is no *us*."

"Not yet." His smile sent a wave of heat from the top of her head all the way to her toes. "But I intend for there to be."

Her heart stopped completely at the determination in his voice and the promise in his eyes. He'd abandoned his earlier excuse of wanting to get to know her better and moved straight to them becoming romantically involved.

The thrill of anticipation skipped up her spine as his gaze held her captive and he slowly lowered his head to brush his lips against hers. But when he settled his mouth over hers in a kiss so tender it robbed her of all rational thought, she forgot all the reasons that taking a chance on caring for Blake could prove her undoing—or that they were sitting in the middle of a crowded casino. Nothing seemed to matter but the sudden heat coursing through her and the need to lean into his embrace. Without a second thought, she raised her arms to circle his neck and tangle her fingers in the silky hair at his nape.

When she pressed herself to his chest, his arms closed around her and he slipped his tongue inside to deepen the kiss. Colorful lights immediately began to flash behind Sasha's closed eyes and it felt as if the world had been reduced to just the two of them when he slowly stroked her inner recesses and coaxed her into responding in kind. But when he effortlessly lifted her from her chair to sit her on his lap, a delicious tingling sensation began to flow throughout her body and a tiny moan escaped her parted lips at the feel of his rapidly hardening body through the layers of their clothing.

"Way to go, man." The sudden sound of a laughing male voice made Sasha's heart stop.

When she tried to jerk from his arms, Blake held her firmly against him as he eased his lips from hers and slowly turned his head to glare at a young man standing a few feet from their table. Blake didn't say a word. He didn't have to. His menacing look was enough to wipe the leering expression from the man's face and had him disappearing into the crowd without so much as a moment's hesitation.

Sasha's cheeks felt as if they were on fire and she couldn't have found her voice if her life depended on it. What on earth had gotten into her? She'd never in her entire life been the type to get so caught up in a kiss that she forgot where she was. Nor had she ever been one for public displays of affection.

Dear heavens, what would have happened if the kiss had been more passionate or lasted longer? Mortified, she buried her face against Blake's broad shoulder. There was no doubt in her mind that she would have made an even bigger fool of herself than she already had.

As if sensing that she would rather be anywhere else than in the middle of a crowded casino, Blake set her on her feet and stood up beside her. "That's enough of the blackjack lessons for one day. It's dinnertime anyway and I'm sure our table is ready."

Before she could find her voice and tell him that what she really needed was to be alone, he took her by the hand and walked toward the Golden Belle. Once they were seated at a small table in a cozy little corner at the back of the restaurant, he reached up to stroke her cheek with his index finger.

"Sasha, I'm not going to mince words." His promising smile sent a wave of excitement coursing through her. "I want you and I'm not going to stop until I make you mine."

Four

Thanking the powers that be for a few moments to herself, Sasha sat in the Golden Belle and thoughtfully sipped her coffee as she waited for Blake to return. He'd been called away on casino business right after they'd finished dinner and it was the first opportunity she'd had to contemplate his bold statement about making her his.

What on earth was she going to do? Did she have the courage to become involved with him?

All of her adult life she'd used extreme caution when it came to relationships. She'd witnessed some of her friends and coworkers suffer through the misery of failure and she'd been determined not to find herself in the same position.

Unfortunately, she wasn't entirely certain she had a choice where Blake was concerned. From the moment she'd laid eyes on him in high school, she'd been attracted to him. And although she'd convinced herself she'd gotten over her schoolgirl crush years ago, she was finding him even more irresistible now than she had eleven years ago.

She sighed heavily as the object of her affection walked into the restaurant, spoke to the hostess, then walked toward her. If Creed was right about Blake, she could very well end up emotionally shattered. But how in the world could she make herself immune to his charms?

"I'm sorry about a being called away," he said, smiling apologetically as he pulled out the chair across from her and sat down. "There was a minor altercation at one of the craps tables and they needed me in the security office to smooth over the situation with one of our whales."

"I hope it wasn't serious."

He shook his head. "The man had a little too much to drink and accused another guest of stealing part of his chip stack."

"Was the guest in question guilty?"

"No." Blake grinned. "The whale's wife had

taken them and cashed them in to keep her husband from losing more than he already had."

Sasha laughed. "I can understand her caution. The thought of losing a lot of money on something as frivolous as a game would drive me insane." Wondering if there was ever any real danger of fights breaking out, she asked, "Do things like a disagreement between two guests ever come to blows?"

"No. My security team is one of the best in Deadwood and they're on top of a situation like this before it ever comes to that." He reached across the table to take her hand in his. "But I don't want to talk about that now."

A warmth began to flow through her from the feel of his hand caressing hers. "W-would you like to discuss my ideas for your promotional campaign?" she hedged, hoping to buy a little more time to sort out what she was going to do.

"No, sweetheart. The last thing I want to do is talk business with you." Lifting her hand to his lips, he kissed the rapidly beating pulse at the base of her wrist. "We'll go over your suggestions tomorrow." He gave her a meaningful look. "I intend for tonight to be all about us."

Sasha swallowed hard. "I haven't exactly agreed to there being an *us*."

His smile caused her whole body to tingle. "Yes, you have."

"I—I don't recall…that happening. W-would you…care to refresh…my memory?" she asked, suddenly finding it hard to make her voice work.

"Your response when I kissed you this afternoon in the casino was all the answer I needed."

His lips grazing the sensitive skin along her wrist caused her to shiver. "I—"

"Don't try to deny it, sweetheart. You're as attracted to me as I am to you." His voice dropped seductively. "You're trembling now from just talking about it."

Sasha couldn't think of a thing to say. What could she say? He was right and they both knew it.

"Come on," he said, rising to his feet and pulling her up to stand beside him. "Let's go upstairs to my suite."

Her heart fluttered erratically. "I'm not sure… that's a good idea."

His low chuckle sent a wave of heat streaking straight to her inner core. "I think it's an excellent idea." He placed his hand to the small of her back and leaning close, added, "Before the evening is over with, I'm going to make sure you do, too."

Try as she might, Sasha couldn't stop the feeling of nervous anticipation building inside of her. No

matter what Creed said about Blake being untrust-
worthy, no matter how foolish it might turn out to
be or how high a price she could very well end up
paying, she was going to follow her heart and see
where it led her with Blake.

She sighed as they left the restaurant. If she was
perfectly honest with herself, she'd have to admit
that she'd never had a choice in the matter.

When they entered his suite, Blake's mouth went
completely dry as he noticed the seductive sway of
Sasha's hips while she walked over to stare out the
window at the street below. The clingy black dress
she wore hugged her like a lover's caress and she
was without a doubt the sexiest woman he'd ever
had the privilege to lay eyes on.

Blake smiled coldly. His brother had been a
damned fool to let her make the trip to Deadwood
alone and it was going to serve Creed right to lose
her. The bastard didn't deserve a woman as special
as Sasha and before the night was over, Blake was
going to convince her of that fact.

But the thought of his brother holding Sasha,
touching her flawless skin and losing himself in her
soft body caused a burning deep in the pit of
Blake's belly and a sudden, uncontrollable need to

stake his claim. Tonight he was going to take her into his arms and make her his.

Walking up behind her, he wrapped his arms around her waist and drew her back against him. "Do you have any idea how beautiful you are?"

She shook her head. "I have too many flaws. My hair is—"

"Gorgeous," he interrupted, nuzzling the side of her slender neck.

"I—I've never liked…my hair," she said, sounding extremely short of breath. "It's always been too hard…to tame."

"You used to wear it down when we were in school," he said, reaching up to release the pins she used to hold it in place. Free of their confinement, the silky curls cascaded over his hands like a cinnamon-colored waterfall. "Your hair is soft and feminine." He turned her to face him and, lowering his head, added, "And it compliments your creamy skin to perfection."

As he fused their lips, Blake slid his hands from her shoulders to her hips and pulled her closer. The feel of her soft body pressed closely to his, the smell of her herbal-scented hair and her sweet taste as she melted against him quickly had him hard with need.

Allowing her to feel his rapidly changing body, he caught her to him and when a tiny moan escaped her slightly parted lips, he seized the opportunity to slip his tongue inside. He explored her with a thoroughness that left them both aching for more. Encouraged by her response, he continued to stroke her tender inner recesses as he slid his hands up to the underside of her breasts.

She stiffened for a split second as if she intended to protest when he used his thumbs to tease the tightened tips through the stretchy black fabric of her dress. Then to his satisfaction, she reached up to put her arms around his neck and leaned into his touch. She might have been resistant to him when she'd first arrived in Deadwood, but her body was telling him all he needed to know about her receptiveness to his advances now.

"So sweet," he said, breaking the kiss to nibble his way down the column of her slender neck. "So damned sexy."

"I—I should go back…to my room," she said haltingly.

"Is that what you really want, sweetheart?"

"N-no. I mean yes." She closed her eyes and took a deep breath. "I can't…think clearly."

He chuckled as he kissed the fluttering pulse at the base of her throat. "Would you like to hear what I think?"

"N-not really."

Leaning back, he gazed into her pretty green

eyes. "I think you need to stay right here with me tonight. In my suite. In my bed. In my arms."

"I can't…do that." Her tone was breathy and not at all convincing.

"Yes, you can." He brushed his lips over hers. "You want me as much as I want you."

She opened her eyes and, staring at him, slowly shook her head. "I—"

"Don't try to deny it, Sasha." He grazed his thumbs over her taut nipples as he pressed himself against her and smiled at the shiver he felt course through her when she felt the hard ridge of his arousal. "Your body is telling me everything I need to know."

"W-we shouldn't."

"Why not?" He nipped at her collarbone. "We're not kids anymore. We're both consenting adults with a desire to find pleasure with each other."

She closed her eyes as she tilted her head back to give him better access. "I've never—"

"This won't be a one-night stand," he interrupted, anticipating what she was about to tell him.

"But that's not—"

"Are you committed to Creed?"

She frowned as she shook her head. "I told you, your brother and I are nothing more than just good friends."

He still had a hard time believing that Creed had spent the last year with Sasha and not taken their friendship to a more personal level. "If that's the case, then there's no reason for you to go back to your room."

Before she could come up with any more excuses why their spending the night together was a bad idea, Blake took her back into his arms and mingled their lips in a kiss that sent a fire racing through his veins at the speed of light. When she sagged against him, he didn't think twice about swinging her up into his arms to carry her into his bedroom.

Cradled against him, her slight frame felt almost fragile and a tenderness he hadn't expected filled his chest. A woman as sweet and sexy as Sasha was meant to be loved slowly, thoroughly, and he had every intention of spending the entire night cherishing her as he was sure his brother never had.

Setting her on her feet at the side of his bed, Blake turned on the bedside lamp, then facing her, gently traced his index finger along her delicate jaw. "I'm going to spend the entire night showing you just how special you are, Sasha."

"Blake, there's something you should know," she said, looking a bit apprehensive.

"Do you want me, Sasha?"

"I shouldn't."

"That wasn't the question," he said, shaking his head. "Do you want me?"

She worried her lower lip with even white teeth a moment before she slowly nodded.

"That's all the answer I need," he said, pulling her to him.

He kissed her forehead, her eyes and the tip of her nose before lowering his mouth to hers. Her lips were sweeter than anything he'd ever tasted and he knew beyond a shadow of doubt that if he wasn't extremely careful, he could become addicted to kissing her.

As his mouth moved over hers, Sasha fleetingly wondered if she was about to make the biggest mistake of her life. But Blake was quickly robbing her of the ability to think of all the reasons making love with him could spell disaster for her and leaving her with nothing but the ability to feel.

"I'm going to love every inch of you, sweetheart," he said as he rained tiny kisses to the sensitive hollow below her ear.

A delicious tingling filled every fiber of her being and her heart began to pound erratically as he slid his hands down her back. Slowly, deliberately, he began to gather the stretchy fabric of her dress in his fists until he reached the hem.

"As sexy as you look in this little number, you're going to look even better out of it," he whispered close to her ear. "Raise your arms for me, Sasha."

Feeling as if she were in some sort of sensuous trance, she did as he commanded and in seconds she was standing before him in nothing but her underwear and a pair of black spike heels. If she'd had the chance, she might have tried covering herself, but Blake took her hands in his and held them out to her sides as his gaze caressed her from head to toe.

His sharp intake of breath, and the spark of need she detected in his dark blue eyes, made her feel more feminine and desirable than she'd ever felt in her life. "Do you always wear a garter belt…and hose?" he asked huskily.

She nodded. "I hate having to wiggle myself into a pair of panty hose."

"I'm glad," he said, grinning. "There's nothing sexier than a woman dressed in scraps of black lace and silk." He glanced down at her feet and his deep chuckle warmed her all the way to her soul. "Unless the woman is wearing a pair of high heels." When he raised his head to look at her, he gave her a smile that sent her pulse racing and caused a delightful fluttering deep in the pit of her stomach. "You're absolutely gorgeous, sweetheart."

Her cheeks heated with a mixture of embarrassment and desire. "At the moment, I'm feeling a little underdressed."

"I fully intend to remedy that," he said, shrugging out of his sports jacket. He tossed the coat onto a chair, then bent to remove his shoes and socks.

When he straightened and reached for the buttons on his shirt, Sasha tried not to stare as he released first one button, then another. But as he slid the oxford cloth from his wide shoulders, the sight of his perfectly sculpted chest, rippling stomach and lean flanks caused her to catch her breath. She'd known he kept himself in good physical condition, but she'd never dreamed that his clothes were concealing a body that could rival that of a Greek god.

As he unbuckled his belt and lowered the zipper at his fly, Sasha abandoned all pretense of nonchalance and simply stared as he slid his trousers down his muscular thighs and revealed the true magnificence of his hard body. Taut and lean, Blake Fortune was perfect in every way.

She swallowed hard when she noticed the straining outline of his erection through his white cotton briefs. He was also unquestionably aroused. The thought that she was the object of his desire caused an interesting and not at all unpleasant tightening in the most feminine part of her.

Unsure of what to do, she started to slip out of her heels, but he shook his head. "Don't. I want the pleasure of taking those off of you." He pointed to her garter belt, bra and panties. "And I'm looking forward to peeling away those little scraps of silk and lace as well."

She shivered with anticipation as she placed her hands on his wide shoulders to brace herself when he bent to remove her heels, then trailed his hands up her legs to the fastenings holding her stockings in place. As he slid the sheer nylon down her calves, Sasha caught her breath at the feel as his palms gently caressing her skin. She'd never in her entire life experienced anything quite so sensual or exciting as having Blake take off her under things, and by the time he removed her lace garter belt and satin panties, Sasha trembled uncontrollably.

He reached for her then, and holding her captive with his heated gaze, unfastened the front clasp of her bra and slowly slid it from her shoulders. "You're absolutely gorgeous," he said as he cupped her bare breasts in his large hands.

Her knees threatened to give way when he lowered his head and kissed first one tight nipple, then the other. But when he took one of the puckered buds into his mouth to tease it with his teeth and tongue, she had to brace her hands on his shoulders to keep her knees from buckling.

"You taste like peaches and cream, sweetheart."

His warm breath feathering over the moistened tip of her breast made it all but impossible to catch her breath. "If you keep that up…I'm not sure… how much longer…my legs are going to support me."

Raising his head, his smile held such promise goose bumps prickled her skin. "Let's lie down."

Before she could move to sit on the side of the bed, he reached down to pull the comforter back, then picked her up and gently placed her in the center of the wide mattress.

"I could have gotten into bed on my own, Blake."

He looked at her tenderly as he stood up and hooked his thumbs in the waistband of his briefs to pull them down. "I like the way you feel in my arms."

She would have told him that she liked having him hold her, but the words died in her throat as he slipped off his underwear and tossed them on the chair with the rest of his clothes. When he turned back toward her, Sasha's heart stalled at the sight of his impressive arousal. Although she'd seen the nude male physique, nothing could have prepared her for the reality of Blake Fortune standing before her fully aroused and looking is if he intended to devour her.

Feeling more than a little intimidated by his size and the strength of his need, she raised her eyes to meet his questioning gaze. "There's something…you probably need…to know."

He shook his head as he tucked a small foil packet beneath his pillow, then lay down beside her to gather her to him. "All I need to know is that you want me as much as I want you." He raised up on one elbow, and leaning over her, kissed his way down the slope of her breast as he skimmed his palm along her side to the swell of her hip. "You do want me to make love with you, don't you, Sasha?"

As she gazed up at him, she knew in her heart that she'd waited for this moment her entire life. She'd had other opportunities to make love with the men she'd dated, but she'd never before been able to share herself. And with crystal clarity, she suddenly realized why. None of them had been Blake Fortune.

"Yes, I want you to make love to me, Blake," she said, surprised at how steady her voice sounded, considering the amount of nervous excitement coursing through her.

He must have detected her lingering apprehension because he gave her a kiss so tender it brought tears to her eyes, then he raised his head and gave her a look that touched her heart. "I don't want you to worry, sweetheart. I promise, I'll never do anything to hurt you in any way."

Before she could tell him that she knew there would be discomfort that neither of them could avoid, he covered her lips with his and she forgot anything she was about to say. Nothing seemed to matter but the feel of his body pressed to hers and the taste of desire in his seductive kiss.

Threading her fingers through the hair at the nape of his neck, she held him to her as his tongue traced her mouth, then dipped inside to stroke, tease and coax. Shivers of delight skipped through her when he withdrew and allowed her to enter his mouth to do a little exploring of her own. She wasn't exactly sure of what she was doing, but rewarded by his groan of pleasure and the feel of his hard erection against her thigh, she decided that Blake didn't mind. Just knowing that she aroused such need in him heightened her own desire in ways she could have never imagined.

When he slowly moved his hand from her hip, down along her thigh, then up to the soft curls hiding her feminine secrets, she went perfectly still.

But the intense impulses that his touch created when he stroked her with gentle care sent a tightening heat straight to her inner core and she couldn't have stopped her moan of pleasure from escaping if her life depended on it.

Finding it all but impossible to lie still, she gripped the sheet with her fists and moved restlessly beneath his hand. "P-please—"

"Do you want me, sweetheart?"

"Y-yes." Waves of heat flowed through her as he continued to heighten her passion, but when he took her nipple into his mouth as his finger stroked her deeply, she felt as if the blood in her veins turned to liquid fire.

"Is this where you need me?" he whispered against her puckered flesh.

Unable to form a coherent thought, much less get any words out, she used her hands to raise his head from her breast and, meeting his questioning gaze, simply nodded.

Smiling, he softly kissed her lips. "That's exactly where I need to be."

As she watched, he reached beneath the pillow, removed the small foil packet and arranged their protection. Then, taking her back into his arms, he used his knee to nudge her legs apart.

When he rose above her and she felt the blunt

tip of him against her moist apex, she closed her eyes and braced herself for what would happen next. Hopefully, the discomfort would be minimal and wouldn't last too long.

"Look at me, Sasha." When she did as he commanded, the blazing passion in his dark blue eyes shook her all the way to her soul. "I don't want there to be any doubt who's making love to you."

Confused by the odd statement and the insistence in his deep voice, she started to tell him she knew exactly who she was giving her virginity to. But her voice abandoned her when he pressed his lower body forward and began to fuse their bodies into one.

"So tight," he said through clenched teeth as he continued to ease into her. But when he met the slight resistance, his eyes widened and he went completely still. "Holy hell. You're a virgin."

Five

Blake didn't move a muscle as he tried to wrap his mind around the fact that Sasha had been telling the truth. She'd never been with Creed, or for that matter, any other man.

"You're a virgin," he repeated, still unable to believe he was the first man to sink himself into her soft body.

"Was," she said, wincing as her tight body resisted the invasion of his. "I don't think that's the case anymore."

"You should have told me."

Moisture filled her pretty green eyes and he

wasn't sure if it was from the physical pain he'd caused her or the harsh accusation in the tone of his voice. Either way, he could have kicked his own ass for being the reason she cried.

"It's all right, Sasha." He gently wiped a tear from the corner of her eye then, brushing her trembling lips with his, added, "Just a little more and the discomfort will start to ease."

It ripped him apart to see another tear slide down the side of her cheek as he pushed forward and completely buried himself in her moist heat. His reflexes urged him to move, to thrust into her and complete the act of loving her, but he remained perfectly still. Her body needed time to adjust to his and he wasn't about to hurt her any more than he already had.

Gathering her close, he kissed away her tears. "No more pain, sweetheart. I promise."

"It's not really that bad," she said, taking a shuddering breath.

"I just wish that you'd let me know." He nuzzled the soft, wispy curls at her temple. "I might have been able to do something to make my entry a little less painful."

"You were so gentle, I don't see how you could have made it any easier," she murmured shyly. "And I did try to tell you."

He frowned. "When?"

Her watery smile did strange things to his insides. "Just before you assured me our lovemaking was not going to be a one-night stand."

He vaguely remembered her telling him there was something that she'd never done, but he'd thought she was going to tell him she'd never been one to engage in casual sex. That was when he'd jumped the gun and interrupted her to voice his assurance that wasn't what he wanted from her. Apparently, he'd made assumptions that were completely off the mark.

But as he continued to stare down at her lovely face, Blake knew as surely as he knew his own name that he meant what he'd said. His seduction of Sasha Kilgore might have started out as an attempt to even a score with his brother, but within the past thirty-six hours his focus had changed and he had no intention of limiting their lovemaking to this one night.

As he felt her begin to relax and accept him as part of her, the strain of holding himself in check became almost unbearable. He needed to love her, to bring her pleasure and find his own in the softness of her sweet body.

"I'm going to make love to you now, Sasha," he said, kissing her slightly parted lips.

He slowly pulled back, then eased forward as he

watched for any sign that he might be causing her discomfort. When he found none, he set an easy pace and in no time he felt her begin to respond, to tentatively move in unison with him.

But all too soon, he felt her tighten around him and he knew she was close to finding the release they both sought. Deepening his strokes, Blake had to grit his teeth to keep himself from unleashing the full force of his need. He was determined to insure Sasha's pleasure ahead of his own, even if it killed him. And as urgent as his need was, it just might.

When Sasha cried his name and he felt her tiny feminine muscles cling to him, then begin to rhythmically contract, he gave in to the demands of his body and thrust into her one final time. His body stiffened and the white-hot light of completion clouded his mind as he gave up his essence and emptied himself deep inside of her.

Drained of every ounce of energy he possessed, he collapsed on top of her and buried his face in the soft cloud of her auburn hair. "Are you all right, sweetheart?"

"That was…the most incredible experience…of my life," she said breathlessly.

Finally summoning enough strength to move to her side, Blake gathered her to him and held her close. "*You* were incredible."

"Is making love always like that?" she whispered, her breath soft against his heated skin.

He hesitated as he tried to put into words what he didn't fully understand himself. He'd found his pleasure with more women than he cared to admit—all of them light-years ahead of her in experience. But nothing could have prepared him for the degree of satisfaction he'd found with Sasha.

Unwilling to admit, even to himself, that what they'd shared was significant and unlike anything that had ever happened to him, he ignored her question in favor of one of his own. "After all this time of waiting to give your virginity to a man, why did you choose me, Sasha?"

"It's absolutely insane and you probably wouldn't believe me anyway," she answered, placing her warm palm on his bare chest.

He liked the way her touch felt on his skin and he covered her hand with his to hold it there. "Why don't you tell me and see if I believe you."

Her sigh feathered over his shoulder and sent an awakening wave of heat straight to his groin. "They weren't you."

She spoke so softly that he wasn't entirely certain he hadn't imagined her confession. "You saved yourself for me?" he asked incredulously.

Raising her head, she met his questioning gaze

directly. "It wasn't a conscious decision to wait for you, but I think I fell in love with you the first time I saw you back in high school. Since then, I've compared every one of my boyfriends to you and found them lacking in one way or another."

"Even Creed?"

"How many times do I have to tell you? Creed and I are just good friends." When she started to get out of bed, he held her to him. "Creed asked me to accompany him to social functions in order to discourage some the more persistent women looking for a great catch. There was never anything more to it than that."

Blake knew all too well the lengths some women would go to in their quest to catch a man with money and social status. "So you were helping him fend off the gold diggers?"

"Yes."

"And you never entertained the thought of becoming romantically involved with him?" Blake asked, needing to know.

She shook her head. "He wasn't you."

The clarity in her guileless green eyes verified her claim and rendered him absolutely speechless. From the moment he was born, he'd been compared to his older brothers and always seemed to fall just short of everyone's expectations. Even his father, the high and mighty Nash Fortune, had held him up to Case and Creed's achievements, both personally and professionally. But for the first time in his life, someone had compared him to one of his older brothers and Blake hadn't come up second-best.

As he continued to gaze at Sasha, a feeling like nothing he'd ever known filled his chest. For reasons he didn't dare contemplate, he never wanted to let her down, never wanted her to find him lacking in any way. Nor did he ever want another man touching her.

The sudden desire to brand her with his kiss became an undeniable need and Blake didn't think twice about pulling her beneath him to once again claim her sweet body for his own. She was his now and he had no intention of ever letting her forget it.

When Sasha went into work on Monday afternoon, she wasn't at all surprised to find Creed standing in her doorway less than five minutes after her arrival. To anyone else his demeanor would probably appear casual and unperturbed. But in the past year, Sasha had come to know him too well. He definitely had something on his mind and unless he'd undergone a radical personality change in the past few days, he was there to let her know exactly what it was.

"Did you enjoy your weekend in Deadwood?" he asked, walking over to ease himself down into the chair in front of her desk. His question was innocent enough and his tone casual, but she knew it was Creed's way of diplomatically bringing up the subject of her time with Blake.

"It was nice to get away for a while," she said, careful to keep her own tone as neutral as possible. Aside from the fact that she didn't feel like listening to Creed's repeated warnings about Blake, it was none of his concern what she did or with whom. "I especially liked visiting some of the museums and learning more about the town's colorful history. It really is fascinating."

He stared at her for several long seconds before his eyes narrowed and he shook his head. "You fell into his trap, didn't you?"

"I don't have the slightest notion what you're talking about," she lied, averting her gaze.

"Damn." Creed rose to his feet and began to pace the length of her office. "I knew I should have gone with you to keep that bastard from pulling a fast one." Stopping suddenly, he turned to face her. "Did you sleep with him?"

Angry with Creed for prying, as well as with herself for being so transparent, Sasha shook her head. "What I do on my own time is none of your business, Creed. And I don't appreciate being treated to the third degree. If you want to keep our friendship intact, you'll drop this right here and now."

He let loose with a creative curse. "You don't know him like I do, Sasha. He's just like his mother—selfish, opportunistic and trouble from the word go." He released a frustrated breath as he shook his head. "The son of a bitch will only end up hurting you and if it's within my power to prevent it from happening, I will."

Sighing, she leaned back in her chair as she continued to stare at her friend. "I appreciate your concern, Creed. But I'm a grown woman and perfectly capable of making my own decisions. I can take care of myself."

As if cognizant of the line he was about to cross with their friendship, he walked to the door, then turned back to face her. "I realize you think you know what you're doing. But becoming involved with Blake Fortune would be a huge mistake."

"That may be," she said, careful to keep her voice as even as her emotions would allow. "But it's my mistake to make, Creed. Not yours."

He looked as if he'd like to argue the point further, then giving her a short nod, he warned as he walked out, "Just be sure to watch yourself around him, Sasha."

Long after Creed had left her office, she continued to stare at the open doorway. She was having
a difficult time believing that they'd been talking
about the same man.

She'd spent the weekend with Blake and found
him to be nothing like the man Creed described. If
Blake was selfish, she hadn't seen it. With her, he'd
been kind, caring and extremely attentive. Her body
heated in a very interesting way as she remembered just how much attention he'd given her.

After learning that she'd come to his bed a
virgin, he couldn't have been more gentle or
understanding. He'd not only been sensitive to the
tenderness of her body and her lack of experience,
he'd assured her pleasure before his own. That
certainly negated Creed's claim that Blake was
self-centered.

And after watching him interact with his employees and guests, it was easy to see why he'd
been so successful with his venture into the gaming
industry. Although he demanded his employees
give one hundred and ten percent to their jobs,
he'd earned their loyalty and respect by asking
nothing more of them than he was willing to give
himself. That didn't sound like a man who took advantage of others.

As she sat there contemplating why Creed felt

the way he did about his brother, Blake entered her office and closed the door. Her heart skipped a beat at the sight of him and she couldn't believe how much she'd missed being with him in such a short time. After flying back to Sioux Falls together on his private jet that morning, they'd parted ways at the airport. And while she'd returned to work, Blake had gone to his family's estate to visit his sister, Skylar.

But something about his expression warned her that things might not have gone well. "Was everything all right at home?"

"I'm not sure." He walked around the desk, pulled her to her feet and kissed her until they both gasped for breath. Then sitting in her chair, he settled her on his lap. "I missed you."

"I missed you, too," she whispered, wrapping her arms around his neck.

They sat in contented silence for several long moments and she could tell he was troubled by something. "What happened?"

He shrugged one broad shoulder. "As usual, Dad and Patricia were off somewhere doing whatever retired couples do."

Nash Fortune had handed over the reins of his thriving enterprise to his oldest sons, Creed and Case, a couple of years before Sasha had come to work at Dakota Fortune. But she'd met the elder Fortune and his third wife on several occasions and marveled at how devoted they were to each other.

"They certainly seem to be making the most of his retirement," she agreed. "But what about Skylar? Wasn't she at home?"

Blake looked pensive as he nodded. "Yeah, but only in body."

"Excuse me?"

"She was there, but her mind was clearly somewhere else," he said, frowning. "I've never seen her so quiet."

Knowing Skylar Fortune from the social and family events she'd attended with Creed, Sasha found it hard to believe that the youngest of the Fortune siblings could be even more reserved than usual. "Do you think she might be ill?"

"I don't think so," he said thoughtfully. He chuckled. "If her appetite is any indication, she's as healthy as one of her horses. She's gained so much weight lately that you never see her in anything but baggy sweaters or sweatshirts."

"Do you know if she's been seeing someone?" Sasha asked.

He looked confused. "What does that have to do with anything?"

She smiled. Like most men, Blake didn't have

the slightest clue the effect a failed relationship could have on a woman. Or what it sometimes compelled her to do.

"Skylar might be nursing a broken heart." She kissed his lean cheek. "Nina in accounting told me that after her breakup with her fiancé, she gained twenty pounds in a month because she went home every night after work and ate a pint of double-fudge chocolate-chunk ice cream."

He was silent a moment before an understanding expression crossed his handsome features. "I do remember seeing Skylar and Zach Manning at Case's wedding reception a few months back. At the time, I didn't think much of it, but I think there was something going on between them."

"Isn't he from New Zealand?"

Blake nodded. "He and our cousin, Max, have partnered up to start a horse-breeding operation in Australia and they've been over here a couple of times to check out Skylar's program." He gave her a smile that caused an exciting little tingle to traverse the length of her body. "But I don't want to discuss Zach Manning, his plans to breed horses or the sorry state of my little sister's love life."

A spark of heat ignited deep in the pit of her belly as Sasha stared at the man she'd fallen in love with. "What do you want to discuss?" She feigned thoughtfulness. "World affairs? The state of the economy? The price of tea in China?"

"None of the above," he said. "In fact—" he brushed his lips over hers "—I prefer action over words."

When his mouth settled on hers, Sasha decided that she did, too. They could talk on the phone after he returned to Deadwood sometime tomorrow. Right now, she was in Blake's arms and from the promise in his heated kiss, having a conversation was the last thing either of them wanted.

"Let's go to your place," he suggested, pulling back to capture her gaze with his.

"I just got here," she said, feeling as if the temperature in the room had risen a good ten degrees. She could feel his rapidly changing body against her thigh and it was creating an answering heat in the most feminine part of her. "And I really should tie up some loose ends on a project from last week."

Groaning, he took a deep breath as he rested his forehead against hers. "I've always admired a strong work ethic, but right now, I'd have to say I think it's a pain."

She smiled, then gave him a quick kiss and rose to her feet. "I said I had a few things to take care of. I didn't say that it would take me the rest of the afternoon." Tugging on his hand, she urged him out of her chair. "I should be ready to leave in about an hour. Do you think you can find something to occupy your time until then?"

"I can't hang out here in your office with you?" he asked as he stood up and wrapped his arms around her waist to pull her to him.

She shook her head. "You're too much of a distraction."

"But I thought you liked the way I distract you," he teased.

Shivers of sheer delight skipped up her spine when he leaned close and whispered the many ways he'd distracted her over the weekend. "I—I do like the d-diversion." She paused and took a deep breath in an effort to steady her voice. "And the sooner you let me get back to work, the sooner we'll be able to leave and you can divert my attention again."

He gave her a quick kiss, then released her and walked to the door. "I'll be back in an hour. And sweetheart, when we get to your apartment, I'm going to show you just how much of a distraction I can be."

When Blake left Sasha's office, he headed straight for the empty conference room at the end of the hall. Holding her soft body against him, kissing her sweet lips and talking about various ways he intended to make love to her when they got to her place had him harder than the Rock of Gibraltar. And unless he found a place to cool off, and damned quick, he'd be the subject of office gossip for days.

Besides, after discussing the possible source of his sister's despondent mood with Sasha, he had an overseas phone call to make. He knew it was probably the middle of the night in New Zealand, but he didn't care. Zach Manning could haul his sorry butt out of bed and explain what was going on between himself and Skylar. And it had better be good.

Closing the door behind him, Blake walked straight to the telephone on the mahogany credenza at the back of the conference room and dialed the Dakota Fortune operator. After instructing the woman to place his call, he waited for the connection to go through.

A few moments later, a sleepy male voice answered after several rings. "What!?"

"Zach? Blake Fortune here."

"Do you know what time it is here?" Zach demanded, his New Zealand accent thickened by sleep.

"Since you're half a world away, it's probably the middle of the night," Blake said, not at all concerned by the man's obvious displeasure at being awakened from a sound sleep.

A guttural curse crackled over the long-distance line. "I assume this isn't a social call. What do you want, Fortune?"

"An explanation." Never one to mince words, Blake couldn't see any reason to do so now. "What happened between you and Skylar when you were here in February for Case's wedding?"

Dead silence reigned for several long seconds and Blake knew he'd discovered the reason behind his sister's withdrawal.

"Why do you ask?" Zach finally responded, sidestepping an explanation.

"She hasn't been herself for the past couple of months and I want to know the reason why."

"Is she all right?"

The concern Blake detected in the man's voice was genuine enough, but that did little to appease his building anger. "Something is bothering her and it's my guess that you're behind it. I also figure you know what that something is and will be able to rectify the situation."

"I'll speak with her," Zach assured him without hesitation.

"Consider yourself warned, Manning. I don't like seeing my sister hurt."

"I'll set things right with Skylar immediately," Zach promised. To his credit the man didn't sound nearly as irritated as when he'd first answered Blake's call. In fact, Zach sounded rather enthusiastic about getting in touch with her.

"See that you do," Blake said, hanging up the phone without bidding the man farewell.

With the matter of his sister's broken heart resolved, Blake smiled as he checked his watch. Sasha's hour was almost up and he had every intention of taking her to her apartment and distracting her until they both collapsed from exhaustion.

Six

Dressed in nothing but Blake's white shirt, Sasha stared into the freezer compartment of her small refrigerator. "What would you like for dinner?"

Blake walked up behind her, wrapped his arms around her and pulled her back against him to kiss the side of her neck. "You'll do just fine."

She laughed as a familiar heat began to flow through her. "You have a one-track mind, Mr. Fortune."

"I can't help it." He tugged the collar of his shirt from her shoulder to allow him better access, and the feel of his firm lips on her sensitive skin sent tiny electric impulses skittering over every nerve in her body. "You bring out the best in me, sweetheart."

"More like the beast," she said, turning to face him.

When they'd arrived at her apartment, she'd barely managed to close and lock the door before Blake had them both stripped of their clothes and had carried her into the bedroom. That had been several hours ago and the passion arcing between them was every bit as strong now as it had been earlier in the day.

His sexy grin caused a familiar fluttering in the pit of her stomach. "If I remember correctly, you weren't exactly complaining when I—"

She placed her index finger to his lips. "Point taken," she said, blushing furiously.

His deep chuckle vibrated against her chest and caused the most interesting tingling in the tips of her breasts. "I love seeing you blush."

"That's apparent." She circled his bare shoulders with her arms and threaded her fingers in the dark blond hair at the nape of his neck. "You've been making me turn as red as a lobster all afternoon."

"That wasn't embarrassment, Sasha. That was the blush of desire."

As if to prove his point, he pressed his lower

body closer and the feel of his strong arousal against her lower belly caused her to go warm all over. "If you keep this up—"

"Interesting choice of words," he said, sliding his hands down to cup her bottom and pull her even closer. "As I'm sure you can tell, that's not a problem."

She gasped from the waves of renewed need that flowed through her when she felt the strength of his arousal against her lower belly. "We're never going to find time to go over my ideas for your promotional campaign."

He kissed her collarbone, then began to unbutton his shirt to nibble at every new inch he exposed. "Is that what you really want to do right now?"

When he parted the garment and covered her breasts with his hands, her knees began to wobble and her heart pounded so hard against her ribs, she felt as if she'd run a marathon. "Wh-what was the question again?"

"Damned if I know," he said as he lowered his head to take her nipple into his mouth.

Teasing her relentlessly, Sasha wasn't at all surprised to feel a delicious need begin to tighten her womb. After making love the entire afternoon, how could they possibly be hungrier for each other now than before?

"This…is insane."

He raised his head and the intensity in the depths of his eyes, the sparkle of heat, told her in no uncertain terms what he wanted. "We're about to go crazy together, sweetheart."

Fully expecting him to pick her up and carry her back into the bedroom, she tightened her arms around him in surprise when he lifted her to sit on the edge of the counter. "Wh-what are you doing?"

"I want you here." Buttons skittered across the tiled floor when he jerked the lapels of his shirt open the rest of the way to give him better access to her body. Then, shoving his boxer briefs to his ankles, he entered her in one smooth stroke. "Now."

The feel of him filling her completely, the heat that threatened to consume her when he began to rhythmically thrust into her and the fact that they were making love somewhere other than the bedroom heightened her excitement in ways she could have never imagined. The urgency arcing between them was more powerful than ever before and Sasha felt as if she would burst into flames at any moment.

Tightening her legs around his slim hips, she clung to him as he relentlessly built the ache of unfulfilled desire within her. All too quickly his body demanded that she give into their fiery passion and she gladly complied as bursts of pleasure shook her to the core.

As she trembled against him, she felt the slight swelling of his body within hers a moment before the moist heat of his release filled her. As she held him to her, tears burned at her tightly closed eyes from the beauty of what they'd shared.

If she'd had any lingering doubts about her feelings for him being the remnants of the school-girl's crush, they had just dissipated like mist under a warm summer sun. She loved him with a woman's heart and belonged to him, body and soul. And no matter what the future held for them, that would never change.

"You want me to do what?" Blake couldn't believe what Sasha was proposing.

"I'd like for you to consider doing a television commercial for the grand opening of Fortune's Gold," she said patiently.

"I have no objections to the concept of buying airtime to run commercials for my hotels and casinos," he said, shaking his head. "I do, however, have a huge problem with starring in the damned things."

Sitting cross-legged in the middle of her bed, wearing nothing but his buttonless shirt and a sweet smile, she looked so sexy and desirable, Blake had to force himself to remember that he'd promised to listen to her ideas for his ad campaign. But if anything could bring him back to reality with a resounding thump, it was the thought of going in front of a TV camera. Just the idea caused a knot in his stomach.

"Blake, you're the natural choice," she insisted. "You're not only the owner of the Fortune Casino Corporation, your enthusiasm and sincerity when you encourage people to visit your establishments will be captured and add a great deal to your advertising. It will make the viewers feel as if you're issuing a personal invitation."

He understood what she was saying and the value of the visual media. But the thought of following the nightly news like some monkey in a sideshow, even for the fifteen to thirty seconds the commercials would run, made him want take off for parts unknown.

"I think a professional actor would be a better choice," he said, leaning back against the pillows.

"I don't." Raising up on her hands and knees, she crawled across the bed to hover over him. "You're handsome." She kissed his chin. "Sexy." She traced the outline of his lips with her tongue. "And you'll have the women flocking to your casinos in droves."

He pulled her beneath the sheet that covered

him from the waist down, then turned to his side and aligned their bodies so they were facing each other. "You really think I'm handsome and sexy?" he asked, slipping his hand beneath the shirt to caress her satiny skin.

"Don't change the subject," she said, sounding less than convincing. "I'm trying to have a serious conversation with you about the marketing strategy for the Fortune Casino Corporation."

Slowly sliding his hand down her thigh, he smiled when her eyes fluttered shut and she sighed softly. "Do you really want to discuss business now?"

"We should."

"Who are you trying to convince, Sasha? Me or yourself?"

When she opened her eyes, the sparkle of desire in her emerald gaze caused his body to harden so fast it left him feeling light-headed. "We're never going to get anything done if you keep distracting me all the time," she complained.

He moved his hand lower to find her receptive and ready for him. "Oh, I think we've accomplished quite a bit."

She poked him in his ribs. "I wasn't talking about our lovemaking."

"That's a shame," he said, kissing his way from her shoulder, down the valley between her breasts to the small indentation of her navel. "You've inspired me more than I ever thought possible and I'm enjoying finding new ways to love you."

"Your creativity certainly has…been working overtime."

The hitch in her voice was an indication of her heightening excitement and, determined to imprint himself in her mind and on her soul, Blake turned her to her back. He held her gaze with his as he moved to kneel between her legs and he knew the exact moment she realized his intention.

"B-Blake, you can't—"

"Yes, I can." He could tell that she was embarrassed by the thought of what he was about to do. "I'm going to give you the most intimate kiss a man can give a woman, Sasha. And when I'm finished, there won't be a doubt left in your mind that you've been loved as thoroughly and completely as it's within my power to do."

Unwilling to allow her to protest further, Blake bent to give to her as he'd never given to any woman and when he kissed her deeply, her soft sighs quickly turned to passionate moans. Her slender body trembled, then suddenly bucked against him and he knew the intense pleasure was about to overtake her.

Relentless in his effort to bring her to the brink,

he smiled from the satisfaction of hearing her cry out his name as the tension released her from its tight hold and she found the ecstasy of her fulfillment. Only then did he move to lie by her side, his chest filling with indescribable tenderness when he realized that she'd drifted off into a peaceful, sated sleep.

As he held Sasha close, Blake stared at the ceiling and mentally reviewed everything that had taken place over the past few days. He wasn't the least bit proud of himself for planning to seduce her as a way to even the score with his brother. Aside from the fact that she and Creed had never been romantically involved, Blake knew now that Sasha was the only one who stood to be hurt in his game of revenge.

He took a deep breath as a wave of guilt threatened to swamp him. She could never learn the truth behind his sudden interest in her after all this time. If she did, the knowledge would crush her. And he'd rather cut out his own heart than ever let that happen.

When he glanced down at her beautiful face pillowed on his shoulder, an emotion that scared the living hell out of him filled every fiber of his being. He knew that they were good together, that he felt more alive and content in her presence than he'd ever felt in his life. But he refused to acknowledge there was anything more to it than two people finding companionship and pleasure in each others' arms.

Satisfied that he'd found an explanation for the unwarranted feeling, he kissed the top of her head. They would continue to see each other until one or both of them lost interest. Then, when the time came for them to part ways, they would do so as good friends who could look back on their time together with deep fondness and no regrets.

Sasha watched the production crew test the lighting and do a sound check in the lobby of Fortune's Gold as they prepared to film the last segment of the commercials for Blake's casinos. She'd finally managed to talk him into being his own spokesman for the ad campaign, but it certainly hadn't been easy. He'd come up with every excuse imaginable, from claiming that he would feel like he was on display to wanting to maintain his anonymity. But in the end, she'd convinced him by showing him the marketing statistics. It had been proven time and again that when the public felt a personal rapport with the owner of an establishment, the amount of traffic increased and ultimately so did profits.

"We're ready for Mr. Fortune as soon as Sally

Ann finishes his makeup," the director said, walking over to stand beside Sasha.

She'd worked with Michael Atkinson on several campaigns for Dakota Fortune and knew his production company was the best in Sioux Falls. By the time the commercials aired in all of the major cities across the Midwest, he would have them edited and tweaked to show Blake and the Fortune Casino Corporation in the best possible light.

"I want to thank you for working this into your busy schedule, Michael." With a little less than two weeks left before the opening of Fortune's Gold, she'd had to scramble to get Michael's company to shoot the commercials, as well as arrange scheduling with all of the television stations to run them on such short notice.

"It's been well worth it, Ms. Kilgore." Michael grinned. "It's not every day that my crew and I get to fly to a shoot on a private jet or have our lunches catered by a master chef."

"Mr. Fortune appreciates your willingness to put your other clients on hold in order to shoot his commercial," she said, diplomatically ignoring the fact that Blake was paying the man double his normal rate to expedite the job.

"Let's get this spectacle over with," Blake groused as he removed the tissues the makeup artist had tucked into his collar to keep from discoloring his shirt.

Once Michael moved away to have a final word with the cameraman, Blake leaned close to whisper in Sasha's ear. "I'm going to get even with you for this."

As he described exactly how he intended to make her pay up, a tingling sensation coursed through her. She started to tell him that she was looking forward to her night of reckoning, but Michael chose that moment to motion for Blake to step in front of the camera, and for the next hour she watched him deliver the ad copy she'd helped him put together.

At first, Blake appeared stiff and extremely uncomfortable. He glanced her way several times and she could tell he was adding to the sensual retribution he had planned for her. But by the last few takes, he appeared confident and completely at ease in front of the camera.

When Michael announced the job was a wrap and he and his crew began tearing down their equipment, Sasha smiled as she walked over to Blake. "That wasn't all that unpleasant, was it?"

Placing his hand to the small of her back, he guided her toward the casino exit. "No, it wasn't as bad as I figured it would be. But I sure as hell don't plan on repeating the experience."

Sasha stopped when she saw Blake's limo waiting outside and realized that he meant for them to leave. "I should probably stay until Michael—"

"I have people to see that Atkinson and his crew get packed up and on their way." He waited for her to get into the limousine, then slid in beside her. With a look that sent her blood pressure soaring, he pushed the button to raise the privacy screen between them and the driver.

"You owe me big time," he said, dragging her onto his lap. "And guess what?"

She laughed when his fingers danced over her ticklish ribs. "What?"

"It's payday, sweetheart."

"Plan on spending the entire week of the grand opening here in Deadwood with me."

Wrapped in plush hotel robes, Sasha and Blake snuggled on his couch as they stared at the flames from the gas log in the fireplace. "I would love to, but unfortunately, I can't take that much time off."

"Why not?"

A wave of goose bumps covered her arms when he kissed the side of her neck and she had to concentrate hard in order to give him a coherent answer. "I have to pay rent, utilities and eat. I can't do either if I don't work."

"Don't worry about it, sweetheart. I'll see to it that—"

"Don't you dare say you'll pay my bills for me." She pulled back to let him see that she meant what she said. "I have never taken money from anyone that I didn't earn and I'm not about to start now."

He shook his head. "Calm down, Sasha. I was going to tell you that I would arrange for you to have the time away from Dakota Fortune with pay."

It was her turn to shake her head. "I can't let you do that."

"Why not?"

From his baffled expression, she could tell he didn't have an inkling as to why she felt the need to refuse. "For one thing, it wouldn't be fair to my coworkers. They work just as hard as I do and they won't be offered time off with pay."

A deep scowl creased his forehead. "Why are you being so stubborn about this?"

"Because it doesn't sit well with me." Trying a different tack, she asked, "Would you pay one of your employees for work they didn't do?"

"No." There wasn't a bit of hesitation in his answer.

"Then why would you think it was all right to do it for me?"

He surprised her when he smiled and shook his

head. "You're wrong, sweetheart. I wouldn't be paying you for nothing."

It was her turn to feel confused. "Would you care to explain?"

"How many hours would you say you've put in on my ad campaign and how many strings did you have to pull to make it all happen?" he asked, catching her hand in his to tug her back down beside him.

She shrugged as she settled back against him. "I don't know. I haven't kept track."

"You worked last weekend to come up with a plan and every night I've called this past week, you've been ironing out the details." He kissed the top of her head. "And correct me if I'm wrong, but I don't remember giving you a single dime for any of it."

She was beginning to understand his reasoning, but that hadn't been part of their agreement. "I don't expect you to pay me. You asked me to do a favor for you as a friend. Which I did."

His frustrated breath stirred the curls at her temple. "All right. I appreciate your efforts and accept that you won't let me compensate you for your time." He wrapped his arms around her and held her close as he pushed her robe aside to trail kisses down the column of her neck and over her shoulder. "But I'm not asking you to be with me for opening week as a favor. As your boss, I'm telling you to be here."

"You can't do that." Desire began to stir within her as his lips continued to move over her skin. But she refused to give in to it. They were having a difference of opinion and she wasn't going to let him distract her until they got it settled once and for all.

"Sure I can." He laid her down on the couch cushions, parted her robe and leaned to kiss his way down the slope of her breast. "I'm the boss. Remember?"

"But—"

"I'll arrange for you to work here opening week, instead of at the Dakota Fortune offices." He took her puckered nipple into his mouth and drew on it deeply, causing ribbons of warmth to swirl to the very core of her. When he raised his head, he asked, "Now, do you have anymore questions, sweetheart?"

"None," she answered, shaking her head. "None at all."

Seven

As Blake and his managers stood in front of Fortune's Gold for the ribbon-cutting ceremony officially opening his newest casino, he scanned the crowd waiting to enter Deadwood's most elaborate hotel. Asking for Sasha's help had certainly paid off. There were twice as many people gathered to try out the gaming tables and slot machines than there had been at either of the openings for his other casinos.

Searching to find her in the sea of people, when he spotted her standing over to the side with a distinguished-looking gentlemen, Blake barely managed to contain his shock. She was exchanging polite conversation with his father, the all powerful Nash Fortune.

Why was he here? He'd hadn't bothered to attend the openings for Belle of Fortune or Lucky Fortune. In fact, his father hadn't visited Deadwood in the six years that Blake had lived here.

But more surprising than having his father in attendance was the fact that Nash was alone. Where was Patricia? His father and stepmother had been inseparable since Nash's retirement and the fact that she wasn't at his side was quite significant.

But Blake didn't have time to speculate about the absence of his stepmother. He had to deliver a short speech, then participate in the cutting of the wide red ribbon officially opening the doors to Fortune's Gold for business.

As happened with the grand openings for his other two hotel casinos, Blake's position as the owner of Fortune Casino Corporation required that he not only preside over the ceremony, but that he be available to greet guests and endure being interviewed by several newspaper and television reporters. Fortunately, it only took a couple of hours for the patrons to settle into their games of choice and the media to move on to whatever else they deemed newsworthy for the day.

Finally free to go in search of Sasha, he found her in the coffee shop seated at a table with his father. Blake's heart lurched when their eyes met. She was, without a doubt, the most beautiful, alluring woman he'd ever met.

"Everything seemed to go quite well," she said when he walked over to join them.

"I'm fairly pleased with the way things went." Unconcerned that his father was watching, Blake kissed her sweet lips, then lowered himself into the chair beside her. "But I'm glad it's over."

"I always hated having to preside over things like this," Nash said, nodding.

A waitress appeared, seemingly out of nowhere to place a cup of coffee in front of Blake. When she moved away, he turned his attention to his father and stuck out his hand in a more formal greeting. "I didn't expect to see you here, Dad."

His father cleared his throat as they shook hands and if he didn't know better, Blake would have sworn that Nash looked a little chagrined. "I thought it was time to see what's claimed my youngest son's attention for the past several years."

An uncomfortable silence followed his father's telling statement. They both knew that Nash had never paid much attention to Blake, nor had he lifted a finger to stop his two oldest sons from pushing Blake out of Dakota Fortune after he'd retired. Then, when Blake had announced he was going to try his hand at the gaming industry, Nash had dismissed it as a waste of time and hadn't seemed to care one way or the other how his youngest son fared with the venture.

"If you two gentlemen will excuse me, I think I'd like to try my luck at the slot machines," Sasha said, picking up her purse.

Blake knew she was leaving in order to give them the privacy to work through their differences. But he didn't hold out much hope of that ever happening. His entire life, he'd tried to measure up to his father's expectations and all he'd received for his efforts was to be compared with his older brothers, Case and Creed. In his father's eyes, Blake always came up lacking.

When Sasha rose to her feet to make her exit, both he and his father stood up. "It was nice seeing you again, Mr. Fortune," she said as she politely shook Nash's hand.

"It was my pleasure, Sasha."

"I'll see you a bit later, Blake." She placed her hand on his arm and gave him an understanding smile. "After you and your father catch up."

"I'll find you," he promised.

As she walked away, he and his father both watched her leave.

"She's a very lovely girl and a delight to be around," Nash said, sitting back down. "She's highly intelligent, too."

"Yes, she is," Blake agreed as he settled into his chair. "She's directly responsible for the day being a complete success."

"Creed speaks very highly of her," his father added. "He says she's done an excellent job in the PR department at Dakota Fortune."

"I'm sure he does think she's quite good at her job," Blake said tightly. He and his father had never had a conversation in which one of his older brothers wasn't mentioned. The sad thing was he doubted his father even realized how it made Blake feel.

They both fell silent for several moments before Blake finally let go of his irritation and thought to ask "Where's Patricia?"

Nash sighed heavily and Blake could tell he was deeply troubled. "She planned on coming with me, but backed out at the last minute."

"That doesn't sound like her. Wasn't she feeling well?" Patricia Blackstone Fortune had been more of a mother to Blake than his own mother ever had and he was genuinely concerned for her well-being.

"I'm not sure." A worried expression marred his father's distinguished features. "Something's been upsetting her lately and I can't think of what it could be."

"Have you talked to her about what's wrong?" Blake asked as he motioned for the waitress to refill their coffee cups.

Nash waited for the woman to walk away before he nodded. "I've asked her several times, but she won't tell me."

Blake frowned. "That doesn't sound like Patricia."

"No, it doesn't." His father hesitated a moment before giving Blake a meaningful look. "I do have a theory though."

"What is it?"

Nash met his questioning gaze head-on. "I think it might have something to do with Trina."

At the mention of his mother's name, a tight knot formed in the pit of Blake's stomach. "What makes you think Trina has anything to do with Patricia being upset?"

"You know how she is," Nash said, shaking his head. "She thrives on upsetting others and if she's not stirring up some kind of trouble or meddling in someone's life, she's not happy."

"But that doesn't mean she's involved in what's bothering Patricia," Blake said evenly.

Trina Watters Fortune was difficult at the best of times and at her worst, a vindictive, unreasonable shrew. But she was still his mother and Blake felt a certain obligation to defend her.

"It didn't even occur to me to suspect that she was until I saw Patricia's reaction when Ivy mentioned Trina's name in passing." Nash lifted his cup and, staring at Blake over the rim, added, "Patricia turned white as a sheet and had to leave the room."

Ivy Woodhouse had been the family's chef as long as Blake could remember, but for reasons he couldn't explain, there was something about the woman that he'd never liked. "What did Ivy say about Trina?"

"It wasn't what she said—it was Trina's name that sent Patricia into a tailspin." Nash set his cup back down on the table and shook his head. "You still have contact with Trina, don't you?"

"Some," Blake admitted slowly.

"Do you think she's behind whatever is wrong with Patricia?" Nash asked point-blank.

Blake started to tell his father that Trina couldn't possibly be responsible for everything that had gone wrong in Nash's life, but stopping himself, he gave his father a meaningful look. "Ever since you threw Trina out for cheating on you and divorced her, I've been listening to you blame her for everything that's gone wrong in our family."

"She's a—"

Blake held up his hand to stop his father. "And on the other hand, whenever I'm around Trina, I have to listen to her tirade about how you ruined her life and how unfair you were to her. And I'm sick and tired of it."

Nash looked taken aback. "I didn't realize—"

"That's because from the time you and Trina split, you've both been too busy using me as a pawn in your little game of revenge and one-upmanship," Blake interrupted. "When I was younger, each time it was Trina's weekend for visitation, I got the third degree about what was going on at home—what you were doing and who you were seeing. Then when I returned to the estate, when you weren't telling me I should be more like Case and Creed, I had to listen to you complain about what a gold digger Trina is and how she tricked you into marrying her after the death of your father."

They were silent for some time before Nash finally spoke. "I understand the position we've put you in. It couldn't have been easy for you or Skylar." Nash wasn't offering an apology, but then Blake hadn't expected him to.

"I survived," Blake said, finally shedding the feeling of being torn between his parents.

His father nodded. "I'd say you not only

survived, but you've done quite well for yourself, son. You've accomplished quite a bit since leaving Dakota Fortune, and you've made quite a name for yourself without my backing." Nash's voice turned gruff. "I'm proud of you, son."

In that moment, Blake felt closer to his father than he ever had. "Thanks, Dad. That means a lot coming from you."

Nash drew a deep breath, scooted his chair back and stood up. "Well, I think I'd better get back to Sioux Falls to see about Patricia."

Blake rose to his feet to walk out of the coffee shop with his father. "Now that you've checked out my operation, you and Patricia will have to come back and spend a little time here in Deadwood."

"We'll do that," his father said, shaking Blake's hand.

"Give Patricia my best."

Nodding, Nash walked out of the hotel and climbed into the back of a waiting limousine.

Stuffing his hands in the front pockets of his suit pants, emotion filled Blake's chest as he watched the long black car pull from beneath the covered entryway and disappear down the circular drive. For the first time in his life, Nash had acknowledged Blake's accomplishments without comparing him to his older brothers…and it felt good.

Perhaps this was the first step in forging a new relationship between father and son.

"Blake, have you seen today's newspaper from Sioux Falls?"

Propped up against the pillows on his bed, Sasha had chosen to read while he watched a baseball game on television. But in retrospect, she wished she'd opted for a nap. Dreaming, even if it had been a nightmare, would have been a lot less disturbing than what she'd just read.

He shook his head without looking up from the game. "No, why? Did they mention something about the opening of Fortune's Gold?"

"You might say that."

Something in her tone must have tipped him off that she was far from pleased with what she'd read because he turned his head to give her a questioning look. "What did they say?"

She pointed to the society column as she handed him the newspaper. "See for yourself."

His graphic curse reverberated around the room the moment he saw the pictures and read the caption. "Where the hell did this gossip monger come up with her information? And who took these pictures?"

"Your guess is as good as mine." Too upset to sit

still, she got out of bed and began to pace the length of his bedroom. "I know we haven't been trying to hide the fact that we're seeing each other. But I certainly didn't expect to see not one, but two pictures of me in the newspaper with a headline that reads Social Climber Sasha Kilgore Ditches One Fortune Brother in Favor of Another."

"The picture of me kissing you was taken in the coffee shop the day of the grand opening," he said, studying the image.

"And the one of Creed dancing with me was taken at Case and Gina's wedding reception in February." She shook her head. "But I don't find the pictures as upsetting as what the columnist wrote about me. She portrays me as a social mercenary trying to play one brother against the other." Thoroughly miserable, tears filled her eyes as she turned to look at him. "That's not me. That's not who I am."

"I know, sweetheart." Blake tossed the newspaper aside, got out of bed and walked over to pull her into his arms. "Anyone who knows you won't believe a word of it."

"But there are thousands of readers who don't know me and they—"

"Aren't important," he said, sliding his hands up and down her back in a soothing manner. "We know the truth and that's all that matters."

As his tender touch chased away some of her tension, she wrapped her arms around his waist and leaned against his solid support. "I suppose you're right. But I can't understand why the columnist had to be so vindictive in the way she reported the story. It's almost like she's trying to use me to widen the rift between you and Creed."

"Scandals sell newspapers, Sasha." His chest rose and fell against her as he took a deep breath. "I was too young to pay much attention at the time, but I've been told that when my parents divorced, newspaper circulation went way up in Sioux Falls."

"Having the details of their breakup being made the talk of the town must have been extremely painful for your family," she said, wondering why the media couldn't respect the privacy of others.

"I'm sure it was for my father, but Trina probably enjoyed the hell out of it. She thrives on things like that."

Sasha leaned back to look up at him. "Why would your mother want to have information like that reported for all to see?"

He rested his forehead against hers. "If you knew her, you wouldn't be asking that question. She's one of a kind. And believe me, sweetheart, that's a real blessing."

Sasha didn't know what to say. She remembered

Creed telling her that Blake's mother was bad news, but she'd thought he'd been exaggerating because of the hard feelings he had for Blake. Apparently, she'd thought wrong.

"But I don't want talk about her, slanderous newspaper columnists or those clueless people with nothing better to do than believe a pack of lies." He kissed the tip of her nose. "I have other, more enjoyable ways to spend our time."

"What did you have in mind?" she asked as he hooked his finger in the spaghetti strap of her satin nightgown.

"Come back to bed and it'll be my pleasure to show you, sweetheart."

Blake held Sasha close as he watched the shadows of night gradually be chased away by the first light of dawn. After they'd made love, she'd drifted off, but sleep had escaped him.

He'd been more bothered by the newspaper article that he'd let on to Sasha. But not for himself. She was the one whose reputation was being called into question. And that's what caused the anger burning deep in his belly.

Blake had long ago gotten used to being fodder for the gossip columnists. Whether any of the Fortunes liked it or not, it went hand in hand with being a member of the wealthiest family in South Dakota. But Sasha wasn't used to having her private life chronicled for the masses to read about over their morning coffee.

Her name had appeared in the newspaper a few times because of the social functions and charity events she and Creed had attended together, but those stories hadn't been based on speculation or been malicious in tone. The article in yesterday's paper had been both and read more like something Trina would write than a reputable columnist.

He closed his eyes in an effort to block out the truth. His half siblings, Case and Eliza, and even his Australian cousin, Max, had had information about them leaked to the press and they'd all accused Trina of being behind it. But surely she wouldn't do the same thing to her own son. Would she?

Blake wasn't so sure. But the next time he stopped by her place for a visit, he had every intention of finding out.

Eight

"Do you have a minute?"

Sasha was surprised, not only by Creed's question, but the fact that he'd even asked it. He never cared how busy she was or what she was doing. If he wanted to drop by her office to chat, he walked right on in. Of course, as co-president of Dakota Fortune, he was her boss and entitled to do that.

"Sure, what do you need?"

An ominous feeling filled her when he held up a news clipping as he reached to close her office door. "We need to talk."

"That's the gossip column that ran in last weekend's newspaper, isn't it?" she asked, wondering if the nefarious story would ever go away.

"Yes." Creed had been out of town on business for the past six days and had apparently just learned about the article.

Walking over to her desk, he slapped the clipping down in front of her. She gasped when she read the sticky note attached to it. "How does it feel to come out the loser for a change?" She looked up at him. "Where did you get this?"

"It arrived in today's mail."

She felt as if she might be sick. "Who would do such a thing?"

"I think we both know who's responsible," he growled.

"Y-you think Blake sent this to you?"

"Who else?"

"You're wrong, Creed." Sasha's fingers trembled as she rubbed at her suddenly throbbing temples. "Blake would never do anything like this."

He propped his fists on the surface of her desk, then leaned forward. "Are you sure?"

Tears filled her eyes as she nodded. "Of course."

"Then who else would be malicious enough to send me something like this?"

"I don't know." She felt as if she were being

interrogated on a witness stand and Creed was her prosecutor, judge and jury.

When she opened her bottom desk drawer for a tissue, then wiped at an errant tear on her cheek, Creed swore vehemently. "I knew he'd do something like this. I just didn't anticipate it happening this soon."

"Y-you're wrong, Creed." Sasha tried to sniff back a fresh wave of tears. "Blake's not like that. What would he have to gain?"

"The satisfaction of publicly humiliating me," Creed stated flatly. "Sending this to me was just his way of rubbing my nose in it."

She couldn't believe what she was hearing. Other than the picture of her and Creed dancing at Case and Gina's wedding reception, his name had only been mentioned a couple of times. She'd been the one the columnist had focused on.

"You think you've been publicly humiliated? How do you think I feel?" she asked, suddenly more angry than hurt. "I'm the one who's been accused of being a social-climbing gold digger."

That seemed to drain away much of his anger and, straightening to his full height, he shook his head. "I never meant to dismiss the effect this has had on you, Sasha."

"But that's exactly what you've just done," she said, saddened that her friend hadn't even considered how the story might have upset her.

They stared silently at each other for what seemed like an eternity, each knowing their friendship had suffered a serious blow.

"Are you going to Deadwood this evening?" he finally asked.

She shook her head. "Blake's flying in later this afternoon to spend the weekend here."

Creed's mouth flattened into a tight line a moment before he nodded, and without another word walked out of her office.

Feeling drained from the confrontation, Sasha began to carefully stack the marketing charts she'd been working on when Creed had shown up. After what he'd just put her through, he owed her the rest of the afternoon off. With pay.

As she retrieved her purse from the bottom drawer of her desk, turned off her computer and left her office, she made a conscious decision not to mention the disturbing incident to Blake. The brothers were already at odds and there was no way she was going to add fuel to a fire that was rapidly growing out of control. Nor was she going to be the catalyst that brought their feud to a head.

* * *

Getting into the shiny red sports car he kept at the airport for his frequent visits to Sioux Falls, Blake started the powerful engine and headed straight for Sasha's apartment. It had been four days since she'd left Deadwood and he couldn't believe how much he'd missed her. He'd called her every night, but phone conversations were a poor substitute for holding her, kissing her and making love to her until they both collapsed from exhaustion.

A half hour later, when he parked the car in front of her apartment building and got out to walk up to her door, he whistled a tune. Life was good. Profits at his three casinos were higher than any of the projections; there hadn't been any more reports about him and Sasha in the gossip columns and he was going to spend the next three days with the most exciting woman he'd ever known. As far as he was concerned, it didn't get any better than that.

When he stopped to dig Sasha's apartment key from his jeans pocket, he smiled. She was going to be surprised and hopefully quite pleased when she came home from work and found that he'd had a caterer deliver a specially prepared dinner for them. She was expecting him to take her out, but after spending the past four days without her in his arms, the last place Blake wanted them to be was in a crowded restaurant.

"It's past time that you and I have it out, little brother."

At the sound of his brother's angry voice, Blake's good mood took a nosedive and he turned to find Creed storming up the sidewalk toward him. "I don't have anything to say to you."

"But I have plenty to say to you and you're going to listen."

"The hell I am." Blake wasn't the least bit intimidated by Creed's menacing expression. "I have plans for the evening and they don't include talking to you."

"I don't give a damn about you or your plans," Creed said, poking Blake in the chest with his index finger. "You're going to listen."

White hot fury invaded every fiber of Blake's being. "Do that again and I'll knock the hell out of you."

Although there were six years difference in their ages, they were pretty well matched in size and build. And if it came to blows, Blake figured he had a pretty good chance of taking Creed in a fight.

"Until today, I couldn't figure out why you'd taken a sudden interest in Sasha when you hadn't so much as given her a second glance in the four years she's worked at Dakota Fortune," Creed growled.

"And you think you've figured it out now?" Blake snapped back.

"Oh, yeah." Creed's smile was filled with loathing. "Because it appeared that Sasha and I were a couple, you decided to seduce her away from me. But you were too blinded by your jealousy of me to see that there was never anything romantic between us."

Guilt coursed through Blake. That was exactly the way his involvement with Sasha had started out. Fortunately, it hadn't taken long for him to realize how special she was and how much he needed her in his life.

But Blake's need to retaliate quickly became stronger than his sense of regret and before he could stop himself, he lashed out. "I figured that out about the same time I took her virginity."

Creed laughed humorlessly. "And she was ripe for the picking, wasn't she?"

"What's that supposed to mean?" Blake demanded, barely resisting the urge to plant his fist in his brother's nose.

"I've seen the way she looked at you over the past year. But being a self-absorbed bastard, I don't suppose you could see that she was attracted to you." Creed gave him a disgusted look. "Although for the life of me, I'll never understand why."

Blake shook his head. "I don't give a damn what you do or don't understand. Sasha's with me now and you're out of the picture." Without thinking, he added, "I win."

"A real man would walk away from this before Sasha ends up getting hurt." Creed raised an arrogant eyebrow. "But then, her feelings have never been your concern, have they? You were too focused on getting back at me to consider what your little game would do to her. And if the truth is known, you wouldn't have cared even if you had."

Blake didn't think he'd ever despised his brother more than he did at that moment. "I've never made a secret of the fact that I'll do whatever it takes just for the privilege of watching you land on your ass. But that's not—"

He started to tell Creed that he'd come to care too much for Sasha to hurt her in any way, but the words died in Blake's throat when he heard the soft female gasp behind him. Spinning around, Blake felt as if he was being torn apart when he saw the devastated expression on Sasha's sweet face and the tears streaming unchecked from her emerald eyes.

Neither he nor Creed had noticed her opening the apartment door, and Blake knew that she'd heard every one of the verbal barbs and accusations that they'd hurled at each other.

Arriving home from the office, Sasha had barely had time to change clothes and feed her cat, Melvin, before she'd heard the angry male voices outside of her apartment door. When she'd peeked out the window to see what was going on, the elation she'd felt at the sight of Blake had quickly turned to desolation. He and Creed had been embroiled in a heated argument and it hadn't taken long for her to realize that she was the subject of their battle.

"H-how could you?" she stammered, unsure which of the Fortune brothers to address first.

"Sasha—"

"Sweetheart—"

They both spoke at once, but she'd heard more than enough. "Don't." She shook her head. "There's nothing left to say."

Blake took a step toward her. "You heard—"

"E-everything," she said, drawing back. If he touched her, she knew for certain she'd shatter into a million pieces.

"I thought you were still at work," Creed said, his expression guarded.

"After our conversation, I didn't feel like staying at the office." She swiped at the tears running down her cheeks. "But don't trouble yourself with firing me for leaving work early."

"I wasn't going to," Creed said, frowning. "Why would you think that I would?"

"It doesn't matter whether you were or not because effective immediately, I'm no longer an employee of Dakota Fortune." When he opened his mouth as if he intended to refuse her resignation, she held up her hand. "I don't want to hear it. I thought you were my friend, Creed."

"I am," he insisted.

She shook her head. "A true friend wouldn't have talked to me the way you did earlier today."

"What did you say to her?" Blake demanded, his fists doubled at his sides.

"It doesn't matter," Sasha answered, staring at Creed. She feared she wouldn't be able to continue if she looked at Blake. And it was extremely important that she let them both know exactly what their feuding had cost them.

"I'm here defending you now," Creed said stubbornly. "If that's not friendship, I don't know what is."

"You weren't defending me as much as you were letting Blake know what easy prey you thought I was." She could tell that her statement shocked him, but it was past time they both heard just how destructive their warring had become and the high price they'd both have to pay for it. "In light of everything that's happened today, I think you'll have to agree that our friendship has come to an end, Creed."

"It's just as well, sweetheart," Blake interjected. "The son of a bitch wouldn't know how to be a friend if his life depended on it."

Sasha finally looked at him and she felt as if her heart broke all over again. "What you did to me is far worse than anything Creed could have ever done." Her voice caught on a sob. "Only the ones you love the most have the power to devastate you."

"Sasha, listen to me," Blake said, reaching for her.

"Don't touch me." She brushed his hand away. "Don't ever touch me again."

"Sasha, sweetheart, you don't mean that."

"Yes, I do." She took a deep breath as she forced herself to push the all-consuming emotional pain aside and dig deep within her soul to muster the last scrap of her tattered pride. "How could you have such little regard for my feelings? Did you even think of what it would do to me when I discovered that you were using me to get back at Creed?"

"If you'll let me explain—"

"I don't want to hear your excuses, Blake." She shook her head. "You win?" she quoted him. "I think that more than sums up the reasons behind your sudden interest in me, don't you?" Sasha held out her hand to Blake. "I'd like my apartment key back, please."

He reluctantly placed it in her hand. "It doesn't have to end this way, Sasha."

"Too late, Blake. It's already over." She glanced from one man to the other through her gathering tears. "I want nothing more to do with either of you." Knowing she was seconds away from losing the last of her control, she added, "Now, feel free to resume your shouting match. But I would appreciate you taking it elsewhere. I have no desire to listen to anything more that either of you have to say."

Her heart breaking, Sasha entered her apartment and closed the door behind her. Shaking uncontrollably, she leaned back against it, then covering her face with her hands, sank to the floor as she released the torrent of tears she'd been holding at bay. How could she have been so stupid? Why hadn't she been able to see past Blake's handsome face and charming smile to the coldhearted man inside?

She should have known there was more behind his excuse than just wanting to get to know her better. He'd had ample opportunity in the four years she'd worked at Dakota Fortune to strike up an acquaintance with her. But he hadn't bothered to look her way. At least, not until Creed had asked her to help him keep the fortune-hunting women in search of a great catch at arm's length by accompanying him to various events.

That should have been her first clue. But she hadn't wanted to believe that the man she'd loved from the moment she'd first laid eyes on him had only noticed her because he thought she was involved with his brother. That was the reason behind his continual questions about her relationship with Creed. He hadn't wanted to make sure he wasn't treading on another man's turf. Blake had been trying to ascertain whether he was seducing the right woman.

Her breath caught and a fresh wave of pain coursed through her. How pathetic she must have seemed to Blake when she'd told him that she'd saved herself because in her mind no man had ever measured up to him.

Hauling herself to her feet, she walked into the bedroom, but when she looked at the bed, she backpedaled and went into the kitchen. Her gaze automatically landed on the counter where he'd made love to her and, rushing from the room, she prowled her apartment in search of something, anything, that didn't remind her of Blake. But his memory was everywhere—holding her, kissing her, making love to her.

When she finally collapsed on the bed, Sasha hugged one of the pillows to her chest as she tried to stop the pain inside of her. How could a heart still beat when it was so badly broken? When it hurt so much? And how was she ever going to survive waking up in the morning without having him in her life?

Seated on a stool at the end of the bar in the lounge at the Belle of Fortune, Blake motioned for the bartender to bring him another round. He'd never been much of a drinker, but in the past few days, he figured he'd consumed enough beer to finance another team of Clydesdales and the wagon they pulled. But no matter how much he drank, Blake couldn't wash away the image of Sasha's tears or her shattered expression when she'd told him she never wanted to see him again.

He'd been a fool to even think of seducing her to get back at Creed in the first place. Then, when she'd repeatedly told him there was nothing romantic about her friendship with his brother, he'd stubbornly held to his plan and taken her to bed. And if that wasn't enough to qualify him for jerk of the year, he'd done the very thing he'd promised Sasha he would never do. He'd hurt her.

But a good case of guilty conscience wasn't his only problem. He still wasn't ready to put a name to what he felt for Sasha, but she had come to mean a great deal to him and he was hurting, too.

How could everything have gotten so far out of control? And what the hell could he do to make things right?

"Why don't you give her a call?" Sam asked, sitting another foaming mug of the amber liquid in front of Blake.

He hadn't told any of his employees about his breakup with Sasha. For one thing, it was none of their business. And for another, as long as he kept it quiet, he could fool himself into believing they weren't really through.

Glancing up from his beer, Blake gave the bartender a warning look. "Leave it alone, Sam."

Sam whistled low. "It's as bad as all that, huh?"

Blake stared at the middle-aged man behind the bar. He'd known Sam a long time and, although they'd never been close friends, he knew he could talk to the bartender and whatever was said would go no further.

"I doubt that she'd talk to me," Blake said, taking a swig of his beer.

Sam gave him an understanding nod. "Women

can be that way sometimes." He chuckled. "But if we grovel enough, they eventually come around."

"Not this time," Blake said, shaking his head. "I screwed up big time."

It was the first time he'd admitted, even to himself, that he'd made a huge error in judgment. But if confession was good for the soul, he hadn't felt it yet. He was still as miserable as hell.

"I don't know what you did, but it can't be all that bad. Have you tried sending her flowers?" Sam asked as he wiped away a spot from the top of the polished bar. "When I get in trouble with my wife, I can usually wiggle out of it with a dozen roses."

Blake grunted. "I could send her enough flowers to decorate every float in the Rose Bowl parade and I doubt it would make a difference."

"Damn, son, you are in trouble."

When Sam walked down the bar to wait on a customer, Blake wondered what he could possibly do to straighten out the mess he'd made of things. He supposed that he could send her flowers. Hell, he was at the point where he'd be willing to buy out a flower shop if that was what it took to get her to listen to him.

"You might try sending candy along with those flowers," Sam offered helpfully when he returned.

"I haven't seen a women yet who can resist a box of chocolates."

Blake nodded as he drained the last of his beer and stood up to remove his wallet from his suit coat. He tossed a hundred-dollar bill on the bar in front of the man. "Thanks, Sam."

"Hey, what's that for?" Sam asked, looking confused. "You're the boss. You don't pay for drinks."

"That's for the advice," Blake said as he left the bar.

He doubted that sending flowers and candy would be enough to mend the rift he'd created between himself and Sasha, but he was going to give it a shot. He wanted her back in his life, back in his arms and back in his bed. And come hell or high water, he wasn't going to give up until he had all three.

Nine

Sasha's stomach churned when she opened the newspaper to see the picture of her and Blake kissing. "Not again," she moaned.

After the nightmare of having her association with the Fortune brothers reported in print, she'd made a habit of checking the gossip column each morning to reassure herself the reporter had lost interest in her. But seeing the same picture next to a caption reading, "Sasha Kilgore rids herself of another Fortune, but will she gain a son…or daughter?" made her feel physically ill.

Where on earth had the columnist come up with

her information? And why hadn't she verified the facts before reporting something so blatantly false?

Sasha wasn't surprised by the report that she and Blake were no longer a couple. Anyone who cared to take notice would figure that out when they were no longer seen together. But why had the reporter added that she might be pregnant?

"Please let me be having a nightmare," she mumbled, running for the bathroom to be sick.

A few minutes later, as she splashed cold water on her face, the telephone rang and she had to abandon the hope that she'd wake up to find it had all been a dream. "Hello?"

"Sasha, don't hang up," Creed said as soon as she answered.

"I thought I told you our friendship is over." Could her day get any worse?

"I just wanted to make sure you're all right." Something in his voice told her that he'd read the morning paper.

"You saw it, didn't you?"

"I couldn't miss it." He paused. "Is it true? Did that bastard make you pregnant?"

She'd been wrong. Instead of getting worse, her day had just hit rock bottom. "No, Creed. I'm not pregnant. But thank you for reminding me that everyone in western South Dakota thinks that I am."

He cleared his throat. "Are you absolutely certain?"

"I'm positive," she said through clenched teeth. Short of assuring him of the regularity of her monthly cycle, she didn't know how to make it any clearer. The sound of the doorbell was a welcome excuse to end the call. "I have to go, Creed."

"Take care, Sasha," he said, sounding as if he'd like to say more.

She broke the connection without saying goodbye, tossed the cordless phone onto the bed and went to see who was at the door.

"Sasha Kilgore?"

"Yes," she said, eyeing the bouquet of purple hyacinth in a cut-glass vase the man held.

"These are for you." He removed a clipboard from beneath his arm. "Sign here, please."

She shook her head. "Not until I know who they're from."

Smiling, the man glanced at the paper on the clipboard. "It says here that Mr. Fortune down in Deadwood placed the order."

Sasha reached to close the door. "I don't want them."

The man looked thunderstruck. "You don't?"

"No."

"What am I supposed to do with them?" he

asked, frowning. "My boss will have my hide if I take them back to the shop."

Sasha sighed and hastily scrawling her name on the delivery slip, took the flowers from him and closed the door. After what he'd done to her, the way he'd used her, Blake thought he could atone by sending her a handful of flowers?

"I don't think so," she said as she walked straight into the utility room to throw the flowers in the trash can.

But the sight of a small envelope on a clear pick in the middle of the bouquet stopped her. A part of her wanted to read the card, to see what message Blake had included with the beautiful hyacinth and savor any connection, no matter small, with the man she loved. Another, more cautious part of her prevented her from doing it. It would only deepen her sorrow and remind her of how miserable she was.

"As if I don't already know," she said, shaking her head.

Leaving the card on the pick, she walked back into the living room and placed the flowers on a table at the end of her couch. She started to walk away, but then, as if in a trance, she sat down and spent the rest of the morning staring at them.

* * *

"You've gone too far this time, Trina," Blake said through clenched teeth when his mother opened her door. More angry with her than he could ever remember, he pushed past her to enter the condo.

Trina hurriedly stepped back to keep from being run down. "Blake, darling, whatever do you mean?"

"You know damned good and well what I mean," he said, waving a copy of the morning newspaper under her nose.

She didn't bother pretending she didn't know what he was talking about. But shaking her head, she gave him a practiced smile. "This really isn't a good time for a visit, darling. I have to go to the gym for my workout with my personal trainer." She touched her bleached blond hair with a perfectly manicured hand. "Then I have a hair and nail appointment."

"Cancel your appointments." Blake wasn't going to leave until he'd put a stop to her vicious game of revenge once and for all.

"Blake, really—"

"Leaking information to the media about Case, Max and Eliza was bad enough, but your own son?" He took a step toward her. "That's going a little far, even for you."

"What makes you think that I'm responsible for the things reported in the newspaper?" She had the audacity to look hurt by his accusations. But Blake knew his mother all too well.

He'd already given her a stern warning about her use of the media to make trouble for the family and she'd denied any involvement. And although he hadn't been entirely convinced, Blake had dismissed the matter. He'd regretted that Eliza and Max had been hurt by having their secrets revealed in print. However, he couldn't have cared less about the effect his mother's activities had on Case.

But now it appeared that he and Sasha had fallen victim to Trina's game of vengeance against the Fortune family, and Blake had every intention of putting an end to it.

"Cut the crap, Trina. We both know that you and this gossip monger attend the same exercise classes," he said, thumping the paper with a flick of his finger. "What I'd like to know is where you're getting your information about the Fortunes."

Abandoning all pretense, a bitter expression replaced his mother's look of feigned bewilderment. "It doesn't matter where I get my information, I'm making Nash Fortune's life as miserable as he's made mine and that's all I care about."

"How the hell do you figure you're making Dad

miserable when it's not the details of his private life you're putting out there for all the world to see?" Blake shoved the newspaper into her hands. "This is my name and that of an innocent woman you're dragging through the mud this time."

"I want everyone in Sioux Falls to know what a fine, upstanding family the Fortunes really are," she said sarcastically. "And why I had the good sense to get out of it."

"Oh, that's rich, Trina." Blake laughed humorlessly. "Everyone from here to St. Louis and back knows that Dad pitched you out with nothing but you're prenup when he found out you were having a series of affairs."

"Nash Fortune ruined my life," she snarled, the angry lines that would normally appear around her mouth nonexistent from her latest BOTOX injection. "He owes me for everything he's put me through."

"No, Trina, *you* were the one who ruined your life, not Dad." Blake shook his head. "And believe me, your prenuptial agreement guaranteed that you were well compensated for anything, real or imagined, that he put you through."

"It wasn't enough," she shrieked. "It will never be enough. I'm having to face the world alone because of him."

"Whatever," Blake said, realizing there was no reasoning with her where his father was concerned. Nor did he remind her that she wasn't entirely alone. She had two grown children. But then, she'd never had more than a passing interest in anything about him or Skylar. "You will cease and desist your efforts to ruin the rest of us through this gossip column."

"I haven't told my friend anything that wasn't absolutely true," she said haughtily.

"That's bull and we both know it." He took a deep breath. "Sasha has never been, nor will she ever be a social climber. And she's not pregnant."

A sudden thought caused his gut to tighten. He'd been careful to make sure they were protected, but there had been that one time in her kitchen when he'd been so hot for her that he hadn't taken the time to use a condom. The chances were remote that he'd gotten her pregnant, but still there was the possibility.

"Are you certain?" Trina asked, giving him a sly look.

"Relatively," he said, remembering that Sasha had a period shortly after the careless incident.

His mother frowned. "But Ivy said—" The moment she spoke the name of the Fortunes' chef, Trina clamped her mouth shut.

"So she's the one supplying you with information about us," Blake said, not at all surprised.

Before his father had divorced Trina, she and Ivy had become good friends. At least, as good friends as two troublemakers could be. Apparently, they'd stayed in touch and Ivy was feeding snippets of overheard conversations to Trina.

"I don't give a damn what she tells you—you will stop reporting our every move to this sleazy reporter," Blake said, pointing to the newspaper. "Either that, or I'll sever all ties with you and you really will be alone in the world."

Before Trina could argue the point further, Blake walked out of the condo and climbed into his sports car. How could anyone be so set on revenge that it became all-consuming?

As he started the engine and backed from the parking slot, he felt as if tiny leprechauns in spiked shoes were dancing an Irish jig inside his stomach. But then, that was nothing new. He could never remember a time that a visit with his mother hadn't made him feel that way.

Steering the car out of the parking lot, Blake set the cruise control as he headed across town to the florist to order more flowers for Sasha. He wondered if she'd seen the gossip column and how she'd reacted to it. She'd been extremely upset by the first report, but this story was far worse, and no doubt, caused her an even greater amount of distress.

The knot in his stomach tightened to an unbearable ache. It wasn't any wonder she wanted nothing more to do with his family. Her association with them had brought her nothing but pain and heartache. And he hated that she'd been caught up in the vengeful games he and his family insisted on playing with each other.

As the realization of what he'd done to her sank in, he took a deep breath against the guilt weighing heavily on his shoulders. His need to even the score with Creed was directly responsible for her recent unhappiness.

Disgusted with himself, he came to the conclusion that he was no better than Trina. His mother had wasted a huge amount of her life trying to get even with his father for the mistakes *she'd* made, not Nash. And Blake was just as guilty of holding a grudge against his brothers, Case and Creed, for reasons beyond their control.

Blake supposed that to one degree or another, all families had their rivalries. But the Fortune brothers had let theirs get dangerously out of control. Case and Creed had always resented Blake, probably because they'd never liked his mother. And for as long as Blake could remember, Trina had been extremely vocal about the differences she felt Nash made between his two older sons and Blake. After years of listening to her harp on the subject, it was no wonder his resentment had built to choking proportions.

But he couldn't lay all the blame at Trina's doorstep. He'd spent more time and energy than he cared to admit nurturing the hard feelings he had for his brothers…and where had it gotten him? Absolutely nowhere. It had been an enormous waste of his energy and spirit and it was past time he let it go.

Besides, he had another, even stronger emotion replacing his resentment and hostilities. It scared the living hell out of him to acknowledge it and God only knew he'd fought valiantly against it, but somewhere between his decision to seduce her and the confrontation with Creed at her apartment, he'd fallen in love with Sasha.

He shook his head as he parked his car in the florist's parking lot. His mind set on what he wanted, he walked into the flower shop. As soon as he arranged for several more bouquets to be delivered to her, he fully intended to go over to her place and if he had to, wear out the knees on his khakis begging her to forgive him and take him back.

* * *

As Blake left the florist, his cell phone rang and when he answered it, he was startled by the sound of his step-sister's frantic voice. "Blake, have you seen my mother?"

A year younger than his sister, Skylar, Maya Blackstone had been raised with the Fortune children when Nash had hired Patricia to take care of them after his divorce from Trina. Blake had always liked Maya well enough, but she'd never seemed to feel as if she were part of the Fortune family. All things considered, Blake wasn't entirely sure he blamed her.

"What's wrong, Maya?"

"We can't find Mother." Her voice shook and he knew she was trying her best not to cry.

"Dad doesn't know where she is?" he asked, getting into his car. It wasn't often that his step-mother left the house without Nash, and when she did, she always let him know where she was going and when she'd return.

"No and he's in a total panic. He had me called out of the class I was teaching to see if I'd seen her."

"Are you still at school?" he asked, steering the little sports car toward Fortune Estate.

"Yes. I have another class to teach and no one to cover for me."

"I'm only about fifteen minutes away," he assured her. "I'll stop by the estate and see if I can find out what's going on."

"Please call me back and let me know what you find out," she begged.

"I will, Maya."

Several minutes later, when Blake drove up the circular drive in front of the estate and got out of the car to climb the steps of the front veranda, Nash barreled out of the front door to meet him. "Have you seen Patricia?"

"No." He'd never seen Nash Fortune panic over anything, but he was certainly on the verge of it now. "What's going on, Dad?"

"I don't know," Nash said, his gaze riveted on the driveway as if he was willing his wife to come home. "It looks like she's left me, son. And I don't know why."

Blake couldn't believe it. Patricia was as devoted to his father as Nash was to her.

"Did you argue?" he asked, trying to make sense of it all.

Nash shook his head. "You know we never disagree."

It was true. In the thirteen years they'd been married, Blake couldn't remember a single time they'd had a difference of opinion about anything.

"Are you sure she's left you? Maybe she's just gone to run some errands or decided to go shopping," Blake offered, hoping that was the case.

"She took some of her clothes," Nash said dejectedly. He lowered himself onto one of the decorative wrought-iron chairs on the veranda. "What am I going to do, son?"

"I don't know, Dad." He knew exactly how his father felt. Since Sasha had told him she never wanted to see him again, it had been the worst four days of his life.

"If I knew what I'd done to upset her, I'd make it right," Nash said, propping his forearms on his bent knees. He stared down at his loosely clasped hands hanging between his knees. "But I don't have the slightest notion where she went."

Blake didn't know where to tell his father to start looking, but he did know where his woman was and he wasn't going to waste any more time finding her to straighten things out between them. "Dad, I'll keep my eyes open and if see her, I'll let you know."

Nash raised sad eyes and the desolation in his gaze shocked Blake. "Please do, son. I don't know if I can survive without her."

Blake knew where his father was coming from and he wasn't about to waste another precious minute getting to the woman he loved. "I have to leave, Dad. But keep me posted if you find out anything."

"I will."

"Oh, Dad, you might want to start looking for another chef," Blake said, remembering his conversation with Trina.

"Why?"

"Ivy's the one responsible for spreading gossip to Trina about everything that's going on around here."

"I'll fire her immediately," Nash said coldly. "Her mentioning Trina all the time might be behind Patricia leaving."

Blake knew there had to be more behind his step-mother walking out on the man she loved, but he couldn't think about that now. He had to get to Sasha.

Leaving his father sitting on the veranda, staring down the driveway as he drove away, Blake called Maya to tell her what he'd found out, then ending the call, he headed back into Sioux Falls.

He felt sorry for Nash and the wretchedness he was feeling. Blake had felt the same way ever since Sasha had told him she never wanted to see him again.

But that was about to change. He was going over to her apartment and he wasn't leaving until he'd made things right with her.

* * *

Closing her apartment door, Sasha turned to search for a place to set the latest bouquet of flowers that had just been delivered. She was rapidly running out of flat surfaces to put them on and would soon have to start setting them on the floor.

After the bouquet of purple hyacinth had arrived that morning, every hour on the hour, the delivery-man was back at her door with another arrangement. There were bouquets of a variety of flowers and in every color imaginable. And tucked into each one was a card with her name scrawled across the envelope in Blake's handwriting. She hadn't opened any of them, but it was getting more difficult with each delivery to resist the temptation of finding out what Blake had written.

Placing the vase of yellow jonquils she held on top of the television, she glanced at the clock on the DVD player. It was getting close to the time for shops to close and, hopefully, it would be the last delivery she received for the day.

But when the doorbell rang, her shoulders slumped. "There couldn't possibly be any flowers left in Sioux Falls," she muttered as she walked to the door. "They're all here in my apartment.

Swinging the door open, she started to tell the deliveryman to start taking them to the local hospital, but the words froze in her throat and her heart pounded so hard against her ribs she was surprised it wasn't audible. Instead of another floral arrangement, Blake Fortune was standing at her door holding a single long-stemmed red rose in full bloom.

Ten

"Go away," Sasha said, reaching to close the door.

Blake looked so good it brought tears to her eyes and she felt as if her heart would break all over again. Even after all that he'd done, she loved him more than anything. But she wasn't fool enough to let him into her life again. Not if she wanted to maintain what little sanity she had left.

"Wait, sweetheart," he said, placing his hand on the surface of the door to hold it open. "I have something I need to tell you."

"I don't want to hear it," she said, shoving at the

door. She was no match for his superior strength, but that didn't keep her from trying to slam the door in his face. "As far as I'm concerned, we have nothing left to say to each other."

"Come on, Sasha. Give me ten minutes."

"No."

"Please?"

"No." She stubbornly pushed at the door. He didn't seem to be expending a whole lot of energy to hold the door open, but she was quickly becoming exhausted from her efforts. "Now, please remove your hand and go away."

Shrugging, he replaced his hand with his shoulder. "Is that more to your liking?"

She shook her head. "You haven't gone away."

"You might as well let me in, sweetheart."

The look he gave her caused her chest to tighten with emotion and she doubled her efforts to shut the door. "What part of 'go away' don't you understand?"

"I'm not going anywhere until you listen to me," he said patiently.

"There's nothing you have to say that I want to hear."

Why was he being so darned persistent? Why couldn't he leave her alone and let her try to put the shattered pieces of her life back together?

Apparently tired of leaning against the door, he used his shoulder to push it open a little farther and entered her apartment. "You might not want to hear it, but I'm going to tell you anyway."

"Haven't you said enough already?" she asked, glaring at him as she closed the door.

He twirled the long-stemmed rose between his fingers as he walked over to inspect the vase of purple hyacinth. "Did you know that the type and color of a bouquet sends a message?"

"I've heard that, but I have no idea what each flower means and right now, I don't really care." Her heart was breaking and he wanted to discuss the flowers he'd sent her?

"You didn't read the cards that accompanied the arrangements, did you?" he asked as he plucked the small envelope from the bouquet.

"No." She wasn't about to tell him that the hardest thing she'd ever done was to resist reading the messages he'd included.

"That's a shame," he said, removing the card from the envelope. "I wrote down the meaning of each one on the cards."

"Are you going to tell me why you're here or give me a lesson in flowers?" The longer he stayed, the harder it would be for her when she had to watch him leave.

"The purple hyacinth says, 'I'm sorry, please forgive me,'" he said as if she hadn't spoken.

"That's nice, but we both know that forgiving you is going to be impossible for me to do." Tears threatened, but she blinked them away. She had more pride than to allow him to see how much she was still hurting.

"Are you certain of that?"

She couldn't believe he had the nerve to ask. "Yes."

He didn't turn to face her, nor did he comment further. Instead, he reached for the card tucked in a beautiful Boston fern. "Did you know that the fern signifies sincerity?"

"Oh, really?" She didn't even try to keep the bitterness from her voice. "I wasn't aware that you knew the meaning of the word."

Instead of responding to her remark, he walked over to another arrangement. "Pink roses ask that you please believe me."

"Why should I believe you or anything you say? I believed you when you said you'd never do anything to hurt me." She shook her head at her own foolishness. "But we both know how that turned out."

He still hadn't looked at her and the only indication that he'd heard her was in the slight stiffening of his shoulders. "Red carnations say that my heart aches for you," he said, moving on to the vase on her coffee table.

"Blake, stop…this," she said, hating the hitch in her voice. The more she listened to him, the closer she got to dissolving into a pool of tears. "P-please, if you have any compassion, you'll leave me alone."

"A bouquet of primrose means I can't live without you," he said, ignoring her passionate plea.

Why was he doing this to her? Hadn't he hurt her enough with his empty promises and insincerity? What made him think that by telling her the meanings behind the flowers he'd convince her to believe him now?

He touched the planter of white violets next to the primrose and stared at it for endless seconds before he spoke again. "These ask that you take a chance on happiness with me."

His relentless continuation was slowly destroying her. "P-please, don't—"

He hesitated a moment as if he was going to face her, then moved on to the final bouquet she'd placed on the television only moments before his arrival. "The yellow jonquils ask that you love me," he said quietly.

Sasha felt as if her heart broke all over again. How could he ask that of her?

"I—I did…love you," she said brokenly. "B-but I can't…" She shook her head. "W-won't put myself…in that position…again."

"Why not?" he asked, his back still to her.

He had to ask? Was he so self-absorbed that he couldn't see how much he'd hurt her?

"B-because I can't let you…hurt me again, Blake," she said, unable to keep her voice from cracking. "I—I can't…go through that again."

Finally turning to face her, he touched a velvety petal on the rose in his hand. "Do you know what a single red rose means, Sasha?"

She swallowed hard as she shook her head.

Walking over to stand in front of her, Blake handed her the long-stemmed rose, then held her hand between both of his. "It means I love you, sweetheart."

His warm touch was heaven and hell rolled into one. "D-don't," she said, forcing the word passed her tight throat. She fixed her gaze on the perfect rose to keep from looking at him. If she did, she knew for certain she'd be lost. "Y-you don't have any idea…what love is, Blake."

He was silent for a long moment. "That was probably true a month ago," he admitted, surprising her. "But that was before you."

Unable to believe him, the rose fell to the floor

as she pulled away. "If you loved me, why did you tell Creed that you'd won?" She shook her head. "Do you have any idea how that made me feel? To know that the man I love with all my heart was only using me in an attempt to get back at his brother?"

He bent down to pick up the rose. When he straightened, he nodded. "I know I've hurt you terribly, Sasha. And if I could, I'd turn back time and do things a lot different."

"Why don't you just come out and say it, Blake?" she asked, drawing on anger born from the emotional pain that seeing him again had caused. "If you hadn't thought I was involved with Creed, you wouldn't have been interested in me in the first place. You would have continued to come and go at Dakota Fortune without giving me a second glance."

They both knew what she said was true and he had the good graces not to refute it.

But when he raised his eyes to look directly at her, the regret in their blue depths stole her breath. "Unfortunately, you're probably right, sweetheart. But it didn't take me long to see how special you truly are."

"Was that before or after I gave you my virginity?" she asked, unable to stop herself.

He took a deep breath and the truth in his gaze

caused her heart to skip a beat. "I don't ever want you to doubt how much that meant to me. Just knowing that you'd always wanted me humbles me in ways you could never imagine."

"Then why…did you tell Creed—"

"That I figured out the two of you weren't involved when I took your virginity?" he finished for her. When she nodded, he shook his head. "Because I was a stupid, selfish bastard, who spoke in the heat of the moment when he should have kept his mouth shut."

"How many innocent victims are you and your brothers going to destroy before you stop this senseless feud, Blake? How far are you willing to go with your game of revenge?" When he took a step toward her, she shook her head. "Please don't."

But as was his custom, Blake ignored her and took her into his arms. "It stops right now, sweetheart."

The feel of his arms around her once again was her undoing and, burying her face in his chest, she gave into the tears she could no longer hold in check. There was no use pretending. No matter what he'd done, she still loved him, would always love him. But could she ever trust him?

"It's okay, Sasha," he said, tightening his hold around her. "You're more important to me than anything else in the world and I swear if you'll give us—give me—another chance, I'll never do anything to hurt you or make you unhappy ever again." His voice grew husky with emotion. "I want nothing more than to spend the rest of my life loving you." He threaded his fingers through her hair and tilted her head so that their gazes met. "I want to make love to you every night and wake up with you in my arms each morning for as long as I live."

"Wh-what are you saying?" she asked, afraid to believe.

The sincerity in his smile and the truth in his eyes couldn't be denied. "I want it all. I want you to move to Deadwood with me. I want us to run our casinos and raise babies together. And when they grow up and leave home, I want us to grow old together."

Lowering his head, he gave her a kiss so soft, so tender, there was no doubt left in her mind that he meant what he said.

When he raised his head there was a suspicious sheen of moisture in his eyes. "I love you, Sasha Kilgore. Can you find it in your heart to forgive me and do me the honor of becoming Mrs. Blake Fortune?"

Her tears fell anew, but this time they were tears

of joy. "Oh, Blake. Do you really mean it? Do you really want all those things?"

"Sweetheart, I've never wanted anything more in my entire life," he said without a moment's hesitation. "Will you marry me?"

"I love you, too, darling." Throwing her arms around his neck, she gazed up at the man she loved with all of her heart and soul. "Yes, I'll marry you."

He kissed her then and the love in that single kiss was more pure and beautiful than she'd ever thought possible.

"You've just made me the happiest man alive, Sasha." His smile caused her chest to fill with such intense emotion it took her breath. "And I intend to spend the rest of my days seeing that you never regret loving me."

"I could never regret loving you, Blake. I gave you my heart when I was fifteen and never took it back."

He shook his head. "And I never intend to let it go."

As they gazed lovingly at each other, she hesitated a moment before she said, "Blake, I want you to do something before we get married."

"Name it, sweetheart, and I'll see that it's taken care of."

"It's not for me," she said softly. "It's for you."

He looked confused. "You want something for me?"

She nodded. "I want you to make peace with your brothers."

To her surprise, he nodded. "I've seen what holding grudges and trying to even scores has done to my family." He touched her cheek. "And what it almost cost me." He gave her a tender kiss. "Revenge for something, whether real or imagined, isn't worth losing the one you love."

Sasha hugged him. "I love you, Blake Fortune."

"And I love you, sweetheart. For as long as I live."

* * * * *

Don't miss the next FORTUNES *book,*
Expecting a Fortune *by Jan Colley,*
available in March from Desire.

Set in darkness beyond the ordinary world.
Passionate tales of life and death.
With characters' lives ruled by laws the everyday
world can't begin to imagine.

NOCTURNE

It's time to discover the Raintree trilogy…

New York Times bestselling author
Linda Howard
brings you the dramatic first book
Raintree: Inferno.

The Ansara Wizards are rising and the
Raintree clan must rejoin the battle against
their foes, testing their powers, relationships
and forcing upon themselves lives they never
could have imagined before…

Turn the page for a sneak preview of the
captivating first book in the Raintree trilogy,
Raintree: Inferno *by Linda Howard.*

Available from next month exclusively
from Intrigue.

Raintree: Inferno

by

Linda Howard

Dante Raintree stood with his arms crossed as he watched the woman on the monitor. The image was in black and white to better show details; color distracted the brain. He focused on her hands, watching every move she made, but what struck him most was how uncommonly *still* she was. She didn't fidget or play with her chips, or look around at the other players. She peeked once at her down card, then didn't touch it again, signaling for another hit by tapping a fingernail on the table. Just because she didn't seem to be paying attention to the other players, though, didn't mean she was as unaware as she seemed.

"What's her name?" Dante asked.

"Lorna Clay," replied his chief of security, Al Rayburn.

"At first I thought she was counting, but she doesn't pay enough attention."

"She's paying attention, all right," Dante murmured. "You just don't see her doing it." A card counter had to remember every card played. Supposedly counting cards was impossible with the number of decks used by the casinos, but there were those rare individuals who could calculate the odds even with multiple decks.

"I thought that, too," said Al. "But look at this piece of tape coming up. Someone she knows comes up to her and speaks, she looks around and starts chatting, completely misses the play of the people to her left—and doesn't look around even when the deal comes back to her, just taps that finger. And damn if she didn't win. Again."

Dante watched the tape, rewound it, watched it again. Then he watched it a third time. There had to be something he was missing, because he couldn't pick out a single giveaway.

"If she's cheating," Al said with something like respect, "she's the best I've ever seen."

"What does your gut say?"

Al scratched the side of his jaw, considering. Finally, he said, "If she isn't cheating, she's the luckiest person walking. She wins. Week in, week out, she wins. Never a huge amount, but I ran the numbers and she's into us for about five grand a week. Hell, boss, on her way out of the casino she'll stop by a slot machine, feed a dollar in and walk away with at least fifty. It's never the same machine, either. I've had her watched, I've had her followed, I've even looked for the same faces in the casino every time she's in here, and I can't find a common denominator."

"Is she here now?"

"She came in about half an hour ago. She's playing blackjack, as usual.

"Bring her to my office," Dante said, making a swift decision. "Don't make a scene."

"Got it," said Al, turning on his heel and leaving the security center.

Dante left, too, going up to his office. His face was calm. Normally he would leave it to Al to deal with a cheater, but he was curious. How was she doing it? There were a lot of bad cheaters, a few good ones, and every so often one would come along who was the stuff of which legends were made: the cheater who didn't get caught, even when people were alert and the camera was on him—or, in this case, her.

It was possible to simply be lucky, as most people understood luck. Chance could turn a habitual loser into a big-time winner. Casinos, in fact, thrived on that hope. But luck itself wasn't habitual, and he knew that what passed for luck was often something else: cheating. And there was the other kind of luck, the kind he himself possessed, but it depended not on chance but on who and what he was. He knew it was an innate power and not Dame Fortune's erratic smile. Since power like his was rare, the odds made it likely the woman he'd been watching was merely a very clever cheat.

Her skill could provide her with a very good living, he thought, doing some swift calculations in his head. Five grand a week equaled $260,000 a year, and that was just from his casino. She probably hit them all, careful to keep the numbers relatively low so she stayed under the radar.

He wondered how long she'd been taking him, how long she'd been winning a little here, a little there, before Al noticed.

The curtains were open on the wall-to-wall window in his office, giving the impression, when one first opened the door, of stepping out onto a covered balcony. The glazed window faced west, so he could catch the sunsets. The sun was low now, the sky painted in purple and gold. At his home in the mountains, most of the windows faced east, affording him views of the sunrise. Something in him needed both the greeting and the goodbye of the sun. He'd always been drawn to sunlight, maybe because fire was his element to call, to control.

He checked his internal time: four minutes until sundown. Without checking the sunrise tables every day, he knew exactly when the sun would slide behind the mountains. He didn't own an alarm clock. He didn't need one. He was so acutely attuned to the sun's position that he had only to check within himself to know the time. As for waking at a particular time, he was one of those people who could tell himself to wake at a certain time, and he did. That talent had nothing to do with being Raintree, so he didn't have to hide it; a lot of perfectly ordinary people had the same ability.

He had other talents and abilities, however, that did require careful shielding. The long days of summer instilled in him an almost sexual high, when he could feel contained power buzzing just beneath his skin. He had to be doubly careful not to cause candles to leap into flame just by his presence, or to start wildfires with a glance in the dry-as-tinder brush. He loved Reno; he didn't want to burn it down. He just felt so damn *alive* with all the sunshine pouring down that he wanted to let the energy pour through him instead of holding it inside.

This must be how his brother Gideon felt while pulling lightning, all that hot power searing through his muscles, his veins. They had this in common, the connection with raw power. All the members of the far-flung Raintree clan had some power, some heightened ability, but only members of the royal family could channel and control the earth's natural energies.

Dante wasn't just of the royal family, he was the Dranir, the leader of the entire clan. "Dranir" was synonymous with king, but the position he held wasn't ceremonial, it was one of sheer power. He was the oldest son of the previous Dranir, but he would have been passed over for the position if he hadn't also inherited the power to hold it.

Behind him came Al's distinctive knock on the door. The outer office was empty, Dante's secretary having gone home hours before. "Come in," he called, not turning from his view of the sunset.

The door opened, and Al said, "Mr. Raintree, this is Lorna Clay."

Dante turned and looked at the woman, all his senses on alert. The first thing he noticed was the vibrant color of her hair, a rich, dark red that encompassed a multitude of shades from copper to burgundy. The warm amber light danced along the iridescent strands, and he felt a hard tug of sheer lust in his gut. Looking at her hair was almost like looking at fire, and he had the same reaction.

The second thing he noticed was that she was spitting mad.

FREE

2 BOOKS AND A SURPRISE GIFT!

We would like to take this opportunity to thank you for reading this Mills & Boon® book by offering you the chance to take TWO more specially selected 2-in-1 volumes from the Desire™ series absolutely FREE! We're also making this offer to introduce you to the benefits of the Mills & Boon® Reader Service™—

    ★ **FREE home delivery**
    ★ **FREE gifts and competitions**
    ★ **FREE monthly Newsletter**
    ★ **Books available before they're in the shops**
    ★ **Exclusive Reader Service offers**

Accepting these FREE books and gift places you under no obligation to buy; you may cancel at any time, even after receiving your free shipment. Simply complete your details below and return the entire page to the address below. You don't even need a stamp!

YES! Please send me 2 free Desire volumes and a surprise gift. I understand that unless you hear from me, I will receive 3 superb new volumes every month for just £4.99 each, postage and packing free. I am under no obligation to purchase any books and may cancel my subscription at any time. The free books and gift will be mine to keep in any case.

D8ZEE

Ms/Mrs/Miss/Mr...Initials ....
BLOCK CAPITALS PLEASE

Surname ....

Address ....

....

....Postcode ....

Send this whole page to:

The Reader Service, FREEPOST CN81, Croydon, CR9 3WZ